UNDERCOVER MAN

The setting of Hans Hellmut Kirst's new novel is
Bonn, capital of the Federal German Republic; the
time near-contemporary. The hero – or non-hero –
is Karl Wander, now a roving, rootless journalist,
but once, an idealistic officer in the post-war German
army who resigned his commission after an altercation
with the Ministry of Defence.

Wander is picked to work under cover for a group
of opportunistic politicians who wish to see the
current Defence Minister ousted and the whole
Ministry revamped. This is to be done by means of
documentary evidence, provided by Wander, of
corruption in armaments contracts. Aided by a
disgruntled munitions tycoon and some successful
industrial espionage, Wander sets about his task.

But Bonn abounds in other kinds of corruption.
Wander literally stumbles on one of these when he
finds a girl beaten almost to death outside his apartment, and discovers that his own former girl-friend,
now a wealthy and unscrupulous Baroness, is up to
the neck in activities that – to put it mildly – smell.

As the two plots gradually dovetail, Wander, aided
by a local chief of police too honest for his own and
others' good, realizes that those anxious for power
are as unsavoury as those already enjoying it. Skilfully
– and unexpectedly - he takes his own form of
revenge.

by the same author

UNDERCOVER MAN

Hans Hellmut Kirst

TRANSLATED BY
J. MAXWELL BROWNJOHN

COLLINS
St James's Place London 1970

Originally published in Germany under the title *Kein Vaterland*

ISBN 0 00 221412 1

Set in Monotype Imprint

© 1968 by Verlag Kurt Desch GmbH München

© 1970 in the English translation by Wm. Collins Sons & Co., Ltd.

Printed in Great Britain
Collins Clear-Type Press
London and Glasgow

'Bonn is half as big but twice as dead as the central cemetery in Chicago.'

An American Journalist's
verdict on the West German
Capital.

'The truth,' he said, 'too readily lulls us into a sense of security; error can often be far more instructive.'

'Everything recurs, and the law is as weak today as it was yesterday—as weak and as strong.'

ALAIN

Chapter 1

She lay sprawled across the corridor, immediately outside the door of his apartment, as if she had been flung there like a piece of cast-off clothing. Her face was hidden by a silky curtain of rinsed-blonde hair, pale and luminous. Something red and sticky was oozing from it.

Karl Wander said: 'Get up. You'll catch cold.'

The girl did not move as he bent over her. She looked as lifeless as a tailor's dummy. A dress of some glossy material was stretched tautly over her prominent buttocks. Her legs reminded Wander of smooth slipways.

He said: 'Out of my way, you've come to the wrong address.'

He heard her groan. She sounded as if she was dying of pleasure, painfully. He was familiar with the sound. It was one of the most saleable items in the feminine inventory. In this junk yard of a world even emotions were delivered COD.

He knelt down to get a better view of her. She smelt, penetratingly and with throat-catching intensity, of cold sweat, urine and blood, mingled with cloying perfume and a sour reek of alcohol. The aroma of the twentieth century.

'These things happen,' he muttered. 'No reason why they should happen on my doorstep, though.'

He took her by the shoulders and turned her over, revealing a pallid face with garishly painted lips like the double lines at the foot of a bill. She was whimpering to herself now, and when he gripped her harder she uttered a faint mewing sound like a distant sea-gull.

'Pull yourself together,' he said. 'It's midnight. I'm not in the market for wine, women and song, so try to keep your mouth shut. You're a pretty unappealing sight at the moment.'

And Wander lugged her, like a lumberjack manhandling a log, into his room. Apartment 204, Koblenzer Strasse, Bonn.

*

The doctor from the casualty department examined the girl and asked: 'Are you responsible for this?'

'I'm responsible for a lot of things,' Karl Wander replied, leaning back in his arm-chair. 'What is it this time – in your opinion?'

'Still glowing with a sense of achievement, eh?' The doctor could not have been much more than thirty, but there was a cold and world-weary look in his eye. His greyish-yellow skin looked like a loose nylon sheath. 'Don't worry, you'll be feeling less cocksure before long. I'll see to that.'

'What do you plan to do?' Wander inquired, swilling the brandy round his glass. Like an opera-goer in a box, he surveyed the scene: the semi-nude girl draped over the bed in his brightly lit bedroom, and, in the doorway, the doctor, watching him.

'I shall submit a report,' the doctor said.

'Submit anything you like,' Wander retorted, topping up his glass. He pushed the bottle invitingly towards the doctor, who ignored it.

'A copy of my report will go to the police.'

'By all means,' said Wander. 'It's nothing to do with me.'

'That remains to be seen,' the doctor said stubbornly.

He eyed his companion with repugnance – the brandy-drinking middle-aged man made an irritatingly casual impression. With a sudden surge of hostility he added quietly, almost in a hiss: 'What makes bastards like you tick?'

'Are you referring to me?' Wander demanded, mildly taken aback.

'Your sort stop at nothing.' The doctor leant forward as if to

8

spit in Wander's face. 'You treat human beings like toys to be played with and thrown away – aids to sexual titillation. Well, you won't get away with it so easily this time.'

'Either you're a TV addict or you go to the cinema too often, Dr – Bergner, wasn't it? You've been seeing too many X-films. Over-indulgence always takes its toll in the end.'

'This girl – ' Dr Bergner indicated the figure lying on Wander's bed – 'has been appallingly knocked about – kicked as well as punched, from the look of her. Half throttled, too.'

'From the look of her, you said?' Karl Wander's expression conveyed polite interest. 'I gather you're not absolutely positive.'

'No amount of quibbling will get you out of this mess.'

'Am I in a mess?' A weary smile flitted over Wander's face. 'The world may be a lousy place but it isn't quite as straight-forward as you seem to imagine – there are shades of grey in it as well. For instance, the girl could have fallen downstairs or something, unassisted. On the other hand, she may have been wounded in the line of duty.'

'A very convenient explanation, but it doesn't commend itself.'

'I once knew a young woman of the same type who used to butt her head against door panels – not walls, mark you. Note the subtle distinction. However hysterical she was, she always spotted the difference just in time. Think of the glorious, bewildering range of alternatives!'

'My job is simply to record my findings, and what I found here was the bruised and bleeding body of an unconscious girl – in your bedroom and on your bed. That seems pretty con-clusive to me.'

'On the contrary, Doctor, you're way off target. I don't know this girl, I've never set eyes on her before, and I've no idea where she comes from or even what her name is.'

'So the fact that she's on your bed is pure coincidence.'

9

'When I got home she was lying in the middle of the passage, outside my door. As if she'd been dumped there by a delivery man. I had to do something about her – I hadn't any choice.'

'Prove it,' Dr Bergner said, 'not to me, though, because I wouldn't believe a word of it. Try to persuade the police you're nothing but a good Samaritan – if you know the meaning of the word.'

Wander put his brandy glass down and got wearily to his feet. He went into the bedroom, picked up the girl's handbag and opened it. Having swiftly checked its contents, he said in a businesslike voice:

'Her name is Morgenrot, Christian name Eva. She apparently lives in this building, Apartment 304. Just a question of wrong delivery, probably the vanman must have got his floors mixed up. That seems to be the answer.'

'She's a neighbour of yours and yet you say you don't know her?'

'There are forty apartments in this block. Approximately seventy people must live here, and they scurry past like ants, if they ever meet at all. Buildings like these aren't designed for communal living – they're a collection of self-contained cells devoted to sleeping, copulation and digestion.'

'But a girl like this – ' Dr Bergner nodded in the direction of Eva Morgenrot – 'wouldn't be easy to overlook.'

'Maybe not,' Wander agreed, 'except that I never had a chance to look her over – I only arrived in Bonn this afternoon. I hope this sort of thing doesn't happen all the time. My idea of fun is quite different.'

*

The door of Apartment 304 was, like all the other doors in the block, an expanse of imitation teak, fashionably dark-hued and provided with a number which aspired to be gold but was really burnished yellow sheet metal.

Karl Wander rang only once. Then, after a few seconds, the door opened.

The woman who thus revealed herself was a tribute to considerable artistic and cosmetic skill. She looked strangely familiar, though he could not place her at first. Hollywood style, he thought, sophisticated comedy department. Not bad for two o'clock in the morning.

'What a surprise,' said the smooth-as-silk apparition, with soft-as-velvet sarcasm.

Wander squinted incredulously into the bright shaft of light that flooded into the corridor. 'Sabine?' he said hesitantly.

'I think you must have come to the wrong door,' she said, turning gracefully so that the light fell on her face, not to mention the well-moulded contours of her body.

It was Sabine – he recognized her.

She was wearing a housecoat of luminous Mediterranean blue. The material might have been glued to her body, a body he had known pretty well at one time. The memory of it sprang painfully to life, even though ten years had passed.

'I never thought I'd see you again,' he said.

'If you're thinking about the old days, forget it,' she said dismissively. Her big eyes gave him a gentle but confident stare, like the eyes of a sacred cow which knows it is safe from slaughter. 'What are you doing here?'

'I thought a girl called Eva Morgenrot lived here,' he said.

'She does.' Sabine's mouth barely moved. Her eyes had narrowed slightly as if she were examining him through a microscope. 'She isn't at home, though.'

'That would be a physical impossibility.' Wander eyed her bosom as he spoke. Like a lot else about her, this seemed to have become considerably more majestic. 'Eva Morgenrot is flat out on my bed precisely one floor below this. Apartment 204.'

'Bugger!' he heard her say.

She said it without a trace of emotion on her orchid-like face, much as she would have said 'hello' or 'sorry' or even 'darling'. She used the same tone of voice for every situation, he seemed to remember, and a single tone of voice was quite enough for her.

'How did it happen?' she asked.

'Somebody confused the numbers, I imagine,' he prompted her instinctively.

Sabine nodded, but not at him. She no longer even looked at him, as if to demonstrate that his existence was of no further interest to her. He accepted the implication. Their time together, a blissfully brief interlude, had ended miserably for him. He felt no desire to resurrect the past.

Sabine – who now went by the name of Wassermann-Westen and was entitled to call herself Baroness, not that he knew that yet – called over her shoulder: 'She's one floor down, Klaus.'

Klaus, who materialized a moment later, was Klaus Barranski, a medical practitioner whose professional success was plain to the nose as well as the eye. He smelled from half a room away of the finest French scent and was at once recognizable as a conscientious product of the male fashion magazine. His artistically shaped silver hair gleamed softly and his green eyes resembled those of a cat with inside information about what happened to the canary.

'How gratifying,' Barranski said in well-oiled tones, 'how gratifying to have found Eva at last.' He had the ideal voice for a Sunday religious broadcast, a voice which combined the unctuousness of a professional church-goer with the blandness of a lonely-hearts columnist. 'We were beginning to get a little worried about Eva. Where is she?'

'Lying on my bed, out like a light.'

Sabine von Wassermann-Westen glanced at Wander briefly, then did her best to ignore him as convincingly as possible.

Dr Barranski lost none of his enamelled urbanity. 'Nothing seriously wrong with her, I trust?'

'Why, what were you expecting?' Wander asked.

'A little information, nothing more.'

Barranski seemed to regard anyone who came his way as a potential patient. This generally induced a state of diffidence because the person so regarded felt fee-conscious. Barranski was not cheap.

'Yes,' he said encouragingly, 'information, and as detailed as possible, if you don't mind.'

'Very well. I found Fräulein Morgenrot lying in the passage just outside my door, like an unsolicited gift. She was pretty badly knocked about so I carried her into my apartment.'

'Did she say anything?'

'What, for instance?'

'So, she didn't say anything.' Dr Barranski made this statement with no outward sign of reassurance. He was a man who seemed equal to any problem that might arise. He gave Sabine a masterful nod and turned back to Wander.

'Kindly take me to her.'

'With pleasure,' said Wander, and led the way.

*

The two doctors eyed each other like dogs vying for the same bone. Barranski had the exotic elegance of a saluki whereas Dr Bergner of the casualty department bristled with pinscher-like irritability.

Wander watched them with mounting interest. 'Please don't restrain yourselves on my account,' he urged them. 'Make yourselves at home.'

'This,' growled Bergner, 'is my case.'

'No one would deny your right to such an opinion, Doctor,' Barranski intoned earnestly and with an air of sweet reason which nothing, apparently, could dim. 'On the other hand, permit me to draw your attention to the fact that this young woman, Fräulein Eva Morgenrot, is one of my regular patients.'

'But not now,' Bergner insisted. 'Not under present circumstances.'

Wander sat down in the far corner of the room and leaned back in his arm-chair to command the best possible view of the proceedings. He gestured through the doorway at Eva Morgenrot, who was still lying motionless on the bed.

'In Bergner's opinion,' he contributed, 'the girl is a victim of foul play.'

'I merely stated my findings,' Bergner said doggedly. 'They permit of only one interpretation.'

'Far be it from me to dispute that, my dear sir. I am simply taking the liberty of expressing certain misgivings.'

The 'my dear sir' sounded courteous in the extreme but was uttered in the tones of a borough engineer addressing a dustman. 'Your diagnosis is correct, I'm sure. Except, of course, that you cannot be conversant with certain facts of which I, as this young woman's personal physician, have long been aware.'

Barranski strode into the bedroom. He bent over Eva Morgenrot, felt her forehead and pulse, pulled her eyelids back, and listened to her heart – all with the swift, deft movements of a switchboard operator. It took only a couple of minutes.

'Very well,' he said, 'I shall now take charge of my patient.'

'In other words, Doctor,' Wander called to Bergner of the casualty department, 'you're redundant.'

'Would you kindly keep out of this?' Barranski requested. He smiled at Bergner, reached into his breast pocket, and produced a visiting card. 'I trust I'm safe in assuming that my name is not wholly unfamiliar to you.'

'It's only too familiar,' growled the younger doctor. He glanced across at Wander as if seeking help, but Wander was examining his finger-nails.

'In that case, Doctor,' said Barranski, 'kindly arrange for

14

Fräulein Morgenrot to be conveyed to her apartment on the floor above.'

Bergner, who seemed to have shrunk two sizes, said: 'She should be in hospital.'

'That may be your opinion, my dear sir.' Barranski's benevolence verged on Christian charity now. 'However, you have very rightly left the decision to the patient's personal physician. I'm sure you would not wish to compel me to get in touch with your superiors. I should regret that exceedingly, from your point of view.'

Dr Bergner hesitated for a moment. Then, hearing sounds in the corridor, he went out and instructed his ambulance men to carry Eva Morgenrot to the floor above. Dr Barranski expressed his thanks in courteous, measured tones and disappeared.

'I need a drink.' Bergner's gaze drifted past Wander to the brandy bottle, which now seemed to claim his exclusive attention. 'May I change my mind?'

'Not yet,' Wander said, leaning back in his chair. 'I want you sober for the time being.'

'God knows what you must think of me.' Bergner perched wearily on the bed where Eva Morgenrot had been lying. 'Do I look as gutless as I feel?'

'Hard for me to tell,' Wander said. 'Who is this man Barranski?'

'A cunning bastard with a big reputation. The two things seem to go hand in hand.'

'I gather you'd like to dent his reputation but he's too well entrenched. Barranski spends five times your salary on silk shirts, I imagine. He's out of your class.'

'You're right,' Bergner said. 'I don't have the fire-power to shoot him down.'

'But it doesn't stop you blasting off occasionally?'

The doctor shook his head. Then he stood up, squared his

shoulders, and walked to the door. 'Anyone who wants to get anywhere in this place has to be durable. Are you?'

*

Somebody rang the doorbell of Wander's apartment – gently, so that it emitted a feline purr. He opened the door and found Sabine von Wassermann-Westen standing there.

'It's me,' she said, and walked into the room with an air of ownership. She brushed past him, sat down in an arm-chair, and said casually: 'I imagine there are still a few explanations needed.'

Sabine, who had now swathed herself in a housecoat of Japanese silk, was a shimmering study in sea-green. At three o'clock in the morning she looked as if she had just emerged from a beauty parlour.

'We don't have to talk,' Wander said. 'Least of all about the old days. They're gone for good – and forgotten.'

'Are they really?' she said softly. She got up, walked straight into the bedroom and sat down on the bed. Then she lay back. Something like languid curiosity gleamed in her velvety eyes. 'Doesn't that jog your memory?'

Wander shrugged. 'Is it meant to?'

'No,' she said abruptly, sitting up. 'We don't know each other and we never met before. And if we do bump into each other again here or elsewhere – which may be hard to avoid in Bonn – we'll be setting eyes on each other for the first time. All right?'

Wander nodded. 'All right. Those few months in Munich don't count.'

'They never happened.'

'Even better.'

'I'm not making the suggestion only for my sake. You'll find that out soon enough.'

'I've no intention of dining out on our murky past.'

16

'I have to be able to count on that – absolutely,' Sabine said. 'It's a deal, then. If either of us goes back on it the consequences could be very unpleasant. Have I made myself clear?'

'Only too clear. If that was meant to be a threat, save it. I'm allergic to threats.'

'All right,' Sabine said soothingly. 'I won't raise the subject again unless I have to. Is that good enough?'

He nodded. 'So much for point one. There's something else I'd like to know, if you don't mind.'

'The latest bulletin on your lady visitor, you mean?'

'Is she still alive?'

Sabine gave a mirthless laugh. 'Obviously you still haven't learnt how much a woman can take before she calls it a day.'

'Why don't you enlighten me?'

Her lashes fluttered like thick fringed curtains. She said, slowly and distinctly, as if she were dictating: 'Eva Morgenrot is a friend of mine – in fact I've more or less taken her under my wing – but she's a pretty complex character for a girl of twenty. Not only has she developed a taste for drink recently, but she isn't too particular about the company she keeps. If I were you I'd stop worrying about her.'

'But whose doorstep will she end up on next time? And why should anyone beat up a girl like her – who'd do such a thing?'

'She had an accident,' Sabine said firmly. 'You'll have to be satisfied with that.'

'But I'm not,' Wander said. 'Another thing. I find it pretty weird that a doctor should have been expecting the girl to be delivered to the door – especially a doctor like Barranski.'

'This conversation is beginning to bore me,' Sabine said. 'We've already said all there is to say, so let's leave it at that. I'm trying to give you some friendly advice.'

'And I refuse to accept it,' retorted Wander. 'I'm a suspicious man – I've become one, rather. It all started about ten years go. Nobody could have been blamed for regarding me as an easy-going fool in those days. Now, quite a few people think I'm a cross between Machiavelli and Cesare Borgia.'

'You don't say.'

'Know what I've been doing lately? Indulging in a sort of intellectual striptease act. I produce journalistic and literary material in almost any style, weight and length required – gay, satirical, ultra-clinical, dramatic. I've turned into a sort of automatic typewriter, and now I've landed here. The reason I came . . .'

'You're drunk.' Sabine spoke like a gas board official reading a meter. 'Never mind, the important thing is to sleep it off. Sleep – that's what you need. Badly, from the sound of you.'

•

Twelve hours later Karl Wander stood looking down at the seated figure of a big man with the build of a St Bernard.

'Remember me, Sandman?'

The big man smiled faintly. 'Your type's hard to forget. I must say, though, I'm a little surprised you're still around. What can I do for you?'

'Just supply me with some information.'

Peter Sandman was, and had been for the past twelve years, German representative of USP, an influential American press agency. His job required him to be based in the Bonn area, but he chose to live in the neighbouring town of Bad Godesberg. 'The air isn't much better,' he used to say, 'but the horizon's a couple of feet wider. You can at least pretend you're out of the rat-race. It's one of the most harmless kinds of self-deception people indulge in in these parts.'

'What brings someone like you here?' he asked.

'A job,' Wander replied evasively. 'One of a number of jobs.'

Peter Sandman leaned back in his chair, looking expectant. 'You've whetted my curiosity. Everything I remember about you tells me you're a dyed-in-the-wool idealist, or used to be. Bonn's no place for professional trouble-makers.'

Wander smiled. 'I'm older than I was,' he said.

'Sure – you must be forty-three or four by now. We're all creeping up on old age.' Peter Sandman grinned back at him. 'I'm about ten years older too, which makes me a candidate for the bone-orchard. I don't understand the world any more, which ought to make me happy. Except that it doesn't. There's too much that stinks round here, and I haven't lost my sense of smell.'

'Perhaps you're too close to your sources of information,' Wander suggested. 'Anyway, you don't look as if you're dying of boredom.'

'I still get a kick out of my work – what else is there? Are you planning to join the Bonn circus?'

'Is that an offer?'

Sandman spread his arms wide in a gesture that looked warmly inviting but was pure habit. 'I'm still in debt to you. You gave me a lot of interesting material that time, ten years back.'

'Material you didn't use.'

'I couldn't, not at that stage. Try and understand me and my country's position, Wander. No nation can afford to tell a prospective ally that its army is a king-size pigsty.'

'Even when it can be proved?'

'Not even then. Added to that, we Americans aren't entirely blameless in the matter of rearmament. You have to think twice before branding our policy a serious miscalculation.'

'Very well, Sandman, keep thinking – I've no intention of disturbing you. I'm not interested in that sort of thing any longer. It's over and done with – finished.'

'Why are you here, then?'

'I don't know yet myself, exactly. All I know for certain is that I badly needed a change and that I was offered a job here.

However, before I start work I'm filling in time by looking into a couple of things I've stumbled on, so to speak.'

'What sort of things?'

'Do you know someone called Sabine von Wassermann-Westen?'

'Listen to him!' the American exclaimed with evident amusement. 'What made you pick that little number? She's way out of your league, Wander!'

'I'm not interested in her as a person – she's more an object of study. What do you know about her?'

'Plenty, but nothing very tangible.' Peter Sandman produced a black notebook from his breast pocket and began to thumb through it. It did not take him long to find what he was looking for. 'Sabine von Wassermann-Westen,' he read, 'ostensibly twenty-seven but probably just over thirty . . .'

'She's twenty-nine,' Wander amended.

Sandman's grey eyes flickered at Wander for a moment before returning to the notebook. 'Originally plain Sabine Wassermann, comes from South Germany, probably Passau, lived several years in Munich, worked in women's fashions, married a Baron von Westen in 1963 and was rapidly and profitably widowed by an accident shortly after the wedding. The Baroness surfaced in the Bonn area three or four years ago. She owns a house in Cologne and an apartment in Bonn.'

'Yes, in Koblenzer Strasse.'

'How do you know?'

'I'm living there too, exactly one floor below.'

'Good,' Sandman said, 'that gives me your address too – or would you prefer me to forget it?'

'I'd appreciate it if we could keep in touch.'

'Contact duly established.' The American smiled at his visitor, this time with an unmistakable air of interest. 'I always enjoy our talks, Wander. Surprises seem to dog your footsteps, and that's an appealing characteristic. But back to your baroness – she ranks relatively high on the local social ladder. You'll soon find out what that means – the theory of social relativity is easier to grasp in Bonn than anywhere else in the world. Anyway, the Baroness is a top-notch lobbyist with a brilliant gift for cultivating ministerial and ambassadorial contacts. She requires careful handling.'

'What about a doctor called Klaus Barranski? Do you know him too?'

Peter Sandman raised his rectangular head an inch or two and regarded Wander with surprise. 'How long did you say you've been here?'

'Since yesterday – I arrived late afternoon.'

'Incredible,' the American observed drily. 'Barranski has a practice in Cologne. He's a society doctor with a batch of important connections, but he also possesses considerable medical skill. His discretion is a byword, and you can bet people take advantage of it. It doesn't matter whether it's an ambassador or a society woman who's contracted an embarrassing disease or a cabinet minister suffering from alcoholic poisoning – Dr Barranski provides swift, effective and confidential treatment. He's reputed to be a millionaire.'

'Know anyone called Eva Morgenrot?'

Sandman pondered the question. 'Should I? Morgenrot . . . Is she young?'

'About twenty. Slim, blonde. Not unattractive in normal circumstances, I'd imagine.'

'I don't have a file on her.' Sandman scribbled the name Eva Morgenrot on a slip of paper. 'As soon as I find anything out about her I'll let you know – be glad to. Any objection to my consulting Jerome? He might have some inside information.'

'Who's Jerome?'

'The man they call "the Wise Monkey of Bonn" – he sees all, hears all, but only says what he thinks prudent. He's one of the luminaries of the US foreign intelligence service, Central

European area – I have the doubtful privilege of being acquainted with him. So, any objection to my calling him in?'

'All I want is some information.'

'Fine. Would you join me for lunch tomorrow, at the expense of the American tax-payer?'

'My first meeting with my new boss is scheduled for tomorrow midday, but we could certainly celebrate tomorrow evening. Just what, I don't know yet.'

'It's a date,' said Sandman. He reached for the slip of paper on which he had scribbled the name Eva Morgenrot and studied it meditatively. Then he flipped a switch on his intercom and said: 'I need all available material on Minister Feldmann, and the same goes for Party Secretary Krug. First, though, get me Mr Jerome.'

INTERIM REPORT No. 1

BY THE MAN KNOWN AS JEROME

on preliminaries which should be greeted with misgiving and preconceived ideas which should be guarded against.

Peter Sandman first 'phoned me on the subject one Saturday late this fall. It was an ideal moment, because Bonn is denuded of politicians almost every week-end.

On week-ends they head for home, or at least for the flesh-pots of Cologne, Frankfurt and Düsseldorf. You can't begrudge them a little relaxation. The fifty or sixty registered prostitutes in Bonn and the immediate vicinity are mediocre at best, and cater solely to the local market.

The grand old architect of the Federal Republic had created an atmosphere which led, among other things, to a certain sexual sterility – in other words, to the sort of rule which provokes exceptions. A number of enterprising foreign embassies were doing their best to counter this, but other interested parties were also making a determined effort to combat the week-end blues of the stay-behinds. This sometimes led to indulgence in certain all too human weaknesses.

In our job we occasionally exploit these weaknesses. By the time Sandman called me that Saturday, however, all our nets had been cast and my men were already assigned to selected targets. It was too early to expect any results, so I didn't hesitate to devote myself to Sandman. Not even I could predict, at that stage, what the outcome would be.

There's nothing much to report on the subject of Peter Sandman. He presumably believed – in all seriousness, on occasion – that he was helping to represent his country's interests in the West German capital. One product of this belief was a sort of sloppy cynicism, but it's quite conceivable that he ultimately got a kick out of it. In the present instance, however, this tendency showed signs of developing into a not entirely harmless craving for amusement.

On that tedious autumn day Sandman mentioned various names to me. The first was Karl Wander. Documentation on Wander was easy to come up with. Nearly ten years earlier he had been the occasion of an official request to us for assistance by the Federal German Constitutional Protection Office. The authorities were deeply suspicious of Wander. With justification, because no incriminating evidence could be brought against him.

Karl Wander was a so-called idealist – always a suspicious feature because the reactions of such people do not lend themselves to prediction or manipulation. Wander regarded the West German army, while he was still serving in it, as a potential breeding-ground for all that was best and most democratic in the new Germany. Needless to say, he was in for a big disappointment.

The file on Wander had never been closed – and quite rightly so, as it soon turned out. He had resigned from the West

German army some ten years before, with a barrage of protests which fell largely on deaf ears. After that he worked, sometimes as a military correspondent but also in other fields, literary included, for a number of newspapers which loudly disclaimed all Party allegiance. But he soon became too much even for them, and went quickly downhill. He openly sympathized with would-be recognizers of East Germany, Peaceniks, militant students, radicals. A confirmed world-reformer, Wander, and therefore to be handled with extreme care.

The next name mentioned by Peter Sandman was Konstantin Krug. This was remarkable, in the context. There could hardly have been a greater contrast. Wander clearly operated with no thought of profit – in fact he accepted the possibility of loss – where Krug, an influential Party Secretary, did business wherever and whenever a business opportunity presented itself.

I couldn't help wondering what these two men had in common.

One thing I already knew, at least. Krug was sailing, apparently of his own free will, in the wake of Feldman, the cabinet minister to whom he owed his present position. Favours tend to obligate a man as well as pay him, almost invariably but not inevitably.

No, not inevitably, because the market price of principles, political convictions and Party loyalty is subject to constant fluctuation, and bids can always be raised. But where did Karl Wander come in?

I should have known that Germany, and by implication the Federal Republic, is a land of boundless possibilities. Even this fact can be exploited if you grasp it quickly enough.

Chapter 2

'I received a sort of summons,' Wander told the desk sergeant at Precinct Headquarters No. 3. The shabby citadel of officialdom in which he found himself was occupied predominantly by filing cabinets. A smell of dust and male sweat pervaded the room.

The sergeant ran his eye over the slip of paper Wander laid in front of him. Then he wagged his doughnut-shaped head reprovingly. 'This isn't a summons,' he amended. 'This is just a request.'

'A request for what? What do you want?'

'Me? Nothing.' The desk sergeant seemed to be hard put to it not to yawn in Wander's face. 'It's a request for information, I expect, but that isn't my pigeon. You'd better wait.'

'What for?'

'For the man whose responsibility it is.'

It took half an hour for the responsible party to appear. He turned out to be a detective chief inspector named Kohl, elephantine of build and stolid of demeanour. His small bright eyes were deeply embedded in the fleshy contours of a bloated face.

'Just the man we've been waiting for,' Kohl said.

'I'm not here by choice. If it's not that important, I'll be only too happy to leave.'

'That would just suit your book, wouldn't it?' Chief Inspector Kohl eyed Wander like a cattle-dealer appraising beef on the hoof. 'Come with me.'

He led Wander into a neighbouring room, which proved to

be a sort of interrogation cell. Traditional German prison décor: penetratingly bleak, harsh grey paintwork, claustrophobically cramped, its only window barred and grimy.

Kohl deposited his bulk on the only available chair, unfolded several sheets of closely typewritten paper, and began to read them with apparent concentration. Then he stared closely at the man standing in front of him, and said: 'You don't look anything like that.'

'How would you like me to look?' Wander inquired obligingly.

'Don't try to be funny. Humour's at a premium in my profession – it gets worn out too quickly.'

'What a shame. Maybe you ought to change your job.'

'You really are a humorist, aren't you?' The policeman gave an indignant snort. 'Listen, only yesterday someone else was standing just where you are – another of the verbal diarrhœa brigade. After an hour he was wringing his hands and begging for sympathy and understanding. Admittedly, he'd just lost his ever-loving mother.'

'Murdered her, I suppose?'

'With a hammer.'

'I lost my mother years ago and I don't own a hammer, if it's any comfort to you. However, I presume that what you're hinting at is my possible involvement in an assault on a person of the female sex – or whatever the jargon is.'

Kohl gave another snort. 'You're not only a humorist, you've got an inflated sense of your own importance. According to the unanimous testimony of several witnesses, you weren't implicated – that much we've established.'

'Then I really don't know what you want me for.'

Chief Inspector Kohl busied himself with his papers once more, then asked, as though reading aloud: 'Are you under the impression that you've brought charges against someone?'

'Should I be?' Wander leaned forward slightly as if to hear

better. 'Was that a hint, or are you simply asking for information?'

'I'm dog-tired, if you want to know.' The policeman's alert little eyes narrowed. 'I spend eight to twelve hours a day mixing with all kinds of trash.'

'Does that include me?'

'Anybody can be trash.'

'Policemen too?'

'Of course,' Kohl conceded. His tone was as impersonal as a newsreader's. 'At the moment I almost feel like trash myself. I ought to button your lip for you.'

'Why not try? I'm no Tarzan and you look pretty robust for your age. What's to stop you from giving vent to your aggressions?'

'I'm due for retirement in five years' time,' said the chief inspector. 'Till then I have to keep myself in check. It comes hard sometimes, particularly in cases like yours, but I'm damned if I'm going to have a punch-up with a rat who's on friendly terms with a cabinet minister. I can't afford to.'

'What did you say?' Wander couldn't have been more astonished if he had heard a TV commercial assuring him that a certain detergent was the worst on the market. 'I don't know any cabinet minister personally, and besides, what's the connection? Who's the great man supposed to be, anyway?'

'You don't think I'm going to name names, do you? It isn't that I'm a coward, Wander. I just don't propose to make a complete idiot of myself, that's all.'

'Perhaps we can do something about this,' Wander said cautiously, ' – together. At the moment, I'm the one who's feeling like an idiot, and it isn't a very pleasant sensation.'

Chief Inspector Kohl's attention now seemed to be focused exclusively on his papers. 'So I've addressed the following question to you: have you preferred criminal charges? Your answer is: no. Am I right?'

'Why don't you come clean and tell me exactly what you're driving at?'

'I repeat: have you preferred criminal charges? No. Are you now preferring charges – yes or no? All right, no. And now make yourself scarce, Wander, before I lose my last shred of self-control and leave my boot up your arse, and, indirectly, up the ministerial arse where you're so cosily installed.'

'Anything else?'

'Yes. If it's any consolation to you, and if it wasn't a physical impossibility, I'd like to spit in my own eye.'

*

'What is it this time?' demanded Dr Bergner, throwing up his arms defensively at the sight of his visitor. 'Haven't you done enough?'

'I'm gradually coming to that conclusion,' Wander said. 'Perhaps you can explain why.'

Dr Bergner worked in the casualty department of his hospital. He had to cope, almost daily, with a continuous stream of emergency cases. At present he was examining a purple-faced child who was wheezing and vomiting. 'X-ray department,' he decreed.

'Was it you who encouraged the CID to lean on me?' Wander asked.

The doctor subjected his visitor to a diagnostic stare but did not appear to reach any satisfactory conclusion. Uneasily, he asked a colleague to stand in for him. 'For about ten minutes – that should give me time enough to deal with this one.'

So saying, Bergner drew his visitor into a neighbouring room, where piles of dirty linen towered ceilingward. A stupefying smell of putrefaction hung in the air.

Wander wrenched the window open and stood there, inhaling deeply. 'I suppose you didn't get anywhere with your accident

28

report, so you chanced an anonymous 'phone call to the police. Naming me.'

Dr Bergner dismissed this with a feeble wave of the hand. 'You obviously assume that I'm a frustrated do-gooder – a fanatical upholder of the cause of justice.'

'It seemed like that last night.'

'Perhaps,' Bergner admitted. He looked even wearier than he had then. 'Even I have an occasional attack of courage – or temerity, I don't know which, exactly, but it never lasts long. Besides, the attacks are getting rarer as time goes by.'

'Are you absolutely positive it wasn't you who set the CID on me?'

'They probably went to the right address, but it wasn't me who sent them.' Bergner was still standing beside the mountain of soiled linen. He was no stranger to the scent of putrefaction. 'What did they want?'

'A mere bagatelle. One of them asked me if I had knowingly preferred charges against anyone. What he wanted to hear was the word no, and that's what he thought he heard. I never got a chance to enlighten him.'

'I know the form. Somebody's covering himself – it's routine procedure.'

'Dr Barranski?'

'You said it – I didn't. However, he's now in possession of a neat official loophole – thanks to your friendly co-operation, Herr Wander. He can now prove that there were no grounds for a criminal charge. That's the way these things are done.'

'Do they happen often?'

'Depends what you call often. With most doctors never, with a few sometimes, with a few others repeatedly. Cases of suicide or attempted suicide are subject to automatic police investigation, as you probably know. Accidents too, at least those involving death or serious injury. Also, any incident which gives rise to suspicions of foul play. If anything of that sort comes to the notice of a doctor he must report it – or cover himself. That sort of jiggery-pokery also comes into the art of medicine these days.'

'And you and your colleagues take it lying down?' Wander demanded angrily.

'Oh, we're indignant when we hear about it, of course – outraged even, sometimes. But we've all got families and jobs and what we choose to call careers and a horde of patients who rely on us. That adds up to a lot of distractions.'

'Don't start indulging in self-pity, Doctor. Instead, give some more thought to the Eva Morgenrot case and whether there's anything to be done about it.'

'Not from my point of view.'

'Then can you at least quote me any other similar cases? Only incontrovertible cases, though – the sort that would stand up in court.'

'You'll be lucky.' Dr Bergner slammed the window shut and flung open the door. 'I really am a doctor, strange as it may seem. If you're contemplating suicide, as you seem to be, don't expect me to help you.'

*

'Open up!' Karl Wander called through the closed door marked 304. 'I'd like to see what you look like under semi-normal conditions, if that's possible.'

'Who is it?'

'Your good Samaritan.'

'The man from downstairs?'

'Yes. Come to pay a courtesy call.'

The door of Apartment 304 opened. Wander saw a much-creased lilac silk housecoat and a tangle of bright blonde hair. Framed by the latter, and doing its best to smile, was the face of a wax doll.

'I'm not really supposed to see anyone.'

'Whose orders?' he asked.

Eva Morgenrot had a high-pitched childish voice. She sounded as if she had been drilled in the art of dumb blondery. 'I pictured you quite differently.'

'And I expected more of a hospital case,' Wander replied. 'You must be tougher than you look.'

'I don't feel a hundred per cent recovered yet,' she assured him with a pout.

'Then get back to bed again.'

Wander walked in, brushing her gently aside, and closed the door. He made for the bedroom without giving her another glance and pointed to the bed, which was turned down. 'If you need another doctor, don't count on me to get you one.'

Eva followed like an obedient child. She lay down with her big eyes fixed on him, pulled the covers over her legs, and stared at him expectantly. 'Do you find me attractive?'

'No,' he said.

'Why did you come, then?'

'To get a closer look at you. I wanted to find out why I'm wasting my time here. How do you feel?'

'Bruised all over,' she said, and closed her eyes. 'Want to climb in beside me?'

'Why should I?'

'Because I like you – isn't that enough?'

'Not for me,' Wander said, almost sternly, bending over her. 'Why were you beaten up?' he demanded. 'Who did it?'

Eva Morgenrot lay there without moving. He waited, not showing any undue impatience, for what seemed like minutes. Eventually Eva raised her moist, shining blue eyes and said: 'Is it so important?'

'I can't judge how important it is until you tell me, but I want to know.'

'It's all so terribly complicated,' she replied slowly. 'Your name's Wander, isn't it? What do your friends call you?'

'Karl, but stick to the point.'

'Then I'll call you Charlie – may I?'

'Suit yourself. If you really want to put me in a good mood, all you have to do is tell me as much as possible about yourself. And your present circle of friends.'

'There really isn't much to tell, Charlie.' Eva stretched seductively. 'I was just born unlucky, somehow – I mean, I'd like to live the way I want and have fun, but I can't. Or maybe it would be more accurate to say, people won't let me.'

'Stop hedging. Who is "people"?'

'Everyone. I'm afraid you'd find it terribly hard to understand – I can hardly understand it myself. I make a lot of mistakes, there's no denying that. But not in your case, Charlie. I can feel it.'

'No more flattery, Eva. It won't work with me.' Wander eyed her as if she were a puppy who wanted to play with him after making a mess on the carpet. 'Don't tell me – you came from a poor but respectable family, felt the urge to better yourself, innocently fell in with bad company and were unscrupulously exploited . . .'

'Stop it!' Eva Morgenrot's voice had suddenly gained strength. She sat up. 'I'm not as dumb as all that!'

'Glad to hear it. Go on.'

'I never knew my mother,' she continued quickly, 'but the man who calls himself my father can lay hands on more money than you'll spend in a lifetime. I can afford to have my fling, and that's what I'm doing. Apart from that, I'm engaged. And as for getting mixed up with the wrong set, I'm in with all the best people here.'

'Sabine Wassermann, among others?'

'What's wrong with that? Sabine knows everybody who's worth knowing.'

'In Bonn, you mean?'

'You don't like her, do you?' Eva gave him a confiding smile.

'Isn't she your type? Do you find me more attractive, or are you just scared?'

'I'm certainly not scared of you.'

'Good, Charlie. Then what are you scared of? Are you afraid I might really tell you who beat me up until I passed out? Would you really like me to tell you?'

He hesitated for a moment and then said decisively: 'Yes, do that.'

Eva laughed. It was a shrill piping sound but not particularly loud. 'I wouldn't do it to you, Charlie – not yet. We hardly know each other, after all, and I'd like to get to know you better. Much better.'

'You're way ahead of me,' Wander said from the doorway. 'God damn it, why should I worry about other people's troubles?'

'You'll be back,' Eva Morgenrot said confidently. She snuggled down in bed. 'I don't know why, but you'll be back. And next time I'll be able to tell myself it's all because of me.'

'Oh, go to hell, girl – if you're not there already.'

*

'Well, Herr Wander, how's it going?' asked a sturdy, cheerful voice. It belonged to a man whose leather coat glinted softly in the light of the street lamps. 'Feeling more at home now?'

Karl Wander had dined in leisurely fashion at a restaurant near the Friedensplatz – dined and wined. Rhine wine, naturally. Now, feeling tired, he was strolling past the cathedral towards Koblenzer Strasse. But the leather-coated man barred his path.

'Don't you recognize me?' asked the man. 'It's Sobottke, your chauffeur. I fetched you from the airport yesterday and drove you to your flat. Don't you remember?'

'I don't forget faces like yours,' Wander said. 'You ought to have stood where I could see you properly.'

'Well, here I am,' Sobottke said, coming closer. 'Glad to see me?'

'Why should I be?' Wander asked cautiously.

'Well, maybe I can put something your way.' Sobottke's wooden features almost splintered with the effort of smiling. 'How about a little trip to Cologne? The car's just round the corner, so we can be there in half an hour. I know some pretty good addresses – you'll be bound to find something you like. Better and safer than here, anyway. How about it?'

'Aren't you taking a bit too much for granted?'

'Not at all,' Sobottke assured him heartily. 'Herr Krug – the man you've come to see – told me to take care of you. Look after our guest, Sobottke – that's what he told me. Entertain him, money's no object and the car's at your disposal. Have yourselves a couple of hours' fun before we get down to business, he said. That's Herr Krug for you – generous to a fault as long as you do right by him.'

'I don't know whether I'll qualify for Herr Krug's generosity, but I'll find out soon enough. Feel like a quick one?'

'Two or three if you like, Herr Wander!' Sobottke cried joyfully. 'All on Herr Krug, too – he'll foot the bill.'

They picked an inn near the Kaiserplatz, where they turned out to be the only customers. A full hour before midnight, Bonn seemed to be sunk in slumber. They stood at the bar and ordered wine, which was served in half-filled tubular glasses.

'Why were you spying on me?' demanded Wander.

'What do you mean, spying?' Sobottke conveyed injured innocence. 'I happened to be passing and I thought you might appreciate a little entertainment. It was a good opportunity, and just what Herr Krug had in mind. He's one of the best, Herr Krug – you'll soon find that out for yourself.'

'What's the idea, though? Trying to sidetrack me?'

'You've got it all wrong, Herr Wander,' Sobottke replied ingratiatingly. He must have been about forty, Wander thought, and looked like an ex-ski instructor. Staunch, straightforward masculinity. 'All I'm concerned with is providing you with a little of the sort of entertainment you won't find here in Bonn. Almost everything in this place is police-registered and it pays to remember that.'

'What are you driving at?' Wander asked.

'Nothing special,' Sobottke replied hastily. 'All I mean is, you're a man and men have certain requirements. Well, you can satisfy them, but not round here. You've no idea the trouble a man can get into in Bonn, so better leave well alone. After all, you're here in search of a job.'

'Tell me,' Wander said thoughtfully. 'You're pretty useful with your fists, aren't you?'

'Some people might put it that way,' Sobottke replied, grinning.

'You'd beat up anyone who got across you, wouldn't you?'

'Like a shot, if necessary.'

'Girls included?'

'That depends. I'm a peaceful type on the whole, but women can behave worse than men, sometimes.' Sobottke grinned again, with relish. 'For instance, I was acting as bodyguard to Herr Krug's minister recently, and some stupid little bitch of a demonstrator kept on shouting him down. Well, it was almost the same as trying to assassinate him, wasn't it?'

'And you beat her up?'

'In a way. There's such a thing as obligations, and obligations have to be taken seriously. But I don't need to tell you that. After all, why else would you be here, except to do your duty?'

'To get a good night's sleep, for one thing. Don't keep me from my bed any longer. I don't care what your reasons are – I don't want to think about them.'

'Let's hope you don't regret it!' Sobottke called after Wander's retreating figure.

35

Wander paused in the bar-room doorway for a moment and said, almost flippantly: 'How can I regret something I don't know about?'

*

'I've been expecting you.' A young man stood blocking the second-floor corridor, immediately outside Apartment 204. 'You are Karl Wander, I suppose?'

'What do you want?'

'If you are Karl Wander, you're a dirty bastard.'

'You could be right,' Wander rejoined. 'I've felt like a bastard myself lately, but there's no reason to broadcast it at the top of your voice, at midnight. After all, why should everyone in the building hear what you suspect?' Wander looked into a tanned face topped by wavy brown hair. The young man's mouth was grim but his eyes were temporarily invisible because he had lowered his head like a ram about to charge.

'I could make mincemeat out of you if I wanted to,' announced the young man.

'Don't be too hasty,' Wander said. He felt exhausted now, and was hungry for sleep. 'Why not think it over and come back tomorrow? – If you must,' he added. He opened the door of his apartment.

The boy stormed past him into the room and braked sharply to a halt. Then he swung round and stood there waiting, legs splayed and crouching slightly. As soon as Wander was inside he kicked the door shut with his heel.

'You're almost in the sugar-daddy class,' Wander's visitor sneered. 'I must have a good twenty years on you.'

'Quite possibly.' Wander did his best to look amused. 'So what?'

'You look overweight to me,' the young man pursued. 'Pretty pasty-faced, too.' He spoke with mounting contempt. 'Take a look at me!'

'I have – not a very enjoyable sight, either. You might have spared me.'

'Training, that's what does it. I'm a first-class boxer and karate expert.'

'Sounds like a pretty tough schedule. Pity you didn't take time off to learn a few manners while you were about it.'

'I could lay you out in three seconds flat.'

'Why should you?'

'My name's Morgenrot, that's why,' announced the human billy-goat. He looked as if he were measuring the distance between them in readiness for an attack. 'Does that mean anything to you?'

'It certainly does,' Wander replied. The word 'unfortunately' hung unspoken in the air. He really did feel drained of energy now – helpless and a prey to unknown dangers. 'All right, so your name's Morgenrot. What am I supposed to do about it?'

'Morgenrot,' the sun-tanned young man explained in a harsh voice, 'is also the name of my sister, whom you know. Her first name is Eva. Mine is Martin. What have you got to say now?'

'Did Eva – your sister – send you?'

'You tried to get your filthy hands on her!' declared Martin Morgenrot. Hatred flared up in his eyes. 'Even though you knew she was engaged. You hurled yourself on her as if she was a common whore, just to satisfy your own disgusting urges!'

'Did Eva tell you that?'

'I know, that's enough.'

'It certainly is enough.' Karl Wander opened the door to the corridor decisively. 'I might feel sorry for you if I didn't think it would be a complete waste of time.'

'Don't try and talk your way out of it, you swine!'

'Listen to me a moment. I hardly know your sister and I haven't the slightest desire to get to know you. Just at present, my only urge is to get some sleep.'

'Sleep, then, and I hope you never wake up!'

Martin Morgenrot swooped on Karl Wander like a hawk descending on a fieldmouse. He slammed one fist into his jaw and the other into his stomach, then kicked him in the groin. Finally, as Wander was already folding up, he brought the edge of his hand down on his neck.

Wander collapsed. He writhed his way across the polished parquet to his bed, where he passed out. His brain had become a soap-bubble, and the bubble had reached bursting-point.

INTERIM REPORT No. 2

BY THE MAN KNOWN AS JEROME

on human and ultra-human potentialities, having regard to circumstances prevailing in the new Germany.

This affair, which was later classified as 'the Karl Wander Case', did not particularly interest me at first. The West German capital offered far more intriguing combinations of circumstances. Compared with them the advent of Karl Wander appeared completely insignificant – just another source of information washed up by the tide of events. However, I was swayed by Peter Sandman's belief in the newcomer's potential. Sandman may be a secret all-American philanthropist, but he's also a newshound with a keen eye and a nose for trouble.

Whether it was that he simply wanted to supplement his own information or, possibly too, to exploit my natural readiness to help, Sandman introduced some other names. The first was Baroness von Wassermann-Westen. Mentioning her to me was like carrying coals to Newcastle because she cropped up all the time. The Baroness was a lone operator of considerable skill. Her speciality: the establishment of contacts. She set up meetings between prospective business partners and cashed in on their deals – a phenomenon common to all centres of political power.

In order to operate like this a person has to have connections, and Sabine von Wassermann-Westen had plenty. These she acquired by arranging select social gatherings and by playing an active personal part in gatherings of an even more intimate nature. It had not taken her long to grasp the basic principle of her profession, namely, that fat profits entail heavy capital investment. She never economized in the wrong place.

Her network of contacts was not so easy to penetrate – that is, I hadn't taken particular interest in it until then. Preliminary investigations disclosed, however, that her favourite business partner was Krug, the Party Secretary. Also to be assumed was an association, possibly intimate and active, with Minister Feldmann. Another name which emerged in connection with her was Barranski's.

Our file on Dr Klaus Barranski was in constant use because we had been systematically using him for many months. We were well aware that he exploited every opportunity for sharp practice which his profession afforded, but his outstanding skill as a doctor seemed to insure him against the possibility of disaster.

We had presented Barranski with an ultimatum some time before: either he co-operated with us for the benefit of the Western world and the American way of life, or he went to gaol. He co-operated, naturally. This enabled us to keep his card index and medical case histories under continuous observation, install microphones in his consulting-rooms, and call upon him for reports. The latter yielded profound and intimate insights into the private lives of prominent individuals of every description.

We could not, of course, allow a goose which laid golden eggs to be slaughtered, but we covered ourselves as a matter of course. I took the precaution of asking him to submit a report, which he promptly supplied. It contained the following passage:

'. . . *I certify that Fräulein Eva Morgenrot was one of my patients for a period of two months. As far as I can recall, she came to me on the recommendation of Baroness von Wassermann-Westen. The complaints for which I treated her were of a wholly trivial nature. On one occasion the patient displayed some bruises which she had, on her own admission, received while accidentally falling downstairs.'*

And that, I must confess, was the point at which I began to sit up and take notice – not sufficient notice, unfortunately. The name Morgenrot rang a bell with me, though its real implications appeared lost on Sandman, not to mention Karl Wander.

From that moment onward I felt inclined to take a personal interest in the affair.

Chapter 3

The office building, which stood equidistant from Bahnhof-strasse, Kaiserstrasse and the Parliament Building, was one of those concrete-and-glass administrative honeycombs typical of the era and area – a gem of Erhardt baroque. A discreet bustle of activity enveloped Wander as soon as he set foot in the entrance hall.

He had no difficulty in finding the suite of offices to which he had been summoned, but the man who occupied it seemed to have entrenched himself behind a stockade of mahogany veneer. Konstantin Krug, forty-two, Party Secretary, member of the Government majority in Parliament and constitutional lawyer, boasted a reception room and two outer offices through which Wander found himself piloted with an equal measure of ceremony and courtesy.

'Good morning,' he said for the third time, having reached the third room. 'My name is Karl Wander.'

'Impossible!' exclaimed a clear, slightly brittle voice.

'I ought to know,' he protested.

'I'm talking about your appearance. Have you been fighting'?

'Someone went for me,' Wander explained helpfully. 'I apparently got involved in a game without knowing the rules.'

'Herr Krug doesn't like that sort of thing,' the female acolyte announced briskly, pointing to the abrasion on his chin. 'Herr Krug sets store by a smart personal appearance.'

She came over to him, a small, dainty creature. Karl Wander found himself looking into a thin face adorned with owlish glasses and surmounted by a helmet of smooth blonde hair.

41

The hand that touched his chin was cool and firm. 'We must do something about that,' she said.

'Are you planning to recommend a good reliable doctor – Dr Barranski, for instance?'

The unapproachable-looking young woman withdrew her hand and walked over to a cupboard. She showed no sign of having heard Wander's remark, but this was one of her best-tried and most effective routines: anything that did not seem to concern her fell upon deaf ears. On such occasions she turned into a sheet of bullet-proof glass.

'My name is Wiebke,' she said, opening the cupboard.

'Christian name?' inquired Wander.

'Wiebke is good enough,' she replied. 'For you and everyone else round here.'

The young woman called Wiebke deposited a metal case the size of a cash-box on her desk and opened it. It contained a first aid kit. Expertly, she selected various items from it. 'Come here,' she commanded, moistening a pad of cotton wool with some clear, pungent-smelling fluid. She dabbed his grazed chin.

'You can't afford to be sensitive in this place,' Wiebke said, when he winced. 'Not openly, that is.'

'You're not being very gentle.'

'It isn't part of my job to be gentle. It isn't in my nature either, and the sooner you realize that the better.' She swabbed his chin once more and stuck a plaster on it. 'There. You may not look any handsomer, but you do look tidier.'

'You seem to be prepared for any eventuality. Are you often called on to act as an auxiliary nurse?'

Once again, Karl Wander noted that Fräulein Wiebke, young, prim, and stubbornly unapproachable, appeared to be totally impervious to hints. She behaved as if she were alone in the room – as if she preferred to be looked upon as part of the surrounding décor.

'So,' said Wiebke, having put away the first aid kit, 'that

42

would seem to be that. Now may I see your identification, please?'

Wander looked amused. 'Don't you trust me?'

'It isn't part of my job to trust people,' she retorted calmly. 'I merely carry out instructions, and since you're supposed to be going to work for us I have to open a file on you. It's the usual procedure.'

Wander handed her his papers. Wiebke took them and started to look through them. The eyes behind the thick lenses sparkled momentarily as she gave a brief glance first at the photograph and then at Wander. Nobody in the office had ever really seen Wiebke's eyes because the glasses were part of her camouflage. She never removed them on duty.

'I advise you to bone up on Herr Krug while you're waiting.'

'I have already.'

'Then do so again, and be thorough.' She pushed a copy of the German *Who's Who* towards him, open at the appropriate page, together with a *Parliamentary Handbook* and a slim file containing newspaper cuttings. 'Herr Krug doesn't like having to explain himself, least of all to prospective employees.'

'You consider this superficial information sufficient?'

'In your case, certainly. I don't think you need to know any more about Herr Krug than you'll find in there.'

Wiebke did not look at him as she spoke. She continued to busy herself with his papers and jot down particulars. Wander leafed through the material he had been given. He knew it all by heart.

'Tell me,' he said coaxingly, 'what about a little inside information – a few personal hints and suggestions?'

'Not from me – it isn't part of my job.' Wiebke looked thoroughly engrossed in her work. 'If you are taken on, you'll deal direct with Herr Krug, nobody else.'

'And what about our own working relationship, Fräulein Wiebke?'

43

'We aren't scheduled to have one,' she said firmly. 'You aren't to submit any form of report to me, nor receive any information from me, nor hand me anything in writing – not even rough notes or newspaper cuttings. As far as you're concerned, I exist merely to connect you with Herr Krug if you have to telephone him and to make any further appointments that may become necessary.'

'I don't even know what anyone expects – or hopes – of me.'

'Herr Krug will tell you that and anything else you need to know. Including, of course, the size of your fee and expense account limit. Ask him about that, not that I imagine you're likely to forget.'

'We're going to get along fine, I feel it in my bones.'

Fräulein Wiebke was spared the need to reply because at that moment the 'phone rang. With routine alacrity she stated her name, listened impassively, and then said: 'One moment, please.' She held out the receiver to Wander. 'A call for you.'

'Why should anyone know I'm here?'

'How should I know?'

'Who is it?'

'Baroness von Wassermann-Westen, and she says it's urgent.'

*

'First,' said Konstantin Krug, 'your fee. You may name the figure yourself in full confidence that we shall endeavour to accommodate you as far as our resources permit.'

'And what do you hope for in return?' inquired Wander.

'Secondly,' said Krug, glancing at his notes, 'basic terms of reference relating to your special assignment. These you will receive exclusively from me or from the Minister on whose behalf I am dealing with you. As to the methods you employ in carrying out your duties, these will to a large extent be left to your discretion. We are interested solely in the results we hope to achieve.'

44

'What sort of results?'

'Point number three. Your activities, which may give you access to confidential records, files, papers, documents and memoranda, will be subject to the Official Secrets Act. I shall therefore have to ask you to sign the usual declaration.'

'Anything else?'

'Just a few minor points. The making of written notes is to be avoided as far as possible. Should this become genuinely unavoidable, such notes are to be handed over immediately for safe keeping. The same applies to any evidence that may be secured. Reports are to be submitted by word of mouth. Should it be considered absolutely desirable to record them in writing, such dictation is to take place here in our offices and nowhere else.'

Karl Wander merely nodded – there didn't seem to be much choice. The man facing him, Krug, Konstantin, native of Franconia, reputed to be politically moderate, Party member of long standing, currently one of the most prominent second-stringers, was not conducting a conversation, he was reciting his homework. He reeled off instructions like a tape-recorder.

'Fourthly, you may count on our full and unqualified support. You will be given access to all the documents which are available to us and which may be necessary to your work. We shall also arrange any contacts you may require – a telephone call will usually suffice. In addition, we are opening a special account in your name to cover any unforeseen expenses that may arise. Initial credit: ten thousand marks. This will be at your personal disposal. Further funds may be forthcoming after consultation.'

Krug ticked off these items in a monotonous voice, his hairless billiard ball of a head never losing its rigid immobility. Only his mouth moved, not his eyes. These stared fishlike at something in the far distance – possibly a ministerial desk.

'Perhaps I ought to start by enlightening you about my previous history,' Wander suggested. 'Before it's too late, I mean.'

'I appreciate your frankness, Herr Wander, but that will not be necessary. Take a look at this file, here on my desk.'

The file in question was bright red and as thick as a man's arm. 'It contains a great many particulars about you, ranging from a copy of your birth certificate, school reports and copies of your military papers to various newspaper articles written by you and sundry other public – and private – statements of opinion.'

'So you're aware of my altercation with the military authorities about ten years ago – or, rather, with the then Minister of Defence?'

'Fully aware.'

'And it hasn't discouraged you?'

'On the contrary, Herr Wander – that's just what appeals to us so much about you. That was precisely the reason we sent for you.'

'Very well. If you've considered it carefully – which I imagine you have – we can get down to brass tacks.'

Konstantin Krug made a suggestion of a movement: he nodded, approvingly. His billiard-ball head glinted as he did so. Then his baritone voice, wholly unchanged in pitch and volume, intoned the crucial details for Wander's benefit. 'This concerns the Federal Army; or, to be more precise, the present Federal Minister of Defence. What do you think of him?'

'My opinion of him, which no doubt figures in your file on me, remains unchanged. If you'll permit me to summarize, the Defence Minister may be an honest man but he's certainly a stupid one. He possesses boundless energy and perseverance but not a spark of imagination, let alone genius. Under his leadership, the West German army shows every sign of turning into a rabble, overfed, sluggish, indifferent and utterly useless.'

Krug nodded again – an extravagant display of emotion. He placed his fingertips together and closed his fishy eyes. 'Just so,' he said. 'That is precisely your point of departure. When the

46

Minister learns what you have just expressed so forcefully, it will strengthen his confidence in you.'

'Which minister?'

'The minister on whose behalf you will be working.'

'And who is that?'

'You'll meet him in due course,' Krug promised. 'All that matters for the time being is that we're agreed on fundamentals.'

'But not on every last detail,' Wander put in cautiously.

'Your fee? Assume that you will be paid the equivalent of a cabinet minister's salary for at least six months. As I told you, we're not niggardly where valuable and effective work is concerned.'

'I'm not worried about the money. It's the army I care about. My ambition is to see it in the proper hands, and I'd be happy to help create a climate in which it can develop along the best possible lines. As things are, morale seems to be on the verge of snapping. There's no form of creative drive or convincing democratic foundation – in fact there's a whiff of pure and unadulterated Nazism in the air.'

'Precisely. I'm familiar with all your arguments and I accept them. The Minister also accepts them. He shares your misgivings. He too wishes to see the Bundeswehr transformed into a democratic force of the first magnitude. That's why we're counting on you.'

'You can, if things are as you say.'

'They are,' Konstantin Krug declared solemnly. 'The Federal Army has a renewed need of men like you, Herr Wander. If we succeed in all that we are trying to do, the Minister believes that you ought to find another permanent position for yourself. The best and most effective place of all, the Minister thinks, would be in the Ministry of Defence itself.'

Wander did not hesitate. 'When do we start, and how?'

'What we expect from you to begin with, as a basis for your

future activities, is an over-all analysis. First, where are the weak points in the present executive structure? Secondly, are there any opposing elements within the present hierarchy which would lend themselves to detachment and mobilization on our behalf? Thirdly, what neutral elements exist and how can their effective co-operation be secured?'

'The present leadership of the West German army is ripe for retirement,' Wander said. 'Too many men have built themselves comfortable little niches and become pure administrators. There are numerous left-overs from the unsavoury past among the middle-ranking officers – they must also be axed as speedily as possible. Conscientious reformers of junior rank should be given a real chance to show what they can do. In other words, let's try to save what still remains to be saved.'

'Excellent,' said Krug. 'You're an idealist, Herr Wander, which is just what we were counting on. The first instalment of your fee is ready and waiting – all you have to do is collect it from Fräulein Wiebke. I look forward to a mutually profitable association.'

✻

'Nice of you to come,' Baroness von Wassermann-Westen declared in a warmly conversational tone as she greeted Karl Wander in the hall of her Cologne house.

She extended a smooth white hand which sparkled as the light played over it – the bracelet on her wrist must have been worth the equivalent of five ministerial salaries. 'I'm dying to introduce you to a few of my friends.'

'You told me on the 'phone that you wanted to speak to me urgently. And alone.'

'You're here, that's the main thing. There'll be time for a chat later.'

She led the way through open glass doors into a room of concert-hall dimensions. Its décor included Empire furniture,

48

tapestries, a Gothic Madonna, and two genre paintings of Flemish origin. Distributed round the room in small groups were a dozen citizens of the Federal Republic. They held glasses in their hands and were conversing with every sign of animation.

'Who are these hot-house plants?' Wander murmured suspiciously.

'A few of my friends, as I told you. You'll have to get used to these people if you want to accomplish anything here. They're part of the scene.'

'Like Eva Morgenrot's brother, I suppose.'

'Are you disappointed I didn't invite him?'

'I can't wait to see him again.'

'We'll have a talk about Martin too,' Sabine promised, adding quickly: 'I trust you haven't taken any action against him in the meantime.'

'No, not yet, or he'd be in hospital by now. Or in the morgue, which is where he'll find himself if he keeps up the good work.'

Sabine von Wassermann-Westen – universally addressed as 'Baroness' – looked relieved. She laughed and drew him towards her guests. When she introduced him it was as if she were presenting a new addition to her collection, and her collection enjoyed quite a reputation among connoisseurs of political objets d'art.

Those present consisted of seven men and five women, all of whom seemed quite at home in the Baroness's retreat: one senior civil servant, two members of parliament, three representatives from the world of heavy industry, and a diplomat. Then there were the ladies of the party: here an unmistakable *poule de luxe*, there a respectable bureaucrat's wife, between them – for variety's sake – a female intellectual, and, finally, two titled whores of boundless experience. All present came from the second rung of the social ladder and were strenuously endeavouring to climb the first.

Wander roamed from group to group. It was evident they all knew each other. Their topics of conversation seemed equally familiar to all, but they did their best to invest them with the maximum of significance.

'One shouldn't underrate the present Chancellor,' said one of the two members of parliament. 'That exaggerated reserve of his is just a shrewd tactical device. At least he isn't a man like Kiesinger, who used to try and sell us compromises between irreconcilable opposites.'

'You're surely not implying,' Wander interposed, 'that Kiesinger came to terms first with the Nazis and then with the Communists? The first course of action rates as largely understandable in this country, wouldn't you say? The second used to be equated with high treason and later, after a few ups and downs, with political stupidity at best.'

'You're really talking about tactical considerations,' observed the first speaker. 'One has to take a broader view of these things – see them in shades of grey rather than black and white. After all, what is involved in such cases is not politics in general but a policy specifically geared to Germany's needs. I, for example, as Chairman of the Defence Committee . . .'

Karl Wander had some difficulty in concealing his surprise. He had carelessly failed to note the politician's name when introduced to him because the man's homely, worried-looking, schoolmasterish face had not struck him as immediately interesting. Now, however, after closer inspection, he established that the man's square jaw might charitably be construed as a symptom of strong character. He decided to jump in with both feet.

'But aren't the procedural methods of your committee typical of the present political climate in this country?' he demanded challengingly. 'You give a permanent impression of well-weighed compromise and cautious neutrality. There's an incessant drizzle of platitudes and well-modulated trivialities, carefully gauged dollops of insurance against every conceivable eventuality – to quote the view of the so-called Radical opposition, a deliberate gamble on the universal power of stupidity.'

The politician's almost benign-looking face coagulated into an expression of uneasiness and dislike, but his voice retained its practised suavity. 'Should such a regrettable impression genuinely have arisen, I can only assure you that it is deceptive.'

'Deceit certainly comes into it somewhere,' Wander retorted with a provocative grin.

The Chairman of the Defence Committee glanced inquiringly at the Baroness, who responded with an encouraging smile. This prompted him to say, cautiously but politely: 'The views you've just put forward are certainly worth discussing at greater length. On another more appropriate occasion, perhaps. What did you say your name was?'

Wander stated his name and excused himself. He manœuvred in the direction of Sabine, but before he reached her he was forced to run the gauntlet of some more polite nothings on the subject of murder and fashion, law and order and left-wing extremism, political morality and modish sexuality. He felt a mounting desire for a large whisky, and got one.

'What else can I offer you?' asked Sabine. 'The general representative of an armaments firm, perhaps, or another member of parliament who considers himself an expert on military matters?'

Wander sank wearily on to a sofa. Sabine, reacting with the swift and unerring instinct of the perfect hostess, smiled round the room, issued instructions to the butler, and then sat down beside him. He studied her like someone examining a suspect banknote.

'For the moment, I'm far too preoccupied to be interested in social chit-chat with political undertones. For instance, I'd be glad to know the answers to two questions: number one, how did you know I was with Krug when you 'phoned me, and number two, what gives you the idea that I might be interested in military experts, notably the Chairman of the Defence Committee?'

Sabine smiled with gracious condescension. 'You sound almost like dear Konstantin.'

'So you know Krug?'

'Lots of people here do – it's only natural.' Sabine tried to broaden her smile. 'It can be a great advantage to know him. It could be for you too, as long as you're a better judge of circumstances and human nature than you used to be. I'd be glad to help you – in fact I'm already doing so.'

'And what do you hope to get from me in exchange?'

Sabine leant back. She scrutinized her guests carefully, but their attentions were satisfactorily diverted. They talked away with their eyes at chest-level, as though gauging the capacity of wallets or the depth of neck-lines. Sabine could therefore devote herself wholeheartedly to Wander.

'Everything has its price,' she said. 'The best bargains are the sort which profit both parties.'

'I don't deal in scrap.'

'Nobody can sell more than he has in stock. You may have plenty to offer, but I doubt if you realize it yet. Till then, your policy ought to be to play safe, and that includes keeping your nose out of things that don't concern you.'

'Are you talking about Eva Morgenrot?'

'A dear little thing, Eva, but she does have her complexes.'

'I would too, probably, with a brother like that.'

'Does that mean you're planning to do something about him after all?'

'Possibly. Is that where our business relationship begins – or began, since yesterday?'

'You're approaching this the wrong way. You haven't the slightest conception of the dimensions of what you're mixed up in.'

52

'Enlighten me, then. I can't wait to hear the full story.'

'You know virtually nothing about Eva – fortunately for you, perhaps. She's a Jonah, poor girl. I'm afraid she's done a lot of harm already, probably without meaning to.'

'Helped by her brother, no doubt.'

'Martin is capable of a lot of things, but he's very fond of Eva. That may account for much of what's happened in the past – and what could happen in the future. Your best plan is simply to forget the whole thing. After all, you have more important matters to attend to here. Why not concentrate on them?'

'And if I don't?'

'I should regret that very much. So would you, I can assure you. The mere thought of Eva's so-called fiancé, Felix Frost...' She paused for effect. 'Steer clear of him, whatever you do.'

*

'You don't look exactly radiant,' Peter Sandman said as they shook hands. 'Didn't you land that job you had lined up?'

'It was handed to me on a plate,' Wander told him. 'A solid gold plate.'

'That gives us something to celebrate, then.'

They had arranged to meet outside the Parliament Building. Now they were heading along the embankment towards a restaurant which Sandman had recommended. A bottle of choice claret, a Château Coufran, had already been brought to room temperature and was awaiting their arrival.

'I've always prided myself on being able to swallow a great deal,' Wander said, 'but I'm gradually coming to the point where I don't have a chance to stand back and admire myself.'

'Endurance is a cardinal virtue in this neck of the woods,' observed Sandman. 'Hang on to it and you'll go places.'

'What places?'

Wisps of autumnal mist crept towards them. The waning

daylight blunted the outlines of the concrete office blocks and transformed them into massive plinth-stones for the cathedral which towered so impressively above the roofs of the city. The road before them, which led to the Rhine Bridge, was a ribbon of harsh light and harsher sound, a conveyor-belt for cars.

'Who's behind Krug?' Wander asked.

Peter Sandman paused to light his pipe, lingering over the operation. Then he said: 'Hard to say, exactly. Konstantin Krug acts as general secretary to his party, and that's worth a good deal. However, you don't just earn a position like that – you also have to fight to keep it. Krug knows that, and so does his current protector.'

'Minister Feldmann?'

'Could be,' Sandman said evasively. 'But what does that mean in practical terms? No reason why the current set-up should be a permanent state of affairs. Besides, it's almost impossible to tell who manipulates whom and in what direction.'

'Minister Feldmann is reputed to be an extremely capable man.'

'No doubt about that, though it would help to know what he's actually capable of. The fact that he's only Minister with Special Responsibility for Displaced Persons and Refugees means little. A fringe ministry of that sort can be either a spring-board to bigger things or a pension plan. Feldmann's the spring-board type.'

They were now standing at the pedestrian crossing west of the Rhine Bridge. The ribbon of light from the road flickered over their faces. Their conversation was overlaid by the roar of traffic.

Wander said: 'Maybe I shouldn't have come here at all.'

'If you hadn't,' Sandman said, 'I'd have been robbed of a treat in store.'

'Recently I've been writing articles for trade journals – butchery, hairdressing, tourism, and so on. They earned me

54

enough to live on, not in luxury, but well enough. I ought to have been content with that.'

The American looked amused. 'Can the diffidence, Wander, it doesn't suit you. Anyway, I'm firmly convinced that you not only want to and will get involved – you're already in something up to your neck. What's more, you've managed to strike oil first time – without realizing it, probably.'

'Why don't you let me in on it, then?' Wander demanded.

Sandman took him by the arm and led him away from the lights and noise. He leant against a wall, deliberately knocked his pipe out and swapped it for another – he seemed to have at least one in each pocket. Then he produced his black notebook, consulted it rapidly, and put it away again.

'You mentioned the name Morgenrot. It sounded familiar but I didn't know why. That was because I was concentrating on the idea of a girl – your Eva – instead of on her father.'

'She isn't my Eva,' Wander said drily.

'Time will tell,' Sandman retorted. 'You haven't found out who her father is yet? All right, get a load of this: Morgenrot, Maximilian, aged 59, industrial tycoon based in the Essen area. Armaments manufacturer specializing in anti-tank rockets. Also produces grenade launchers, small-calibre cannon, automatic rifles. A pretty extensive business with scope for further expansion, but geared to the export market. In practical terms, that means no direct links with the Ministry of Defence – yet.'

'So that's what I've walked into!'

'Yes. A pretty remarkable coincidence.'

'But no more than a coincidence.'

'Do you plan to take advantage of it – or have you already started to without realizing it?'

'Heaven forbid! I've had more than enough of the girl as it is, or at least of her brother Martin.'

'He isn't her brother,' Sandman said. 'Morgenrot and his late wife adopted Eva when she was a baby. Martin was born a couple of years later. They aren't blood relations.'

'And you think that explains a thing or two?'

'Maybe. At least, it could provide one more possible explanation – among many.'

INTERIM REPORT No. 3

BY THE MAN KNOWN AS JEROME

on the subject of guesswork and the dangers inherent in those who refuse to observe the rules of the game.

Sandman may have had some good qualities – exceptional ones, even – but he wasn't a good poker-player. When he thought he was holding good cards he failed to disguise the fact, at least from me. His reactions were an open book.

There was no mistaking his special interest in Karl Wander. He wanted all available information about him, and the information was easily obtainable. Wander belonged to the happy band who never try to hide anything, presumably because they think they have nothing to hide. A common fallacy, viewed from our angle.

For instance, Sandman wanted to know if Wander was what is known as an honest man. He was. Also, if there were any suspicious features about his past. Absolutely none from the legal aspect but plenty from our side of the fence. Confirmed idealists like Wander are infinitely susceptible, easily exploited by anyone who throws the right switch at the right moment.

Talking to Sandman one night, I asked him precisely what he thought Wander was capable of. 'Anything and everything,' he said tersely. 'Even murder?' I asked. Sandman didn't dismiss the idea, just shrugged. That was smart of him. He couldn't have found a more effective way of whetting my curiosity.

Over the second bottle of brandy I asked Sandman to be a

56

little more explicit. He started by quoting Goethe's admission that there was no crime of which he had not felt capable, given the right circumstances. I didn't argue. Then he said: 'Wander isn't a pathologically inclined criminal, of course, but he's a pretty complex character. It would probably take a whole chain reaction to activate his destructive urge.'

Well, it was true. Anyone can become a criminal – without exception. We can all be induced to commit crime almost automatically by a particular combination of circumstances. 'Wander has had to swallow a lot of accusations in his time,' Sandman said. 'What throws me is that he doesn't evade them – he positively seeks them out. Without wanting to, perhaps even without knowing it, he leaves a trail of disaster behind him.'

Even I couldn't fail to be impressed by so much sympathetic interest. Besides, it struck me as an ideal training assignment for junior agents, so I put a couple of beginners on the potential case. Nothing fragile around for them to smash, or so I thought. Pretty dumb of me.

In fact, it didn't seem to be anything more than a jigsaw puzzle at first. My conscientious young agents raked together everything they came across. Much of it useless, but that was only to be expected.

For instance, there were some excerpts from one of Baroness von Wassermann-Westen's diaries – carefully gauged chit-chat, obviously, committed to paper for insurance. One passage referred to Eva Morgenrot: '. . . dead drunk, looked dazed . . . suspect she'd taken some kind of drug . . . consider it vitally necessary to consult a reliable doctor . . . always these frightful, dangerous relapses . . .'

Then some comments by Karl Wander's former superiors while he was still in the army. Their gist: highly intelligent but extremely independent; good at dealing with the lower ranks but occasionally over-familiar with them; incapable of developing a feeling for certain refinements of meaning – for instance, unable to distinguish precisely between obedience and discipline. Conclusion: as a subordinate, far from easy; as a superior officer, completely undesirable.

We also managed to photocopy a letter from Eva Morgenrot to a girl-friend. Pert exaggerations indicative of extreme youth. For example: '. . . what beautiful people . . . like a gilded pigsty . . . perfumed shit . . . dear Sabine sometimes acts like a whore-house madam . . .'

Nobody in our line of work takes such things seriously. However, one of the agents I had assigned to the case did turn in a report which alerted me. He submitted a virtually clean sheet on Konstantin Krug. There was hardly anything to report on the man, and nothing could have aroused my suspicions more.

I immediately checked with records. All that emerged at first was this: Krug, Konstantin, respectable middle-class background, previous history irreproachable. Dutiful son, star pupil, reliable public servant, took to politics like a duck to water. No known hobbies, no discernible enthusiasms, no demonstrable interest in women, nor in men; apparently an art-lover, but within limits; devoid of private life. Ergo, the sort of neuter that makes your flesh creep.

Neuters titillate my imagination. My imagination isn't over-developed but I can't entirely suppress it. But then, who doesn't have his occasional little weaknesses?

Chapter 4

'The Federal Army lacks an image,' declared Minister Feldmann. 'It has no real spirit, no character – nothing capable of transforming it into a dynamic force. I mean that in the democratic sense, naturally. Are we agreed so far?'

'Entirely,' said Wander.

They were lunching at the Hotel Rheinhof, at the corner table on the left of the terrace. The river flowed sluggishly past the broad windows. Beyond the sound-proof panes, Rhine barges glided noiselessly along like ghost-ships.

'Too many opportunities have been missed already,' said the Minister, dissecting his salmon. 'The army has turned into a bloated administrative machine, a uniformed welfare organization, a government-approved scrap-heap for obsolete equipment.'

'That was one of my arguments, too,' Wander said.

'We're familiar with them,' observed Krug. He was the third member of the party, not – as Wander had noted – that this prevented the conversation from being a duologue. Krug could become no more than his Minister's shadow or echo when the occasion warranted it.

Minister Feldmann made a dignified impression. He had the brow of an academic and the facial contours of an actor. His voice matched his appearance, but his grey-blue eyes were slightly disturbing to those privileged to inspect them at close range. They might have belonged to a racing-driver or possibly a boxer – keen, alert, and always focused on a specific target. The current target was Wander.

'The Federal Army,' Feldmann continued, 'must be jolted out of its present lethargy. More of the right kind of self-confidence – that's what it must develop if it is to function properly. Our army must assume its rightful status – become a refined and perfected instrument. Increased efficiency and a new spirit, that must be our slogan.'

It dawned on Wander what the Minister wanted him to say. 'Exactly. Radical changes entail radical measures. To mix metaphors, since the present leadership certainly won't change its spots or fade away of its own accord, it must be removed or, shall we say, dismantled before it can be replaced.'

Minister Feldmann looked reasonably satisfied. He said nothing because saddle of venison was now being served. When the waiter had gone he said: 'You might describe the process I have in mind as changing the guard. However, what matters is how we commend it to as wide a section of the public as possible.'

'But does this fall within your sphere of responsibility, Minister?'

'That question, Herr Wander, is wholly immaterial,' Krug cut in quickly. 'It has nothing to do with your assignment.'

'I shall answer it nevertheless,' said Feldmann. 'However, please regard what I am going to tell you as highly confidential, Herr Wander.'

Krug cleared his throat. 'Herr Wander has already signed a document committing him to absolute secrecy.'

'A pure formality, I trust.' The Minister laid his hand on Wander's arm with an air of friendly intimacy. It was a surprisingly heavy hand, almost like a block of wood, and the fingers were vice-like. 'Well, then. My colleague the Chancellor is deeply concerned. In his view, the true value of the Federal Army is grotesquely disproportionate to the vast sums that have been spent on it.'

'And that,' Krug said softly, 'is our real basis of action.'

'Allow me to add one other point,' said the Minister. 'I am far from delighted with the situation that has grown up, but I feel indebted to the Chancellor – as a personal friend, apart from anything else. He has asked me to perform this service for him, and perform it I shall.'

'What about possible changes in personnel?' inquired Wander.

'That,' he was promptly assured, 'is a matter for the Chancellor. That is to say, the final decision rests with him. We are simply endeavouring to create a situation ripe for change. You understand?'

The Minister pushed his empty plate aside and continued: 'To come to the point, Herr Wander, you must already have formed one or two definite ideas on this subject. My friend Krug informs me that he broached the matter to you yesterday.'

'Well,' Wander said, 'you'll probably have to take a closer interest in the present Defence Minister yourself. He belongs to your own party, and that means you have better access to confidential documents than anyone else. I doubt if there's much against him from the purely human angle, nor very much from the professional or administrative angle either – he's such a colourless figure. The political angle is more promising. For instance, a number of his recorded statements have been blatantly self-contradictory, and he's said some more than embarrassing things in the past.'

The Minister nodded. Krug made a note and said: 'That sort of thing isn't very remarkable in itself, but it might lend some additional substance to our campaign.'

'Thanks, presumably, to some wire-pulling by you, Herr Krug,' Wander continued, 'I've managed to make contact with the Chairman of the Defence Committee. My personal impression seems to confirm what everyone already knows. The man positively exudes eagerness to please. His principle is never to offend anyone, that stands out a mile. However, I'll be glad to take a closer look at him. The same goes for the present Defence Commissioner. One or two unsavoury rumours are already circulating about him, and it should be possible to confirm them.'

Krug's tone was admonitory. 'Just so we understand one another from the outset, Herr Wander: your job is to procure evidence, nothing more. The evaluation of that evidence is my – our responsibility alone.'

'I fully appreciate that,' Wander assured him. 'What's more, I have a pretty clear idea of how you intend to go about things. For instance, if I manage to rake evidence that the Defence Commissioner is corrupt, that he's an alcoholic or homosexual who is exploiting his position or being exploited himself, you will decide whether it's used to make him toe the line or to shoot him down in flames.'

'For heaven's sake, Herr Wander!' Krug exclaimed, deigning to show temperament. 'In future, kindly refrain from using barrack-room slang. This is hardly the place for it.'

'But I'm on the right track, aren't I?'

'Please continue, Herr Wander,' said the Minister. Coffee and a cigar seemed to have put him in an exceptionally mellow mood. 'Let us proceed to the next salient point – the Inspector-General.'

'He and the Defence Minister are a team. That means they'll have to be axed simultaneously. It shouldn't be too difficult – at least half a dozen generals are itching to step into the Inspector-General's shoes, and at least two are better qualified to wear them.'

'But will they be prepared for a trial of strength if it comes to one?' Once again, it was Krug who seemed willing to confront the issue for his Minister, even if he did it delicately.

'There's at least one man who will,' Wander assured him.

'I'm referring to the leader of the officers who call themselves traditionalists, or sometimes patriotic conservatives. Their counterparts are the self-styled innovators, the hopelessly romantic theorists of reform.'

'Of whom you used to be one,' Krug added in a soft voice.

Wander nodded impassively. 'In the meantime I've been forced to the conclusion that too many of these so-called reformers are a dead loss – they're so damned decent and diffident they never achieve anything. They aren't genuine innovators or revolutionaries, they're just dreamers. You won't create a new Federal Army with them. A completely fresh start is the only solution left – that's why I approve of your campaign.'

'But it's our campaign, not yours,' warned Krug.

'Of course. I'm simply supplying the ammunition.'

The Minister had leaned back in his chair, presumably to get a better view of his table companion. His eyes were slightly closed in a way which made them look deceptively mild. He motioned briefly to Wander to proceed.

'The present Inspector-General swings to and fro between the rival camps like a pendulum. He sometimes goes up to the pseudo-reformers and pats their puny shoulders with every appearance of fellow-feeling, but he takes good care to humour the ultra-conservatives at the same time. General Keilhacke is the biggest fire-eater on the active list. You might do worse than turn him loose on the Inspector-General.'

'First-rate soldier, Keilhacke,' mused Krug. 'A battle-hardened tank specialist from the Rommel and Guderian stable. Plenty of dash – involved in the Hitler bomb plot, too.'

'Very much so,' said Wander. 'He helped to betray at least three of his brother officers to the Gestapo – out of the most honourable motives, of course.'

'Enough said,' decreed the Minister. 'That is irrelevant to the point at issue.'

'No gentleman makes capital out of Germany's tragic past,' Krug supplemented. 'It isn't done.'

'Keilhacke,' the Minister said in a tone which implied meditation. 'Not a bad choice. As it happens, I myself have been devoting consideration to him for some time now.'

Wander winced. 'Not as a future Inspector-General, I trust.'

'You may safely leave such decisions to the Chancellor,' Krug interposed hastily. 'That isn't under discussion.'

The Minister took in Wander's reaction at one swift glance. He smiled, then said in an understanding tone: 'The fact that generals have their uses doesn't necessarily mean that they gain concessions as a result. Their expectations are one thing, how we exploit them is our business. If Keilhacke actually succeeds in obliterating the present Inspector-General, so much the better for us. We shall not incur any binding commitments whatsoever.'

'Our sole concern is for the army,' Krug put in. 'Concentrate on that idea throughout this operation, Herr Wander. After all, the interests of the army are very close to your heart, are they not?'

'I'm sure they are,' the Minister said amiably. He smiled again. 'Tell us what else you have in mind.'

Wander hesitated for a moment, then continued: 'The complex system of arms procurement offers another promisingly vulnerable area of attack. The methods and practices currently employed in placing arms contracts will no doubt give you some scope for action. The same applies even more strongly to extravagant expenditure on experimental projects.'

'Very awkward material to handle,' Krug observed. 'Factors affecting the defence budget are exceptionally intricate and involved. To gain a full picture of them we should need a whole team of scientists and arms experts. We aren't stingy, but we simply couldn't afford them.'

'It needn't cost the price of a packet of cigarettes if you press the right button.' Wander said. 'Take Bölsche's of Munich, for instance – their weapons research is directly financed out of defence funds to the tune of several million marks a month. There's another firm of similar size and capacity which doesn't receive any subsidy at all. I think it's highly probable that companies which don't enjoy that sort of financial favour would be happy to get hold of as many of their competitors' plans as possible and hand them over to us – simply as proof positive that a mint of public money has been irresponsibly thrown away.'

'Have you a firm in mind?'

Deliberately, Wander replied: 'Yes, Morgenrot's of Essen.'

The Minister sat hunched in his chair in stony silence. Krug raised a warning hand like a traffic policeman. 'We mustn't rush things. I think that will do for today.'

'Precisely,' said the Minister. His cool, keen, racing driver's eyes were wide open now. They might have been seeing Karl Wander for the first time.

*

'No,' Wander said firmly. He had just opened the door of his apartment to reveal Eva Morgenrot. 'You're not coming in – not while your brother's around.'

'He's in Cologne,' she whispered. 'Please, I have to speak to you.'

'Not in your flat or mine. Preferably outside, in the middle of a football crowd.'

'But I'm not allowed to leave the building – my doctor said not.' She smiled at him almost shyly. 'I ought really to be still in bed.'

'Then get back there, and don't expect me to climb in beside you.' He eyed her, wavering. 'I'll see you to your door.'

'But I don't feel well,' she announced, tottering towards him.

Reluctantly, Karl Wander stepped aside. The girl walked past him with exaggerated languor, not forgetting to smile at him again, gratefully this time. 'Don't go perching on my bed, though,' he snapped. 'You've got me in enough trouble as it is.'

Eva Morgenrot sat down on his bed and gazed up at him. 'It's a shame I didn't get to know you earlier, really it is.'

'I'd call it a cause for self-congratulation,' he said. 'Let's get one thing straight. I didn't invite you in – you came of your own accord. I didn't want to let you in but you insisted. Is that clear?'

'You honestly needn't worry about Martin. He really is in Cologne and he won't be back for a while.'

'Are you sure?'

'I spoke to him on the 'phone a few minutes ago.'

'Did he call you or did you call him?'

'I called him in Cologne.'

'In that case we can count on no interruptions for at least fifteen minutes. Your brother would take about half an hour to get here from Cologne, even if he drove like a maniac. Well, why did you come?'

'To see you, Charlie.'

'All right, so you've seen me.'

'I wanted to apologize. I'm so sorry about everything.'

'You mean you're sorry you gave your beloved brother my address?'

Eva gave a childlike laugh. Then, from one moment to the next, she became serious again, at least outwardly. 'He isn't really my brother, you know.'

'He behaves more like your lover.'

'That's just what he'd like to be. I wasn't much more than a baby when I was adopted. I grew up with Martin, never suspecting a thing, never imagining that he'd try to treat me as

66

anything but a sister. Well, he's been after me for years now, and recently he's become more and more of a handful. It must run in the family – his father behaved the same way.'

Wander pulled a chair up to the bed and sat down. 'You have a pretty vivid imagination – I've noticed that before now.'

'I'm not lying to you Karl – Charlie, I mean – and I'm not imagining things either.' Confidingly, she reached for his hand. 'I'll never get out of this mess unless someone helps me. Will you help me? Please – I trust you.'

'Don't give me that,' Wander said brusquely, pulling his hand away. 'Your personal problems have nothing to do with me.'

'But it's not only my brother and father – I'm as good as engaged to someone called Felix Frost. Does that name ring a bell?'

'Oh, come off it, Eva! You might as well save your breath – melodrama makes me feel sick. You give a nice enough impression at first glance – blonde inside and out. Also, there are times when you arouse my protective instinct.'

'So I do attract you after all?'

'No. I demand something more than that. Sincerity, for instance. You may not be lying, Eva, but you're hiding a hell of a lot.'

'I can't tell you everything – not yet – but some day you'll understand why.'

'I can hardly wait,' he said drily. 'Unfortunately, patience isn't one of my virtues. How about a little confidential information on account concerning your relationship with Baroness von Wassermann-Westen, for example?'

'Sabine is about the only person I can really trust,' Eva replied eagerly. 'She always helps me whenever she can. I don't know what I'd do without her.'

'Either you're lying to me, Eva, or you're even more naïve than I thought.'

'You don't know Sabine or you'd never say such a thing.'

'If it wasn't you who set Martin on me it must have been her. It can only have been one of you two.'

'You're wrong, honestly you are.'

'What makes you so sure?'

'It's like this,' she said, avoiding his eye. 'Martin is convinced he saw me going into your apartment late that night.'

'But that's ridiculous!'

'Of course it is, but he's absolutely positive.'

Wander felt uneasy. He rose and walked to the centre of the room. 'Look, Eva,' he said, 'just what *is* going on round here?'

*

Detective Chief Inspector Kohl looked up from his desk with elephantine deliberation. 'Were you sent for again, or are you simply at a loose end?'

'I'd appreciate a word with you, Chief Inspector – off the record.'

'I'm on duty, Herr Wander.'

'After office hours, then, if you prefer.'

The policeman closed the file in front of him and got up. 'Office hours are over,' he said. He reached for his raincoat and walked to the door. Wander followed him, a little surprised. In the outer office the big man called out: 'Routine inquiries, as usual. If I'm needed urgently you can contact me at Mutter Jeschke's.'

The constable thus addressed gave a familiar grin and chalked up a thick 'J' beside Kohl's name on the personnel board.

Outside, Kohl stood still for a moment, sniffing the air like a gun-dog. Then he pulled on his raincoat, stuck his hands deep into his pockets and walked off, shoulders slightly hunched.

Wander caught up with Kohl and fell into step beside him. 'I'm surprised we're still on speaking terms.'

The policeman laughed raucously. 'You summed up my curiosity correctly, and that's a point in your favour.'

'Are there any others?'

'Your stupidity,' replied Kohl. 'It could also be a form of decency – they're hard to distinguish sometimes. I propose to do what I do every evening and drink a glass of beer – only one, mind you, but a big one. I'm not standing you a drink so don't take it into your head to stand me one. I only allow friends to do that, and I don't have any friends at present – haven't had for years.'

They crossed the main square and entered a small cavernous bar near the mouth of Brüdergasse. The few customers inside were sitting, singly for the most part, at small round tables fashioned out of wine-barrels. Their attention seemed to be focused entirely on the glasses in front of them.

Lurking behind the counter was a lady wrestler with a fat cheerful face and a brass voice – evidently Mutter Jeschke herself. As soon as she caught sight of Kohl she drew a large glass of beer with ceremonious care.

'I'll have the same,' Wander said.

They drank independently of each other, the burly policeman with deliberate enjoyment, Wander quickly and with a hint of nervousness. Putting their half-empty glasses on the counter, they contemplated them as though lost in thought.

Eventually Karl Wander asked: 'Why did you bring me here?'

'Wanted you to try this beer,' Kohl said slowly. 'It comes direct from Dublin, Ireland. Not everyone likes it.'

'Me included,' said Wander. 'However, I'm not much of an expert on drink.'

'Nor on human nature, I'd say.'

'Seems not. Why don't we sit down properly at a table?'

'Let's just stand for the time being, Herr Wander. The main

reason why we're standing here at all is that I've checked the statements you made recently at headquarters. They appear to be correct.'

'Why did you check them?' asked Wander. 'Routine or just boredom?'

'I've had over thirty years of boredom in my job – complete and utter boredom. Daily contact with criminals soon bores people – people like me, anyway. It isn't often I come across someone who gives me food for thought.'

'Are you sorry you can't pin anything on me?'

'Perhaps I ought to be. I may have fired a warning shot across your bows just in time. You seem to be sailing pretty close to the wind.'

'Perhaps I've already gone too far. Let's assume I realize that, and let's further assume you realize it too. Why are we still rubbing shoulders at this bar?'

'Most people are downright uninteresting,' replied the policeman. 'You're different from most, Herr Wander – more dangerous too, maybe, but from whose point of view? Time will probably tell.'

Karl Wander drank some more of his heavy, creamy, heady Irish stout, and started to enjoy it. He drained his glass and asked Mutter Jeschke to refill it. Kohl did not exceed his regular ration.

'Could you get hold of some information for me?' Wander asked point blank.

Kohl shrugged. 'I could, but on one condition.'

'Name it.'

'Tell me what you want first.'

'Information on Eva Morgenrot. Anything you can dig up. Is that possible?'

Kohl sniffed the rich brown contents of his glass, keenly. Then he said: 'Give me two or three days. I'll call you.'

'And the quid pro quo?'

'Indirect assistance to the police. Let's call it that, anyway. I'm anxious to get a look at some documents I can't lay hands on, not as a policeman – that's to say, not through normal channels.'

'Who are you gunning for?'

'Dr Barranski,' said Kohl.

*

The male fashion-plate who had introduced himself as Felix Frost smiled as if he were laying siege to a woman. 'I really must apologize for intruding, Herr Wander,' he said. 'I wanted a little chat with you.'

'Chat away,' said Wander, and sat down in an arm-chair.

They had met in the foyer of the Hotel Excelsior in Cologne, near the cathedral square, after a brief telephone call from Frost. The rendezvous was not only neutral but luxurious. The Excelsior was rated the best hotel in the square.

'As you're no doubt aware,' Frost began, almost cordially, 'I am unofficially engaged to Fräulein Eva Morgenrot.'

'Did she give you my 'phone number?'

'Good heavens no!' The young man's tone implied that he had been accused of some grave indiscretion. He raised his dainty hands in entreaty. 'Eva and I maintain the most broad-minded relationship imaginable.'

'If that's the case,' Wander said, 'we may as well dispense with the rest of this interview.'

'I wish we could. However, I must admit I'm worried.'

'On account of her brother? Are you afraid he may work off his aggressive urges on you, or has he already done so?'

'Certainly not! Martin and I are friends – very good friends, actually.'

This surprising revelation left Wander temporarily speechless. He was seized with a hilarity which he found hard to account for until he tried to visualize Martin, the foster-brother, and Felix, the unofficial fiancé, arm in arm.

'Martin is just as worried about Eva as I am,' Frost continued in his ballad-singer's voice, 'though probably for different reasons.'

Karl Wander stared past him at the glossy elegance of the hotel foyer. No one seemed to be taking any notice of them. The people sitting there, drifting past or standing side by side were like islands, like pack ice, like trees that refused to knit into a wood. They were safe from interruption.

'Martin Morgenrot's theory,' said Wander, 'is that I'm sleeping with his sister, molesting her and exploiting her physically, mentally and financially – something like that. Is that your opinion too?'

'Of course not!' Frost assured him hurriedly. He smiled like a toothpaste ad. 'Apart from anything else, I'm extremely broadminded – from every angle, I might add . . . No, what worries me is a certain tendency towards irresponsibility on Eva's part.'

'In what respect?'

Felix Frost put his hands together and massaged them tenderly. 'Have you often been with Eva?' he inquired.

'If you mean what I think you mean, never.' Wander feigned amusement. 'I found her outside my door, semi-conscious. Since then she's spoken to me twice.'

'What about, if I may ask?'

'Well, about how unhappy she is, for example. In spite of her plutocratic father, her muscular and devoted brother, her film-star of a fiancé . . .'

Felix Frost took this as a well-deserved compliment, but his face froze into a smiling mask as he said: 'The thing is, neither Eva nor I can afford a scandal of any kind.'

'Are you afraid I may cause one?'

Frost's tone was deliberately casual. 'I'm not a poor man

by any means. I can afford to pay for anything worth buy-ing.'

'And you think I may have something to sell?'

'I wouldn't dismiss the possibility – circumstances being what they are.'

'Then make me an offer,' Wander urged. 'And don't forget to say what for.'

Felix Frost glanced round the foyer. The smile had left his choir-boy's face. His right hand fingered the collar of his snow-white shirt, then slid down the aquamarine Windsor-knotted tie that adorned it. He said: 'Did you search Eva's handbag? Did you find something and pocket it?'

'What, exactly?'

'Something, as I said. A sheet of paper, for instance – a document. Have you anything like that in your possession?'

'No.'

Frost closed his eyes briefly – he had long and luxuriant lashes which might have been false but were, in fact, genuine. 'I don't expect you to confide in me immediately, Herr Wander. Think it over and take your time. Not too much time, though, please. And bear one thing in mind: you'll have a hard time finding a higher bidder. Kindly remember that for Eva's sake as well as your own. Things could go badly for her if you don't.'

*

'An army isn't a nursery-school,' declared General Keilhacke. 'Troops dislike being molly-coddled – they want to be trained, disciplined, prepared for action. Men and their equipment must be welded into a single tightly-knit fighting unit.'

The General was standing on a pile of debris at the edge of the training area, watching tanks manœuvring across the moor-land. The members of his personal entourage – his ADC, a regimental commander and his adjutant, a weapons expert wearing major's insignia, and a civilian technician – hovered in

73

the background, within call. Only Karl Wander enjoyed the enormous privilege of standing next to the General.

'There's only one training objective worth striving for,' Keilhacke said firmly. 'To test men to the limit of their capabilities. That's taken for granted in my sphere of command.' He gave Wander a vigorous nod. 'Tell that to your Minister.'

General Keilhacke was a man of medium height but looked infinitely taller. He usually strode along with body erect and chin slightly raised, and his movements had the power and precision of a machine. His piercing gaze would have graced an eagle and his voice a drill sergeant. All in all, he was leadership personified.

'All this foolishness about citizens in uniform is threatening to undermine morale,' he pursued. 'I'm all in favour of democracy, of course, but my first duty is to prepare soldiers for battle.'

'Train them for defence,' Wander amended discreetly.

'Which amounts to the same thing.' General Keilhacke was not a man to be weaned of his personal convictions, but even he had learnt that certain new-fangled ideas had to be taken into consideration. He looked upon their mastery as an unavoidable military stratagem.

'Let's run through the whole thing once more!' General Keilhacke commanded his entourage in robust tones. 'Get those tanks back to the starting line and have them advance in the same formation. And speed it up this time – squeeze all you can out of them!'

The regimental commander approached with due caution. 'The engines haven't been tested sufficiently, sir. We don't know the extent of their capability. Also, the racking of live ammunition . . .'

'High time we found out!' Keilhacke barked impatiently. 'Even if the fur does fly as a result!' he added. 'The Federal Army isn't a holiday camp and the tank corps is still the pick

74

of the bunch. We owe it to ourselves to show what we can do.'

Recalled by radio, the tanks withdrew into a small wood, where their engines continued to drone. Then they raced forward again, lurching over the rutted ground, cavorting like captive bears, shuddering as they sped along. The General hardly seemed to notice them.

'Effeminacy,' he said to Wander, 'that's the deadly poison we're exposed to these days. It starts with trifles – hairstyles, for instance, or shaving-cream, or those poster-sized masturbation aids purveyed by filthy magazines which nobody has the guts to ban in barracks except me. Well, I'm not going to have my men ruined. He-men are what we need, not tailors' dummies!'

'The public haven't been made sufficiently aware of that yet.'

'High time they were!' declared the General. 'Our politicians have a lot of ground to make up in that respect. So far, the dominating mood has been one of civilian sluggishness, not to mention weak-kneed consideration for our self-styled allies – in short, lack of national awareness!'

'Things will change, I'm sure,' Wander said.

'God grant they do!' Keilhacke exclaimed, almost devoutly.

'It's largely a question of personalities – in the Minister's view.'

As though in deference, Keilhacke bowed the rugged head which conveyed such strength of personality. 'Anyone who elects to become a professional soldier chooses the path of self-sacrifice. I have always accepted that, honestly and without reservation.'

He paused deliberately, then continued: 'As a young officer I drafted some of the more important aspects of Guderian's master plan and did not begrudge him the successes that stemmed from it. My draft schemes also played a modest part in Rommel's desert operations, not that they always received the credit they deserved. That, my dear fellow, is public service.

75

The true patriot never lusts after honour and glory but is nevertheless worthy of recognition, however belated.'

The tanks were now bounding powerfully across country, their engines howling like a pack of tormented wolves. The General's entourage surveyed the dismal landscape in spellbound silence. Keilhacke, scenting opportunity, continued to devote himself to Wander.

Wander said: 'I'm only here as a sort of co-ordinator, an indirect liaison officer and public relations consultant, if you like. I do know, however, that the Minister is pinning his hopes on you – quite justifiably, in my humble opinion.'

'I've never let anyone down yet,' Keilhacke assured him. 'Nobody who put his faith in me ever lived to regret it.' He glanced swiftly at the lurching tanks. 'Full speed ahead!' he commanded. 'Get those egg-boxes moving!'

'The time has come to speak out, plainly and unmistakably,' Wander declared, in accordance with instructions. 'For instance, it ought to be stressed that the West German army is neither an American subsidiary, nor a loosely integrated band of European mercenaries, nor a plaything of the Russians, but a completely independent body.'

'I've been advocating those views for years,' General Keilhacke growled. 'The trouble was, no one listened.'

'Times are changing. A television team will be calling on you in the next few days to report on you and the armoured corps. One of the mass-circulation dailies is showing a lively interest in personal details, and the best-known news magazine is even said to be considering the publication of a controversial interview with you. On top of that, a leading German weekly intends to publicize your attitude towards the Soviet Union.'

'That,' exclaimed Keilhacke, 'is crystal clear!'

'And you've demonstrated it in practice, if my memory serves me correctly,' observed Wander. 'You were decorated with the Knight's Cross, way back in the days of the Russian campaign.'

76

'I won the oak leaves later on,' the General said reminiscently, 'during the Ardennes offensive against the Americans. To a soldier, war experiences are a capital investment which ought to carry a high rate of interest. The Americans know perfectly well that they need us if they're to cope with the Russians, believe me. On the other hand, we mustn't let ourselves be exploited – that we can do without.'

Wander proceeded to produce his trump card. 'The present Inspector-General evidently fails to share your view. There doesn't seem to be much prospect of changing his mind, either.'

'I deplore his flabby theories.' Keilhacke now deemed it appropriate to reveal himself as a sage but practical tactician. 'The Inspector-General is a fine officer – always was – but far too amenable to compromise. His present attitude is wrong, dangerously wrong.'

'Are you doing anything about it?' Wander asked.

But General Keilhacke appeared to be temporarily distracted. He was observing the terrain through his field-glasses. His gaze had come to rest, not on the tanks but on a radio truck parked near some undergrowth, and, in particular, on the radio operator.

'The man's eating!' he exclaimed with barely suppressed delight. 'Eating on duty, before my very eyes!'

He turned to the regimental commander. 'Have that gluttonous swine relieved at once! Institute disciplinary proceedings and report to me within twenty-four hours.'

'Yessir,' the regimental commander replied automatically.

Wander knew from hearsay that he had just been privileged to see the General at his favourite pastime. Keilhacke seized every available opportunity to promote discipline and good order in a way that lent itself to rumour. It was part of his personal legend.

Instantly, the General resumed his conversation with Wander. 'I shall open fire with every gun I've got. I intend to brief your Minister in person, especially as I plan to ask him for one or two additional objectives of a more concrete nature. Anyway, Wander, you're acceptable to me as a civilian liaison officer.'

General Keilhacke gazed meditatively across the training area. Suddenly, one of the racing tanks transformed itself into a dazzling yellow ball of fire. It disintegrated like a nut crushed with a sledge-hammer, was engulfed in luminous red flames, and started to give off dense clouds of acrid smoke. Nothing but a smouldering scrap-heap remained.

'What's the meaning of this shambles?' Keilhacke bellowed at his regimental commander. 'I want a thorough inquiry held at once, and make sure you check whether all safety regulations were observed.'

'Yessir,' said the regimental commander.

Keilhacke turned to Wander. 'There, you've seen it for yourself. These are the sort of sacrifices we're forced to make. It's time we were told why!'

INTERIM REPORT No. 4

BY THE MAN KNOWN AS JEROME

on the snares and temptations of eternal woman, in other words, the most natural thing in the world.

The really fateful feature of the whole affair – though it only emerged subsequently – was Karl Wander's incredible naïvety. He was still the typical German youngster at heart: he yearned to believe in something, so he believed in the sense of duty natural to German leaders, in the ultimate triumph of goodness, nobility and decency. All that mattered, he thought, was to further that triumph as best he could.

At the same time, Wander did undoubtedly develop a certain scepticism, a modicum of healthy distrust and a semi-service-able sense of reality. His experiences with the West German army were still fresh in his mind.

He could not bring himself to take the decisive hurdle, however, and that was why he came to grief. What finally threw him was that dominant German national trauma, the ineradicable respect for authority. It was enough for a cabinet minister to demonstrate carefully gauged confidence in him at a personal level.

Feldmann had discreetly developed into a power-tactician. After years of intensive preparation, he was launching his first political operation of any size and note. He had allowed for the fact that a number of people would want to share in the spoils, and not even a man like Wander could seriously distract him. This is evidenced by a report that came into my hands.

The source was Konrad Kalinke, a waiter at the Hotel Rheinhof in Bonn. He had served Feldmann during the crucial conversation over lunch with Wander and Krug. The Minister's concluding remark, which Kalinke overheard, was: 'That man (Wander) could be extremely useful, but we must be on our guard. Let's hope we haven't bought ourselves a potential trouble-maker.'

This remark was testimony to Feldmann's judgment, just as the answer he received was indicative of Krug's exceptional skill as a manipulator of men. Krug's reply was:

'I think I've pretty well covered us from that angle. Wander couldn't go sour on us without dishing himself.'

This turn of phrase ought to have made me sit up and think, but I wasn't sufficiently familiar with Konstantin Krug and his methods at that stage. Instead, I concentrated on the Minister and his possible weaknesses. Everybody has his failings, and one of Feldmann's – but not the only one, as it turned out – was Baroness von Wassermann-Westen.

I have to admit that for quite a while I found the lady in question a dark horse. Women who try to meddle in our kind of

79

business are always surrounded by queries. The Baroness was probably self-employed. She no doubt thought she could reconcile her own interests with those of her country and her firm, but the devil alone knew when one or the other motive predominated. Her main centre of interest was probably located below the navel.

It wasn't only that, though. Any attempt to plumb the depths of a human being can turn into an adventure, and even I succumb to temptation occasionally.

Chapter 5

'So you know my daughter Eva,' said Morgenrot senior, rubbing his hands as if they were cold. 'Do you know her well?'

Wander shook his head. 'I've only met her a couple of times. I'm a neighbour of hers – temporarily.'

'Are you here because of her?'

'Not directly.'

'You have some information about her?'

'Plenty of information,' Wander replied, moderately amused. 'Nothing that would warrant blackmail, though. I imagine that's what you're thinking, but I can set your mind at rest on that score. I'm merely the man you were told to expect by Herr Krug or his Bonn office.'

'Why didn't you say so right away?' Morgenrot gave a relieved laugh. 'Sit down, make yourself comfortable. Can I offer you a drink?'

The chairman and managing director of Morgenrot's was a small, bony man who moved with the speed and agility of a monkey. He quartered the room almost incessantly, shuttling back and forth between desk and filing cabinets, windows and door. He paused only when he spoke. His practice on such occasions was to place his palms together and cock his bald head as though listening to himself. His amber-coloured eyes radiated a gentle warmth.

'Your daughter's a decorative girl,' Wander said.

'Have you been to bed with her?' Morgenrot inquired, relishing the surprise evoked by his question. 'Not yet, from the look of it. Never mind, she's a great disappointment.'

'How would you know?' Wander asked, swiftly and instinctively.

Morgenrot came to an abrupt halt as though he had been
brought up short by a plate glass window. For two full seconds
he neither moved nor spoke. Then he chuckled. 'A man can
learn quite a lot about his children if he makes the effort.'

'Effort? In what direction?'

Morgenrot looked hugely entertained. 'Perhaps you ought to
sleep with Eva,' he said without a trace of embarrassment. 'You
could even embark on a lengthy affair with her – I wouldn't be
averse to subsidizing it financially. It's just what my daughter
needs at the moment. She wants someone not only to satisfy her
physically but blow away the cobwebs, otherwise she'll go on
indulging in stupidities which even I can't afford.'

'Your son thinks Eva should be taboo where I'm concerned.
He tried to impress that on me the other day – pretty forcibly,
I might add.'

Morgenrot whipped himself into a paroxysm of mirth.
'Martin's still sowing his oats – completely off the track
sexually, too. Chases around after his own sister like a tom-cat.
He tried it as a child, but in those days it was simply a joke.
The thing seemed to have subsided for a while, but he's been
acting like a madman lately, particularly these last few months.
Sometimes I think he's only play-acting, but there are other
times when I get the impression he's ripe for an asylum.'

'You don't seem to derive much pleasure from your children,'
Wander said.

'On the contrary! I get a great deal, but in my own way.
They realize that.' Morgenrot kneaded his hands with increas-
ing rapidity, then clapped them together. 'It's the old, old story.
My wife died early on, soon after the boy's birth, and I became
wedded to my work. I made money while the children ran wild.
Well, what's the use of crying over spilt milk?'

'Eva isn't quite as wild as you seem to believe.'

82

'No? Isn't she really? Are you positive? I hope not. I'd hate to think Krug had sent me a gullible idiot. However, I've more faith in his judgment than that. All right, let's get down to business.'

Morgenrot scurried behind his desk and sat down. As he did so he pushed a silver-framed photograph slightly to one side with an ultra-gentle, almost caressing movement. It was evident that he wanted a full and unobstructed view of his visitor.

Wander's eyes travelled from the heavy, dark, well-worn furniture to the thick red velvet curtains, then down to the threadbare carpet. Nothing in the room harmonized, nothing looked expensive – indeed, much of the décor looked cheap. It was a setting more appropriate to a provincial quack than a successful captain of industry.

'I imagine,' Wander began tentatively, 'that Herr Krug gave you some idea of my business on the telephone.'

'But only an idea,' Morgenrot replied. 'He plays his cards pretty close to the chest. In the old days he'd have been a cattle-dealer, but politics and cattle-dealing have a lot in common, don't they – or am I wrong? Perhaps you can enlighten me.'

Wander realized that there was no need to make any diplomatic detours – it would have been a pure waste of time. He said: 'We should appreciate certain information about the planning and financing of arms production.'

'Those are trade secrets, I'm afraid.'

'We were thinking of some firm other than your own – Bölsche's of Munich, for example.'

Morgenrot senior stared at him with positive gratification. 'Does that mean you expect me to indulge in industrial espionage?'

'Herr Krug dislikes that sort of terminology – he would no doubt prefer to call it a request for expert advice based on sound documentary evidence.'

'For the use of whom? Minister Feldmann?'

'Why ask? I assume you know the object of the exercise perfectly well.'

'I like to see confirmation of what I know,' retorted Morgenrot. 'A profitable operation calls for thorough spade-work.' He jumped up from his chair and resumed his monkey-like scampering, pausing briefly from time to time. 'These things cost money. I shall have to invest a packet in bribes, staff recruitment, confidential inquiries and whatever else proves necessary.'

'You've got the picture,' Wander said. 'Always remember this, though. This is an investment which could double if not treble the size of your order book – and the same applies to your net profits.'

Morgenrot was hovering by the door now. 'You can tell your employers this: I agree in principle, whatever the scope of the operation. On the other hand, I should require certain guarantees, notably direct confirmation from the Minister himself. Meanwhile, I'll give you a few concrete facts and figures to take to Feldmann – as a sort of hors-d'œuvre, let's say. Wait here.'

Morgenrot disappeared, leaving Wander seated in front of the desk. He leant forward slightly to get a better look at the silver frame which Morgenrot had so tenderly pushed aside. He picked it up and studied the photograph.

It was a studio portrait of Sabine von Wassermann-Westen.

*

Karl Wander parked his rented car in a side street round the corner from his temporary address. Glancing up at the third-floor windows, he saw lights burning in the living-room and bedroom of Apartment 304. Eva Morgenrot was at home. Almost reluctantly, he headed for the main entrance.

A tall shape detached itself from the shadow of a tree. It was

84

not hard to recognize Peter Sandman in spite of the dim lighting.

'I just happened to be passing, as they say.' Sandman chuckled as briefly as his modest joke deserved. 'So I thought I'd come and see what kind of slum you're living in.'

'It's the height of elegance,' Wander assured him, leading the way to the lift. 'Rent-free, too. I could hardly afford a luxurious pad like this on my income, especially as half of it goes towards a pension scheme.'

'A life insurance policy might be more appropriate,' Sandman observed.

They entered the apartment and Wander switched on every light in the place. Sandman emitted an appreciative whistle. His bloodhound's nose led him unerringly to the liquor cabinet. It contained half a dozen assorted bottles of branded liquor – French cognac, Scotch whisky, American bourbon, English gin, Calvados and Kirschwasser.

'It's all part of the décor,' Wander said invitingly. 'I'm lucky to have such a generous host.'

'A host who knows what two and two make, I'd say.' Sandman chose the Calvados. 'This handsome little piece of real estate and another like it are managed by an agency which is a subsidiary of a construction firm which in turn belongs to a finance house. One of the senior partners of the finance house is a man named Konstantin Krug. Ever heard of him?'

'If that's a joke, tell me another.'

'I can think of at least one more,' Sandman said.

'Perhaps you'd better save it. Don't you really have anything better to do than take a burning interest in my affairs?'

'Not right now.' Sandman sniffed his Calvados. 'Anyway, it's your fault. I already know the kind of circle you've gotten mixed up with.'

'But you don't propose to use what you know, if I understand you correctly. Not for the moment, at least.'

85

'You understand me perfectly,' said Sandman. 'I can afford to be generous when I feel like it, especially to friends.'

'If you really consider yourself a friend of mine, Peter, I'd prefer it if you left me to get on with my work here in peace.'

'I know you well enough to feel optimistic, Karl – not only optimistic but curious.'

'So I won't get rid of you that easily?'

'Do you want to? You're not a born loner, not the sort of man who's hell bent on going down in solitary state with all flags flying. You've got too much common sense for that.'

'All right, Peter, but it's your fault if you're disappointed. Well,' Wander went on brightly, 'what are you selling me?'

'A blackmailer. He'd fit your current scheme of things like a glove.'

'How did he come your way?'

'He was offered to me by one of the Defence Commissioner's assistants. Don't look so innocent, Karl – that sort of thing isn't so rare. They call it covering fire. Journalists can be very useful – only influential ones, of course. An ambitious sidekick who wants to go places fast can't do better, in certain circumstances, than shoot his boss down in flames. Don't act as though you've never heard of such a thing – you of all people.'

'You know perfectly well why I'm not bursting with enthusiasm, Peter. I don't like your having such a clear idea of what I'm up to.'

'I'm not sure I do have such a clear idea, and some time I'll tell you why. To start with, though, concentrate on the crumbs that drop from my table. The Defence Commissioner's office has received a communication from a soldier stationed in the Coblenz area. He makes certain rather arrogant demands, I gather. What's more, he adds an unmistakable threat that if his suggestions, as he calls them, aren't implemented by those higher up, he may be compelled to publicize his knowledge of

86

certain embarrassing facts. And that is an equally unmistakable dig at the Defence Commissioner himself.'

Wander looked sceptical but quickly realized that his scepticism merely amused Sandman. 'Well, what does this – this assistant to the Defence Commissioner propose to do about it?'

'Go through the usual administrative rigmarole to start with – i.e. file it for routine attention, which should take three to four days in my experience. That gives you time enough.'

'For what?'

'To disarm the bomb. You can then decide when to detonate it, if ever. There may be no need to detonate it at all. It depends which suits you better.'

'Who suggested all this – the supplier of the explosive?'

'Certainly not. That gentleman – who holds the rank of senior administrative adviser, let's say – simply invited me to come over for a talk. During it he mentioned several items of accumulated correspondence which he described as curious. They included this one. He had no idea what to do about it, he told me with a wink – it struck him as completely absurd.'

'I get you. It was his way of informing you indirectly.'

'And of covering himself at the same time. Anyway, he had to leave the office soon afterwards and left the open file within reach. Here's the address you want.'

*

Karl Wander opened the door leading to the pocket-sized balcony of his apartment. He stepped out on to it and looked down at the chains of light threading the dark canyon of Koblenzer Strasse. The sky gaped above him like a gigantic yawn. It was midnight.

Sandman was making his way along the floor of the canyon. He turned his head in Wander's direction – a pale indistinct blob, round and moonlike. Then he vanished into the night.

Wander smiled at him, raised his hand in farewell, and immediately wondered a little at having made such an uncharacteristic and totally superfluous gesture. It dawned on him that he felt friendly towards Sandman – a luxury he could hardly afford. After all, he was being employed as a sort of bloodhound.

He leant over the parapet, listening intently, and peered up at the windows of Apartment 304. They were still lit as they had been two hours ago, but now the curtains were not drawn. He could just make out a narrow strip of purple wallpaper.

'Eva!' he called in a subdued voice. He felt sure she would hear him, but she didn't, even when he called her name again. Louder.

Wander went back into the living-room without closing the balcony door. He picked up the oblong card beside the telephone listing the numbers of the various apartments in the building, found that of Apartment 304, dialled, and waited. The monotonous beep-beep seemed to grow in volume, increase in length, rise in pitch. Nothing else happened.

He dialled once more with an equal lack of success. Then he replaced the receiver and went out. He hurried up the staircase that wound round the lift-shaft like a huge serpent. Outside the door of Apartment 304 he halted and listened for some moments. Then he rang the bell.

'Eva,' he called after a brief pause.

He rang and knocked simultaneously.

Then, as he listened again, he seemed to hear a suppressed groan – perhaps only a deep sigh. It might have been the night breeze drifting in through an open window, but it wasn't.

He knelt down and squinted through the keyhole. It was obscured from the inside by a key. Again he knocked, this time hammering at the door with his clenched fist. He did not wait for an answer but raced to the lift and rode it down to the basement. Here he rang and knocked the porter into a state of wakefulness.

'Come with me, quickly! We must get into No. 304.'

The porter yawned at him. His pudgy hamster-like face swam torpidly above a brown and black striped dressing-gown. 'What's all the fuss about?' he growled. 'Why should you worry about what goes on in other people's apartments?'

'Don't waste time!' Wander snapped. 'There's something wrong.'

'Like what? A lot of things happen round here, but it's none of my business. Besides, No. 304 belongs to the Baroness, and she's in Cologne. I'll have to call her before I do anything – she's very particular.'

'Either you get your pass-key at once or I break the door down!'

'All right, all right,' grumbled the man. 'You take the responsibility, though. I'll have to report a thing like this to the management straight away.'

Wander hurried back to the lift and held the door open until the porter reappeared. They travelled up together. Outside No. 304 the man in the dressing-gown bent down and poked about with his pass-key until he had cleared the lock. 'Practice makes perfect,' he remarked smugly. Then he opened the door.

Wander elbowed him aside and rushed into the apartment. All the lights were on. Eva Morgenrot was lying in the bedroom, pale as wax, soaked with sweat and breathing stertorously. Her yellowish eyeballs stared into space and her hands lay clenched upon her chest.

'What is it this time?' the porter demanded plaintively. 'That girl gives nothing but trouble.'

*

With trembling fingers, Karl Wander rummaged in his wallet

for a slip of paper covered with names and numbers. As soon as he had found it he went over to the telephone, snatched up the receiver, and dialled. An unemotional male voice said: 'Casualty department.'

'Dr Bergner, please.'

The doctor was on the line in less than a minute. His voice sounded sleepy. Wander stated his name and asked hurriedly: 'Do you remember me?'

'Unfortunately, yes.' Bergner said no more.

'I'm with Eva Morgenrot. She's lying on her bed, breathing in a funny way. There's an empty bottle on her bedside table – sleeping pills, presumably.'

'Are you capable of giving first aid?'

'I know the normal treatment for symptoms of poisoning. I'll do what I can.'

'Right. I'll send an ambulance at once.'

'Why not come yourself?' Wander asked.

'I've no desire to renew our acquaintance. Apart from that, I'm only on stand-by tonight. A colleague of mine is responsible for outside emergencies.'

'Can't you swap with him?'

'Why should I?'

'Stop hedging!' Wander shouted furiously. 'Get over here – I need you.'

Dr Bergner cleared his throat. 'Are you involved in any way? I mean, is there a chance someone will try to hold you responsible?'

'Not directly, I imagine,' Wander replied cautiously. 'Indirectly perhaps. Is that good enough for you?'

'I'm on my way,' Bergner said, and slammed down the receiver.

The ambulance drove up less than fifteen minutes later. Wander, who was waiting at the main entrance, saw Bergner jump out.

90

The doctor told the ambulance men to wait below but hold themselves in readiness. Then he walked up to Wander and asked formally: 'Was it you who dialled Emergency?'

Wander replied, loudly enough for the ambulance men to hear: 'Yes, I thought it necessary.' This concluded the official part of the performance.

Accompanied by Wander, Bergner took the lift to the third floor. On the way he said: 'Are you sure you were right to ask for me personally?'

'Positive, if you're half the doctor I think you are.'

'I wouldn't put it past you to shove a cuckoo's egg under me and expect me to hatch it.'

Wander opened the lift gate. 'We evidently suffer from the same allergy, Doctor – when something smells bad we both want to throw up.'

'All right,' Bergner said, squaring his shoulders. He walked into the apartment and bent over Eva Morgenrot. Her breathing had dwindled to a faint whisper.

*

'I thought so,' said Wander, who was standing by the window. He looked down into the street, now an opalescent cavern through which the dying night still dragged its weary way. A steel-blue Cadillac had drawn up outside the block. 'We have a visitor – Dr Barranski.'

Bergner, massaging Eva's cardiac region, paused almost imperceptibly. He gave Wander an accusing and contemptuous glare. 'So that's it,' he said. 'You found time to call the man – I should have known.'

'You're wrong, Doctor.'

'If you didn't, who did?'

'The porter, probably. He notified the Baroness and she must have alerted Barranski. I admit I might have guessed but

I couldn't have known for sure. Anyway, I know a little bit more than I did.'

'And you expect me to do your dirty work for you, I suppose?'

'Let's say I expect you to behave like a doctor. I thought that's what you were – correct me if I'm wrong.'

Bergner stared down at the inert form of Eva Morgenrot with an expression of mournful bewilderment. Then he said: 'I sensed it when we first met, Wander. You're the sort of man who likes riding tigers, and you don't care who gives you a leg up.'

Dr Barranski made his entrance. Every light in the apartment seemed to be focused on him. He gave the impression of having just stepped, well rested, out of a refreshing bath. A discreet aura of scent enveloped him. His suit was of a softly luminous midnight-blue which toned exactly with his Cadillac.

He greeted them perfunctorily, seeming to ignore Wander and merely note the presence of Dr Bergner. Going over to Eva Morgenrot, he examined her eyes, felt her pulse, listened to her heart. 'Bad, very bad,' he said.

Then, but not before, he turned his attention to Dr Bergner. 'How do you come to be here?'

'An emergency call,' Bergner replied, coolly matter-of-fact.

'And your diagnosis?'

'Acute poisoning,' Bergner replied, more to Wander. 'Probably an overdose of sleeping tablets.'

'In other words,' said Barranski, 'attempted suicide.' An expression of sorrow settled on his well-tanned features. 'Have you already made a written note to that effect?'

Bergner shook his head. 'There's no reason to at this point. My diagnosis is only a provisional one – it needn't be accurate.'

'But it is,' declared Barranski.

'Why so sure?' Wander blurted out. 'Because it suits you?'

'I should appreciate it,' Barranski said, frigidly polite, 'if you would keep out of this. It might lead to awkward misunderstandings – awkward for you, Herr Wander.'

'Why only for me?' Wander demanded belligerently. 'Why not for you too – or for the lady who sent for you? Why was she so quick off the mark?'

Barranski remained impassive. 'Because she knows that this young woman happens to be a regular patient of mine. I have been acquainted with Fräulein Morgenrot for some time now, and I'm familiar with her moods of depression. This suicide attempt doesn't surprise me.'

'I see no conclusive proof whatsoever that this is attempted suicide,' Bergner said.

'I do,' Barranski replied in a tone of dignified restraint. So saying, he removed his fingers from Eva Morgenrot's wrist and very carefully laid her arm across her body. Then he looked up with an expression of infinite melancholy.

'What is more – and it grieves me deeply to have to say this – her attempt at self-destruction has succeeded. Eva Morgenrot is dead. I must ask you to leave me alone with her.'

*

'What the hell am I supposed to think of myself now?' Dr Bergner demanded as he strode into Wander's apartment. 'I always felt I had the makings of a doctor, if nothing more, but you and that fellow from Cologne seem determined to demote me into a quack.'

'And you don't feel there's anything you can do about it?' Wander forced himself to say. His face was pale and his hands trembled slightly.

Bergner slumped into the nearest arm-chair. He said wearily: 'If you keep any form of liquor which approximates to neat alcohol, I could do with some.'

With an unsteady hand, Wander placed the bottle of Kirschwasser on the table – hundred per cent proof spirit distilled in the Black Forest, clear as morning air and sharp as a razor. He poured out a glass the size of a man's fist. The liquor overflowed the rim and trickled on to the table, where it formed a widening circle. A stupefying smell rose to their nostrils.

'That swine Barranski!' Bergner muttered. 'I've been coming across him more and more often recently – literally tripping over the man. He needs cutting down to size, but I can't do it.'

'Eva Morgenrot wanted to survive,' Wander said. 'I'm sure she did. All she went through, all she was made to go through, was like a transitional stage to her – a stepping-stone to a fresh start.'

'Did you notice the cocksure way Barranski produced his suicide theory? He could be right, of course – in fact it's the most likely explanation – but there's no way of proving it. That bastard simply stated it as fact. All right, so it was poisoning, but it needn't have been sleeping-pills only. No reason why another substance shouldn't have contributed to her death.'

Wander took a pull at the bottle. 'Why does life have to be an unbroken series of surrenders?'

'She was his patient,' Bergner went on. 'Barranski will confirm my diagnosis and issue a death certificate. An unsupported suspicion on my part won't change anything.'

'Eva can't have killed herself,' Wander said. 'I'm sure of it.'

'Were you a friend of hers – more than a friend, maybe?'

'I don't know,' Wander said, more to himself than Bergner. 'Sometimes – like now – I wonder if I know anything at all. The best policy would be for everyone to build a wall round himself, with electrified wire on top and dogs behind it. That's the only way of securing a life of your own, even temporarily.'

The doctor shook his head wearily. 'And I thought you'd help me to nail Barranski – I can't do it on my own. All right,

94

I'll make out the usual report and they'll enter it in the hospital records.'

'A couple of sheets of paper, is that all? A couple of sheets of paper buried under a mountain of files? We might as well give up!'

'My report will note that the symptoms of poisoning were exceptionally acute – so acute that the ingestion of sleeping-pills in the quantity presumed to have been taken might not have been enough to account for them on its own. That's all I can do.'

'What if I get hold of a detective, Doctor? A shrewd character named Kohl who would be only too delighted to investigate the whole affair?'

'I doubt if he'd be able to scotch the suicide theory – it's too damned plausible. Anyone who's prepared to accept the circum-stances at only half their face value will accept it as a matter of course.'

'What aroused your suspicions, then?'

'Barranski doesn't rule out the possibility of foul play – I sensed that immediately – and he's doing all he can to gloss things over. That sort of behaviour not only arouses my sus-picions, it makes my gorge rise.'

'You're one of the world's unfortunates, Doctor,' Wander said. 'So am I.'

*

'I know this isn't your office and I realize you're not on duty, but I must speak to you.'

Fräulein Wiebke gave Wander a short and searching stare. 'Come in,' she said. 'The bathroom's through there – a little cold water wouldn't do you any harm. Also, your hair needs combing. I'll make you some black coffee.'

Her voice was as immutably businesslike in the small hours as it had been in broad daylight. Her cool, smooth face showed no traces of fatigue. She moved around her sparsely furnished one-roomed flat just as she did in Konstantin Krug's office.

'I have to talk to someone,' Wander said, when he had finished in the bathroom. He sat down at the table uninvited and watched her preparing coffee in the kitchenette. Her pleasantly natural manner soothed him. 'Something terrible has happened.'

'To you?'

'To Eva Morgenrot. She's dead – she died two hours ago.'

The girl, now with her back to him, put down the coffee-cups abruptly. She seemed to freeze for a moment, then turned to face him, wide-eyed.

'How did it happen?'

'An overdose, probably.'

'Suicide?'

'That's the theory.'

Fräulein Wiebke resumed her activities. She placed a coffee-pot and two cups on a tray and carried it across to the table. 'Are you involved in some way?'

'You're the second person to ask me that.'

'So the answer's no. Good.' She put a cup in front of him and filled it with black coffee. 'Any other likely candidates?'

'Are you expecting to hear a particular name – a name you know, for instance?'

'I'm not expecting anything, Herr Wander. I don't imagine you came here to cry on my shoulder. I know enough about you to know you'd spare me that. You don't know me at all, on the other hand, or you'd never try to pump me so crudely. I can't think why else you're here.'

Wander drained his cup without pausing for breath. He pushed it across to the girl, who refilled it. Then he said: 'Have you ever watched someone die?'

She didn't answer, just looked at him in a reappraising way. 'Why should her death affect you so much?' she asked at length.

'Because I feel so helpless. When I was a youngster I was put in charge of a dog. It was run over in front of my very eyes. I ran across to it and held its head in my hands. It whimpered and fought for breath, and all the time it looked up at me with an expression of infinite trust. I couldn't do a thing to help. It died in agony. I'll never forget that. I ought to have taken better care, you see.'

'Drink up your coffee,' she said brusquely. 'Then you'd better get some sleep – use my bed if you like. I can stay with a girl-friend who lives upstairs. The best thing you can do is leave tomorrow. Go back to writing – the climate here obviously doesn't agree with you. I'll dream up a plausible excuse.'

'What if I don't want to?'

'Think it over carefully. Sleep on it and you'll see it's the best solution.'

'What if I can't?'

A trace of bewilderment passed across the girl's face. 'What are you really after?' she asked. 'Money? That would be one likely motive, I grant you, but it might cost you a bit too. Or do you feel you're here to carry out a sort of mission – a self-imposed one? That can be just as expensive, especially for people like you. You seem prepared to invest a lot of personal feeling in your work. Fancy doing that in this place! Can't you really think of anything better to do?'

'But you're here too. Why?'

'I landed here without giving much thought to places and personalities. I don't invest anything in the way of private emotion or political conviction – I just do a routine job. There's nothing more in it, not for anyone. Don't you understand?'

'And yet I'm sitting here with you.'

'That doesn't have to mean anything, neither to you nor me.'

'I accept that,' Wander assured her. He succumbed to the temptation to put his hand on hers, and left it there. 'May I come again if I'm feeling really low?'

U.M.–G

'Don't tell me you're planning to make a habit of it,' she said, sounding almost amused. 'All right, if you insist on playing the wolf in sheep's clothing . . .'

'What's your first name?' he interrupted her. 'You do have one, I suppose?'

She hesitated for a moment. 'Well, I suppose a little mild amusement wouldn't do you any harm – my name's Marlene.'

'It suits you,' Wander said gravely.

Marlene Wiebke ran her fingers through her short straw-blonde hair. She looked suddenly resentful, and tried unsuccessfully to inject a maximum of formality into the atmosphere. Rising to her feet, she said: 'It's high time you got some sleep.'

'I'm on my way,' Wander replied, not moving. 'Thanks a lot for your tempting proposition – offering to give up your bed, I mean. Some other time, maybe. It can't be soon enough for me. I'm feeling better than I did.'

'You'll feel even better when you've shaken the dust of Bonn off your heels, take it from me.' Marlene Wiebke went to the door and opened it. 'On the other hand, you may genuinely be a hopeless case. Who knows?'

'Who knows?' Wander replied, getting up. 'I may only just have become one.' He reached for his raincoat. 'Please don't try to understand me – I abandoned the attempt myself quite a while back.'

'You're not leaving tomorrow?'

'No.'

She gave him her hand. 'Try to forget tonight – our conversation, I mean. And if you can't forget that girl's death you might bear this in mind: every suicide, fake or genuine, is automatically investigated by the police. It all depends who conducts the investigation.'

'Of course,' Wander replied absently, still holding her hand. 'But it's pure routine.'

'In every case? Even when the man in charge is someone like Detective Chief Inspector Kohl?'

'Why bring his name up?'

'He called the office yesterday and asked to speak to you urgently. Said he had something for you, and would you contact him.'

'I'll do that,' Wander said. 'Kohl's an avenging angel at heart. I know he doesn't seem like one – not with that avuncular voice and comfortable waist-line – in fact he may not realize it himself, but . . .'

'Pack your bags!' Marlene Wiebke spoke with a vehemence which surprised her as much as Wander. 'I've never given anyone advice here, but I'm making an exception in your case. Just get out of Bonn and don't ask me why. And don't get any wrong ideas, either. In your position you can't afford to.'

'Good night, Marlene,' he said. 'No matter what happens, try to stay the way you are.'

INTERIM REPORT No. 5

BY THE MAN KNOWN AS JEROME

on the function of mistakes which seem so inevitable that they pass for the obvious.

There has never yet been a case which permits full and straightforward comprehension or precise reconstruction. Not even the crudest dilettantes of my profession, the couriers and contacts, are immune from dangerous complications, and the more varied the motives, personalities and ideas involved the greater the scope for error.

Blind alleys are frequently mistaken for freeways. However vital, a key document may come into our possession before we can assess it properly. Once the game has run its course and the result is known, we naturally know more – but not everything.

No operation goes off without a hitch. This naturally encourages us to take such errors for granted from the outset, even when one or other of them has to be paid for in human lives. However, there is nothing to be done about forces of which one has no knowledge or conception.

I did not originally regard the affair as anything more than a form of private entertainment – a personal favour to Peter Sandman. In addition, it presented an opportunity of training junior agents. The real facts of the matter were not recognized in time.

What really interested me and dominated my attention was the Feldmann-Krug-Wander combination, which seemed to offer a prospect of some fierce in-fighting. We thought we had secured ringside seats, and in a certain sense this was true. The only trouble was, our seats did not provide a view of the fighting behind the scenes, and what went on in the dressing-rooms was just as much of a closed book to us.

My provisional assessment was as follows: Eva Morgenrot's death was comparatively unimportant – suicide and nothing more. These things occur with unhappy regularity, even in the best circles. Sandman agreed with me. Only Wander refused to go for the suicide theory.

I was not annoyed by Wander's guesses, conjectures and suspicions, especially as it came out that Wander, as I myself suspected, had a weakness for the girl. His interest was probably of a very personal nature but may only have been exaggerated sympathy. People like Wander react that way.

It was also Sandman who drew my attention to Detective Chief Inspector Kohl, whom I already knew. Kohl was doing his best to reach pensionable age with a minimum of fuss. To the best of my knowledge, he had – until the time in question – been doing just that.

On the other hand, Kohl was undoubtedly a top-notch detective, a fact which enabled him to work swiftly and smoothly from the purely technical angle. He seemed to have no personal, let alone individualistic, ideas about the criteria and methods of his profession. His superiors described him as a model subordinate. As a result, the surprise he pulled came as twice as much of a shock.

We might have foreseen it, even so. It would have been enough to realize that Kohl represented a not insignificant piece in the game of chess that was being played simultaneously on several boards. All we needed to have done was to visit a bar belonging to one Frau Jeschke, talk with Kohl's fellow-detectives, question Dr Barranski a little more thoroughly, or sound out Wander himself.

Frau Jeschke did talk later on. The following are extracts from her observations on Kohl: 'Knew him for twenty years or more . . . came and had a beer every evening – only one, mind you, and didn't talk much . . . brought that man Wander along one day – started drinking and talking after that . . . sometimes made remarks like: "We're always running away, and with luck we don't get caught. I've never had much luck, though." That sort of thing.'

But we missed all this at the time and thought we could afford to be amused by very different things – for instance, a newspaper clipping Sandman had dug up. Taken from a leader written by Karl Wander ten years before, it ran: 'For us, the year 1945 was zero hour. We had been given the greatest opportunity world history has to offer: a chance to make a completely fresh start. What was more, we had been taught a lesson more precious than any which had ever been learned before – a lesson purchased with millions of dead and the ruins of our cities and private lives.

And where do we stand now?'

That sort of cry from the heart tickles me – in fact, one or two of my closest associates found it a comic masterpiece. But Sandman remained sceptical. He took Wander seriously on this point because he felt convinced that Wander himself was being dead serious – that he meant exactly what he wrote.

To me, this was just one more indication that we were dealing with a confirmed do-gooder, and do-gooders always have tickled my sense of humour.

One more mistake!

Chapter 6

'There you are at last,' said Detective Chief Inspector Kohl.
He eyed Wander challengingly. 'If you hadn't come of your own
accord I'd have sent a squad car and a couple of men to fetch
you.'

'What is it this time?'

Wander was at Precinct Headquarters No. 3. The policemen
in the big room took little notice of him. To them he was just
one of the three or four dozen problems to be dealt with daily.
He could safely be left to their veteran chief inspector.

'Come with me,' Kohl commanded, and set off down the
cavernous corridor leading to the interrogation room. On this
occasion he motioned Wander into the only chair and remained
standing by the door.

'Well?' he said.

'Be a bit more explicit,' Wander prompted. 'How can I know
what's going on inside your head?'

'Eva Morgenrot's death – why didn't you notify me right
away?'

'I was just going to.'

'Too late,' said the policeman. 'Why?'

'Is this a conversation or the third degree?' Kohl's abrupt
manner began to make Wander feel ill at ease. 'Don't tell me
we're back at square one. Surely you're not suggesting that I
had anything to do with it, are you?'

'Not directly,' Kohl replied. He sounded almost regretful.
'Nor indirectly either, from the look of it. Seems more likely

you've battened down the hatches. Hear no evil, see no evil, speak no evil – is that it?'

'I was out of Bonn all day yesterday.'

Kohl nodded. 'I know, you were visiting Morgenrot senior in Essen.'

'Anything wrong with that?'

'Not necessarily. You can take it that I've simply noted the fact. You're the proud possessor of a watertight alibi, or so I gather from Mr Sandman.'

'Who else have you talked to?' Wander asked. 'Baroness von Wassermann-Westen, maybe, or Martin Morgenrot?'

'Don't they appeal to you?' Kohl inquired softly.

'They nauseate me.'

'That's understandable,' said Kohl. 'I've spent a little time on those two myself – of necessity. The Morgenrot girl's suicide, potential or ostensible, appears to have followed a schedule of its own. To be precise, the poison – presumably sleeping-pills – needed two hours to take effect. Furthermore, vital importance attaches to the time prior to the ingestion of the fatal dose because that was when she decided to commit suicide. However, both Wassermann-Westen and Morgenrot junior state that they spent the entire day together, or at least the afternoon. In Cologne.'

'You mean they're covering for each other?'

'Perhaps. It's hard to crack an alibi like that. God knows what their relationship's based on, but it exists.'

'Martin Morgenrot is a handful – he worked me over a few days ago.'

'So I'm aware. That's another thing you might have told me earlier. As it was, I had to waste nearly a whole hour worming it out of the boy. He alleges – with some conviction – that he worked you over because he saw his sister entering your apartment in circumstances warranting only one interpretation . . .'

'That's absolutely ridiculous!'

'But hard to refute. The only person who could confirm your story is dead.'

'Are you planning to make something out of it?'

'You didn't stick to our agreement, Wander. I told you how much I wanted to get Barranski. If I'd been able to confront him on the spot, with the girl actually lying there, I might have been able to make trouble for him. Now it's too late.'

'So you don't believe her death was a conventional suicide either?'

'What do you mean, either? Who else finds it hard to believe?'

'Barranski himself.'

Kohl was genuinely surprised and showed it. 'How do you figure that out?'

'Dr Bergner came to that conclusion, not me. I called him and he turned up before Barranski arrived. According to his findings suicide was entirely possible – probable, in fact. Even so, Barranski's stubborn insistence on taking over the case made Bergner feel sure that he didn't exclude the possibility of murder.'

'I must speak to this Dr Bergner of yours.'

'I can fix that – be only too happy to.'

'Then be quick about it.' Kohl opened his briefcase and removed a sheet of paper. 'Incidentally, here's the address of Eva Morgenrot's mother, together with details of her birth and adoption. Would you care to pay her a visit?'

Wander nodded. 'I will, but it'll be anything but a pleasure in the circumstances.'

'And this time,' Kohl said, 'make sure you notify me promptly of anything you find out.'

*

'You wrote to the Defence Commissioner,' Karl Wander began, adding quickly: 'Is what you say in the letter true?'

The army corporal, Fünfinger by name, whom Wander had met in a bar near Coblenz station, looked puzzled. 'Are you part of his outfit?'

'No.'

'Do you belong to a similar outfit?'

'Wrong again, Corporal.'

'Police? Special Branch? Something in that line?'

'I'm here on a semi-unofficial basis, for personal reasons,' Wander explained, heading for the bar. 'What are you drinking?'

'Speaking semi-unofficially,' the Corporal replied, 'I fancy champagne. Would your personal reasons run to that?'

Wander nodded and placed the order. The landlord kept a stock of Veuve Clicquot in his ice-box for the benefit of female regulars whose regulars wore uniform. Champagne was their favourite form of refreshment between spells of duty.

Corporal Fünfinger scrutinized the man who had invited him to have a drink. 'How do you know I wrote a letter at all?'

'These things get around.'

'Get around where?'

Fünfinger was a short, fat man. His face resembled a gnarled potato adorned with a pair of shrewd, watchful little eyes. His hands looked just as gnarled, but the voice in which he launched his shafts of cheerful sarcasm possessed gentle, almost caressing undertones.

Wander pushed a brimming glass of champagne towards him. 'My suggestion is this: you request the Defence Commissioner's office to return the letter you wrote him and hand it over to me.'

'Christ,' said Fünfinger, 'you've got a nerve. What makes you think I'd do anything of the kind. Why should I ask them to send my letter back?'

'For two reasons,' Wander replied. 'In the first place, my information is that your letter could be construed as blackmail. You accompanied your demand with a threat.'

'Bullshit,' retorted Fünfinger. 'I simply made a complaint and piled it on a bit, that's all.'

'In your opinion, maybe, but your opinion doesn't necessarily carry any weight with the people who received your letter. You didn't sound off according to regulations – that's why they've got you by the short hairs. The Director of Public Prosecutions doesn't like attempted blackmail.'

The Corporal reached for his glass and drained it with every appearance of pleasure, never taking his eyes off Wander. 'Listen,' he said in an obliging voice. 'Whatever you do, don't take me for a fool. I suppose it was the Defence Commissioner who marched you off to see me – you probably owe him a favour or something. All right, tell him this from me: as far as I'm concerned, he can have fun whenever, wherever and however he likes. I'm not interested in his little affairs. All I want him to do is follow up my complaint and make it snappy.'

'But what exactly do you expect the Defence Commissioner to do, Corporal?'

'Help me get rid of someone – someone I don't like.'

Wander had some difficulty in marshalling his thoughts. He refilled their glasses with deliberation, playing for time. His gaze travelled round the tawdry bar-room and was intercepted by a come-hither stare from a female customer. Fünfinger sent her a glass of champagne coupled with a message to the effect that she was a distraction, and would she sit farther away. She complied.

'What if the Defence Commissioner declines to help you get rid of your pet hate?'

'Then I'll finish him instead – it's as easy as that.'

'Is it really?'

'Of course,' said Fünfinger. 'I suppose you're wondering what I've got up my sleeve. OK, I'll tell you, just to show you and your boss which way the wind's blowing. The thing is, there's this mate of mine who works as a floor waiter in the

Hotel Splendide. My mate has a mate who works as a bellhop in the same high-class whore-house. That's where the Defence Commissioner stops off when he has things to do here, and he seems to have a lot of things to do here when he wants to. Coblenz is a garrison town, so there's plenty of scope – for the Defence Commissioner as well as the lift-boy.'

'Are you making allegations of homosexuality?'

'Allegations?' Fünfinger looked almost hurt. 'I can produce evidence – plenty of it, and nothing that wouldn't stand up in court.'

'Why are you so obsessed with the idea?'

'Are you hard of hearing or something?' The Corporal's tone carried a hint of impatience. 'I told you, I don't care who does what or where. Anything goes with me, just so long as nobody tries to pin the same sort of thing on me.'

'Very tolerant of you.'

'As far as I'm concerned, this big shot and his boy-friend can – well, no, let's just say they're welcome to each other, especially as it's more of a mental thing with them – kinky poetry and art books and so on, even if they do use a hotel bedroom as a base. Well, why not? Let them, as long as I see the last of Drau.'

'Who's Drau?'

'My CO,' Fünfinger explained. 'Major Drau, a leathery old sod with plenty of war service but a right bastard into the bargain – mentally disturbed, probably, because they haven't promoted him fast enough. He reckons he should have been a colonel long ago, in the normal way. The fact that he isn't almost reconciles me to wearing this bloody awful uniform. Anyway, Drau – we call him Dirty Drau – works off his inferiority complex by using filthy language all the time. He talks the way normal people shit.'

'And that's the only reason why you're out to get him, Corporal? I wouldn't have credited you with so much sensitivity.'

'Shows how wrong you can be.' The Corporal grinned broadly. 'Don't waste any more time trying to find out what makes me tick. That dirty old sod Drau could have raped my mother, my sister, my girl-friend or me - who cares? The fact that he exists is an insult to the human race and that's good enough.'

'I don't follow you,' Wander said. 'The use of foul language is frowned on officially, I grant you, but it isn't a punishable offence. I doubt if you'd get very far with your complaint. However, just suppose I managed to get rid of Drau. Would you be prepared to hand over your evidence on the Defence Commissioner to me?'

Corporal Fünfinger pulled the champagne bottle towards him and studied it attentively, then tipped the remainder into his glass. 'I would, but how do you plan to get Drau?'

'Do you think he'd be particularly hard to get rid of?'

'Not if you went about it the right way. Apart from all the things he's done over the years, it isn't just his vocabulary that'd make your hair curl – he always carries the latest additions to his pornography collection around in his briefcase. What's more, he's even been known to read them aloud in the mess.'

'All right,' Wander said. 'I'll make you a present of Drau and you surrender your evidence. It's a deal.'

*

'I don't understand,' said the woman sitting opposite Wander. 'I've never been married and I've never had a child.'

The scene was Frankfurt, where Wander had stopped off on the way back from Coblenz. He was in a dress shop near St Paul's Church. The proprietor's office doubled as stock-room and emergency bedroom, and contained a broad couch screened by bolts of garishly coloured material.

'Your daughter was called Eva, wasn't she?'

'Forget it,' the woman said dismissively. 'We're only wasting time, and that would be a pity.'

There was little doubt of her readiness to regard Wander as a kindred spirit. She made an unusually femine, gently sensual impression. The full mouth dominating her face parted readily to reveal her teeth, and her eyes resembled a cat's, languid but alert.

'I don't like problems,' she said, leaning back against a mountain of silk cushions. 'There are better ways to spend one's time – nicer ways. A man like you shouldn't concentrate on a woman's past – not when he's actually with her.'

'Your daughter Eva,' Wander pursued, 'was born on the fifteenth of July nineteen forty-nine. Father allegedly unknown. She lived at first with her grandmother in Bremen. In November nineteen-fifty, when she was a little over twelve months old, she was given a home by the Morgenrots, who adopted her legally soon afterwards.'

'How do you know all this?' She raised herself on one elbow and stared at him with mounting uneasiness, then gave an unconvincing laugh. 'What's it to you, anyway?'

'More than you can guess. I knew your daughter.'

'Well? Are you having an affair with her?'

'No,' Wander replied curtly.

'I wouldn't put it past you, but maybe Eva's too young – too young for you, that is. Anyway, it's nothing to do with me.'

'I've also met Eva's adoptive father, Herr Maximilian Morgenrot.'

'I see!' She lost her feline languor and a shrill note crept into her voice. 'Was it him who gave you my address? What did he tell you about me? Don't bother – I can guess. I hope you didn't believe a word of it. You don't have to be a mind-reader to see through that man.'

'All the same, he adopted Eva with your consent.'

'Not him, his wife! And if he told you anything different he's lying as usual. I was a distant relative of his wife, so when they didn't have any children to begin with she took care of Eva for me. I was in a pretty bad way at the time. Besides, I'm not the motherly type. Adoption was the best solution – for all of us. It paid off, too.'

Wander, who refrained from looking at the woman, did not reply. Rising to his feet impatiently, he walked over to a pile of bales and leant against them. 'But the Morgenrots' marriage didn't remain childless,' he said, ignoring the last remark.

'No, the boy arrived a year or two later. God knows how Maximilian Morgenrot produced a son! Maybe it wasn't his – I wouldn't have put it past that cousin of mine. She didn't live long, but it's my opinion that marrying that man was the thing she regretted most. I can sympathize, too. What do you think he is, a gentleman?'

'He's a cynical egoist and a shrewd businessman,' Wander said, not without calculation. 'There are plenty of his sort around, though – they think their methods are the done thing these days. On the other hand, Morgenrot may only have become like that recently. We all progress in one direction or another.'

'He was always like that!' she blurted out. 'It wasn't obvious at the start, but my cousin soon found out what kind of man she was stuck with. That's why she took precautions.'

'Precautions? How?'

'By adopting Eva, of course. The factories belonged to her – she brought them with her when she married. Morgenrot was just a senior employee, an executive director or something similar, so it was a marriage of convenience for the firm's sake, mainly. Then, when Morgenrot became more and more of a big businessman, my cousin hit on the adoption idea. She made it a provision of her will that if she died prematurely Eva would inherit half her estate when she came of age, cash and all other registered assets included.'

III

'In just under two years' time, in other words.' Wander pulled up a chair and sat down. 'And you didn't take any interest in Eva throughout the time she was forced to spend in Morgenrot's house?'

'That was the agreement. I kept my part of it, too.'

'In return for what?'

The woman in front of him spread her arms wide in a grandly proprietorial gesture which embraced her entire surroundings. 'The price was this business – one of the best in town. Besides, who was I to stand in the way of my daughter's happiness? Eva had everything a girl could want.'

'Life without a mother, not even an adoptive mother, and Maximilian Morgenrot for a father.'

'What are you on about?' the woman exclaimed defensively. 'Another couple of years and it'll all have paid off. Eva will be a millionairess.'

'No she won't,' Wander replied. 'Eva is dead.'

*

'I'm quite tame today.' Martin Morgenrot's grin was almost familiar. 'You don't have to worry – I don't have any plans to take you apart for the moment. Not unless you force me to.'

'How did you get in?'

'Through the door.'

Morgenrot junior was sitting in the middle of Apartment 204 as if it belonged to him. He had slumped into an arm-chair and propped his legs on the table. The ashtray beside him contained a whole cemetery of cigarette-ends. He had evidently been waiting for some considerable time.

'Who let you in? Do you have a key? If so, where did you get it from?'

'What difference does it make?' The boy stared contemptuously at Wander, who was standing just inside the door. 'You've got more pressing problems on your plate right now.' His right hand knotted itself into a fist. 'After all, I'm the brother of a girl who killed herself – probably with your help.'

'That's enough,' snapped Wander. 'Clear out!'

'Take it easy,' said the boy. 'I know you've got an outsize chip on your shoulder because I can have any sports car and all the women I want. If you want to know, women make me sick. All they're after is my monthly allowance, which runs into four figures.'

'What's that compared to the seven-figure sums – the millions of marks – you'll get out of Eva's death?'

'No more cracks like that,' Morgenrot junior said in a low voice. He looked as if he were about to spring to his feet. Almost simultaneously, he made an effort to laugh and actually succeeded. 'I'll inherit from the old man some time or other, so who cares about a few million marks either way? I've already got more money than I can spend.'

'So in fact there was no need for Eva to die from your point of view?'

'That's just what I'm trying to tell you, Wander. Eva was a stupid little cow at heart – she couldn't even give milk properly, just bullshit, but that didn't stop everyone wanting to milk her.'

'Me included, you mean?'

'Of course, and nobody slaughters a cow they plan to milk. They give it the best treatment they possibly can.'

'I begin to understand,' Wander said. 'You don't hold me directly responsible for Eva's death. In that case, who's your candidate?'

'Any suggestions?' The boy watched him attentively.

'You want me to be specific?'

The answer came back like a whiplash. 'Certainly I do. It's the only chance you've got, Wander. Either you tell me who was responsible for Eva's death, which shouldn't be too difficult, or . . .'

'Or what?'

'Or I hold you personally responsible. You can take your pick.'

*

The rally of the Displaced Persons' Union took place in Kennedy Park, known formerly as Liberation Park, earlier as Adolf Hitler Park, and earlier still as Kaiser Wilhelm Park. Apart from the name, nothing much seemed to have changed over the decades. The Germanic love of public ceremony blossomed on the same soil like a perennial.

Men formed the majority of those who had been drummed up for the occasion, but the participants also included a scattering of elderly women, docile children and patriotic adolescents. None of them had anything against the name Kennedy, just as Kennedy had voiced no complaints about displaced persons. The DPs consequently regarded him as one of their patron saints, the more so because there was no prospect of his setting the record straight.

They paraded in a mood of total tranquillity. Fanfares rang out, guards of honour froze to attention, heads craned inquisitively to catch a glimpse of the politician responsible for the DPs' welfare, Minister Feldmann.

Wander lurked in the background. He had propped himself against a tree from which a brace of loudspeakers hung suspended like two ripe fruits. Next to him a banner fluttered in the gentle breeze. Emblazoned upon it was a coat of arms, heraldic symbol of one of the provinces lost in the aftermath of a lost war.

The crowd, which had flocked in from far and wide, began to evince gratitude and enthusiasm. Everyone clapped, and one or two were sufficiently moved to cheer. Their plaudits were directed at Minister Feldmann, who had now mounted the platform.

Feldmann, dignified as ever, seemed moved himself. He gave

a paternal nod and raised the hand that held his hat, possibly as a means of fanning himself in the overripe heat of early autumn.

'Big Brother in person,' said a sonorous voice beside Wander. 'Big Brother with paternalistic undertones, though – he's already in a transitional phase of development. Paternalism always works – not only in Germany, but better here than elsewhere.'

Wander identified his neighbour without looking round. 'What are you doing, Peter, warming your cold heart in the white heat of popular enthusiasm?'

'Popular enthusiasm lost its effect on me a long time ago,' Sandman replied. 'I've produced several dozen articles on functions like this, and I could see my readers yawning while I wrote – at least in recent years. People have become blasé about these things. As long as no blood flows, everything looks rosy.'

Near the platform, a television reporter was surrounded by stewards and ushered – to use the accepted term – outside. This meant in practice that he was borne forcibly away in response to shouted orders. The conductor of the association's brass band, prepared for such eventualities, launched his bandsmen into the march 'Old Comrades'. The Minister continued to chat, undistracted, to the chief organizer of the rally. The Shadow Minister, who was also present, studied his fingernails with extreme and visibly nervous concentration.

'It's a disgrace!' Wander shouted at the stewards as they marched the unwelcome television reporter towards the gates. 'A disgrace, that's what it is!'

Sandman laughed. 'What are you complaining about? The bouncers don't beat up disruptive elements on the spot, and some people might call that a sign of progress. Even these lads have learnt – or it's dawned on them, at least – that you don't have to exterminate a man to put him out of action.'

'You mean you can still laugh at this sort of thing, Peter?'

'I can still read,' the American replied serenely. 'What's more, I have a pretty useful memory. It was functioning this morning, when a draft of the speech the Minister's due to deliver today fluttered on to my desk. You know the routine – Sunday hand-outs are the usual way of giving journalists advance information so they can splash it by Monday morning at latest.'

'I'm not interested in how you get your information,' Wander said. 'Anyway, it doesn't matter what you suspect – you'll never be able to prove it.'

'Of course not. Feldmann would never admit publicly that someone else had been tinkering with his draft. In this case, you.'

'Come off it. These Sunday sermons are all alike – just so many peas in a pod.'

'Except that this isn't a Sunday sermon. We're just about to be treated to something strangely reminiscent of those manuscripts you left with me ten years ago. At least, some of your phrases recurred more or less verbatim in Feldmann's draft.'

Wander did not reply. He seemed to be listening to the crackle and roar of the loudspeakers. The rally organizer was followed by a regional chairman of guaranteed reliability, then another and another. Silesians, Pomeranians and East Prussians took the floor in turn, also Sudeten Germans.

All spoke of undying loyalty to their unforgotten homeland, of unbreakable ties and sacred obligations, of inviolable human freedoms. What was right for the inhabitants of darkest Africa, namely, self-determination, was right for them. Was it not time at this late hour, to take positive action?

Next came the solemn boom of Feldmann's voice. He welcomed and thanked all present, not only on his own behalf but also on that of the Chancellor, who was unfortunately detained. While still at the preamble stage, he assured them of his heartfelt sympathy. He asserted his complete understanding of the unbreakable ties and sacred obligations to which expression had just been given. He promised – indeed, vowed – to remain steadfastly aware of them. Let no one take them in vain!

'World history,' Feldmann now declared, reading from his draft, 'must have a purpose, otherwise we should not be standing here today.'

'A gem of a phrase!' Sandman murmured delightedly to Wander. 'Was that another of yours? I could forgive you a great deal, just for that.'

Wander shook his head. The Minister's voice rose a decibel: 'The interests of people who have been robbed of their homeland in defiance of international law and morality must never be forgotten!'

'That routine drivel certainly isn't mine,' Wander said.

'Hardly,' replied Sandman, 'but what about the next bit?'

'Courage in the face of destiny, genuine faith and unadulterated conviction,' declaimed the Minister, 'merit something more than fine words; they merit and demand the will to form clear-cut decisions, to adopt an unequivocal and realistic stand – indeed, to take final and conclusive action!'

Slowly and laboriously, the Minister worked round to his pet subject, the West German army. First he spoke of sympathy for the interests of those in need of protection. Then it came: 'We are all in need of powerful and reliable protection, of a pacifying force in which we can put our faith. In practical terms, we must have at our disposal a Federal Army which is wholly and unmistakably filled with a genuine sense of responsibility. Reluctant as I am to ask the question, does our army satisfy these requirements?'

It was clear that the Minister did not think so, and he proceeded to demonstrate his unbelief at due length. True, he praised the spirit of 'honest endeavour' animating the troops – almost all of them splendid men and many of them admirably public-spirited, but deplorably lacking in assured knowledge of the things that ultimately count. And why? 'Because our soldiers have not so far been fortunate enough to find the trail-blazing leaders they deserve.'

'Let's cut the rest,' Sandman said, drawing Wander out of the charmed circle of the loudspeakers. He did not stop until they were close to the wire fence. 'What does it all mean? Is Feldmann planning to take over the Ministry of Defence by force?'

'I doubt it,' Wander said. 'After all, the present Minister of Defence is one of Feldmann's oldest friends in the Party.'

'So what? People who want to get to the top generally tread on other people, even when they belong to the same party – hadn't you heard?'

'It could also be that he's acting on direct instructions from the Chancellor,' Wander protested. 'The Chancellor wants to see conditions in the Federal Army changed – they're capable of improvement, God knows. Why shouldn't I help, instead of standing aside? It's my belief that the army needs a firm ideological foundation – you know that.'

'And you think a character like Feldmann is qualified to make your fantasy come true?'

'At the present time,' Wander said, 'nobody seems better qualified than Feldmann to initiate genuine changes, and that's the prime requirement now.'

Peter Sandman leaned against the wire fence. Almost pityingly, he said: 'What if Feldmann isn't interested in constructive change, Karl? Just for a moment, try to imagine that he wants the West German army for his own private purposes, as an instrument of policy? Don't you think it's possible?'

'No,' Wander replied firmly. 'I can't believe it. He's acting on the Chancellor's behalf.'

'And yet there are a couple of things I find highly suspicious. There's his speech today, for one. Coming from him on such an occasion, some of those remarks sounded ambiguous, to put it mildly. Added to that, two big Sunday papers have published interviews with General Keilhacke. Keilhacke doesn't pull his punches – he's obviously trying to sell himself as the next Inspector-General. And what then? Do you genuinely think he'd allow himself to be manipulated, him and his men? No, Karl, it's a dangerous game. Do you really feel up to it? Another thing: they've just published a sizeable edition of an excellently produced and handsomely illustrated pamphlet – Feldmann's life-story, or as much of it as he chooses to reveal. The perfect political gentleman, the loving and devoted paterfamilias, the meritorious statesman who combines great future promise with a modest sense of duty, the courageous front-line soldier, sympathetic to the anti-Hitler resistance movement but not actually involved – and so on. If that isn't a cold and calculating power bid, what is it?'

Wander shook his head impatiently. 'All you've done is shoot an arrow and paint a target round the place where it landed – anyone can score a bull's-eye that way. As I see it, Feldmann has more integrity than most of the leading politicians around today.'

'It looks that way on the surface, I know. He combines the country gentleman image with the vitality of a bull – in other words, he has all the most important attributes of his predecessors. Taken in conjunction with his marked inscrutability and ambiguous statements, it makes an alarming mixture. And as for his integrity, which you seem so ready to accept, you obviously don't know much about human nature. He has his vices, like everyone else.'

'I can't believe that.'

'No? You've settled pretty close to his source of supply – Sabine von Wassermann-Westen, I mean.'

'Tell me more.'

'Not right now,' Sandman replied with gentle mockery. 'First, you're due for a little lesson in contemporary politics.

Far be it from me to disillusion you ahead of time.' He described a sweeping gesture at something behind Wander's back.

Turning round, Wander saw the stewards who had earlier dealt with the television reporter. They were now bearing down on him. The men ranged themselves in front of him, fat, fleshy and powerful. Meanwhile, the assembled throng were already singing the German National Anthem, but only the first verse.

One of the stewards lowered his head and trumpeted: 'You swore at us!'

'I merely said it was a disgrace.'

'Meaning us.' The men surrounded Wander. They gripped him under the arms. 'That's an infringement of democratic order and discipline, and we make the rules round here.' So saying, they hustled him to the exit.

There, one of them aimed a vigorous kick at the seat of Wander's pants. He dodged, threw himself to the ground and rolled out of the way. A cloud of dust rose.

Peter Sandman helped him to his feet. 'I'm not saying you deserved it, Karl, but I'm gradually coming to the conclusion that you ask for these things.'

*

'Well, here I am!' announced Sobottke, Krug's driver, indefatigably cheerful as usual. He shook Wander vigorously by the hand and gazed round Apartment 204 as if planning to move in. 'What shall I do, boss?'

'Anything you like, so long as you leave me to work in peace.' Wander indicated some sheets of manuscript paper and said, with discreet sarcasm: 'For Herr Krug. I'm sure you wouldn't want to disturb me.'

'Not on your life!' Sobottke assured him. 'Far from it. My job is to protect you from outside distractions so you can get on with things.'

'What things?'

'Well, your problems, in a manner of speaking.'

Wander pushed his papers aside. Sobottke's crude geniality got on his nerves. 'I see. If I follow you correctly, Herr Sobottke, you're not here to deliver a message or a written report or to collect anything of the kind from me. Equally, you're not here to pay a social call.'

'Right first time!' Sobottke grinned admiringly and added: 'You've got brains, Herr Wander. Be a pity if someone tried to knock them out – Herr Krug thinks so too.'

'You mean he's worried about me?'

'Not any more. Not now that I'm with you.'

'I don't remember indenting for a watch-dog.'

'You didn't need to, Herr Wander. Herr Krug always knows what a person's short of. Sobottke, he said to me, Herr Wander has a tough and responsible job to do – we must make it easier for him. That's why I'm here.'

Wander pushed his chair back as though seeking support from the wall behind him. 'How do you see your duties?'

'Simple – in future, I tag along wherever you go, as a sort of escort.'

'As a sort of spy, you mean.'

Sobottke looked appalled and raised both hands in supplication – hands like steel pincers. 'But Herr Wander, whatever gave you that idea? Fancy misjudging Herr Krug like that! You mustn't even think such a thing! My job is just to follow you around in case you need me.'

'If I do I'll send for you.'

'But what if you couldn't get hold of me right away? You'd be up the creek then, and Herr Krug would never forgive me. What's the matter – have you got something against me?'

Wander deemed it advisable to reply in the negative. 'I'm a lone wolf, Herr Sobottke,' he explained. 'I can't work properly unless I'm on my own.'

'I won't interfere, believe me. I won't offer advice or butt in when you're talking to people. I'll even keep two paces to the rear – you only have to say the word. Besides, I can drive your car when you want me to, carry your briefcase, book tables in restaurants and so on, even take care of more personal arrangements – girls, for instance. I told you already, I've got some lovely addresses in Cologne . . .'

'Thanks, but I'm still all right in that respect. Apart from which, I like driving, I don't carry a briefcase, and nobody yet found it necessary to book me a table in a restaurant. Thanks again for your kind offer.'

'But what if something happens to you?'

'What, for instance?'

'Well, somebody might take a crack at you – you never know.'

'So that's it,' Wander said thoughtfully. 'Your main job is to protect me, not keep me under surveillance. Krug is providing me with a bodyguard. Does he really think I need one? What gave him that idea?'

'You're making a big mistake,' Sobottke cried. 'Herr Krug is really worried about you, Herr Wander, and all you do is suspect him.'

'Do I? How would you know?'

Sobottke was evidently at pains to cut short a conversation which had begun to embarrass him. 'Orders are orders – they still are to me, anyway, especially when they come from Herr Krug. Sobottke, he said to me, you put yourself at Herr Wander's disposal as of now – he's your boss from now on. That's what he said, and here I am.'

'All right,' Wander said briskly. 'If I'm your boss now – to quote Herr Krug – my orders are as follows: get lost and stay out of my sight until further notice. If I need you I'll send for you.'

'But Herr Krug . . .'

'You tell Herr Krug this: I may be working for him along

lines laid down by him, but either I use my own methods or I quit. That's all. And now goodbye, Herr Sobottke, and give my best regards to Herr Krug.'

*

'You're enough to put a man off his Guinness,' Detective Chief Inspector Kohl said, catching sight of Wander. 'This is my second, and I'm ordering another. See how low I've sunk, thanks to you?'

'Keep a clear head,' Wander advised, joining him. 'I need you. Besides I know a couple of things that may cheer you up.'

'I'm fed up with you and your crazy stories,' Kohl growled. 'You've landed me in the shit up to my nose, Wander, and the smell's getting on my nerves.'

They were facing each other over a pock-marked table in the far corner of Mutter Jeschke's bar. A lamp like a storm-lantern hung above them. The proprietress was polishing glasses, but otherwise they were alone.

'Who do you really work for, Mutter Jeschke?' the policeman demanded. His voice was provocatively loud.

Without pausing in her movements, the woman replied placidly: 'Myself and my customers.'

'Not for the Constitutional Protection Office or one of the secret service departments? It doesn't matter which – they're all crap. What about armaments firms, party headquarters, news agencies – do you pass information to them?'

'Nonsense!' Mutter Jeschke said firmly. 'Looks as if you really can't take more than one glass of beer.'

'You're in for a big surprise,' Kohl declared. 'I'm going to get stinking today. I not only need to – I can afford to. I've been suspended until further notice. Leave – that's what they call it.'

'Did you get into trouble?' Wander asked.

'Yes, after I made some. Seems like it, anyway.'

Mutter Jeschke reached for a glass, gave it a superfluous rub with a clean cloth, filled it with creamy Irish stout, and put it down in front of Kohl. 'If you really want to know, Herr Kohl, I do sometimes work as a police informer, but only for detective chief inspectors named Kohl.'

'That's all right,' Kohl said. He snorted vigorously. 'I'm sorry.'

Wander turned to Mutter Jeschke. 'Our friend here was unloading his suspicions on to you, but they were aimed at me.'

'You're dead right,' Kohl grunted. 'Know something, Wander? I have a sneaking suspicion that the only reason you came to Bonn was to do me out of my pension. If not, what else are you up to?'

Wander shrugged. 'All right, if you're so keen on knowing, why shouldn't I tell you? I'm working for Konstantin Krug, the Party Secretary. My job is to carry out research into army administration.'

'You expect me to believe there's no more to it than that?'

'It's quite enough for me.'

'What about this business I stumbled on? What about the Morgenrot girl?'

'Pure coincidence, so far as I can see.'

The policeman slowly drained his glass. 'Another of the same,' he called. 'And another for Herr Wander too. I want him to feel as lousy as I do.'

'I hope you'll bear in mind,' Wander said, 'that I could only tell you what I knew myself – or thought I knew.'

'Point taken,' Kohl replied. 'However, I've come to the conclusion that I didn't interrogate you properly. I should have questioned you far more thoroughly about Morgenrot senior.'

'Was it Morgenrot who arranged this holiday for you?'

Kohl gave an almost embarrassed nod. 'I ought to have been more careful.'

'I didn't think you were careless.'

'Anyone can make mistakes. For instance, I never thought you'd stab me in the back.'

'Try to go on thinking that way,' Wander said. 'Is it so difficult?'

'You promised to arrange an interview with that Dr Bergner of yours. Why didn't you?'

'He got cold feet, but I'm working on him. He won't be able to suppress his decent impulses for ever.'

'Dammit, Wander!' Kohl exclaimed. 'What sort of man are you? You're always hell-bent on meddling in problems that don't concern you.'

'They pursue me,' Wander replied with a shrug. 'I can't do much about them, though. That's why I rely on you. You're the expert.'

'Some expert!' Kohl shook his head sadly. 'I'm just a pimple on the so-called arm of the law. All right, I did go through Eva Morgenrot's belongings – examined them pretty thoroughly too. I searched everything – her clothes, her suitcase, the whole apartment. As it turned out, Wander, I found something which may well interest you. It was a key, and stamped on it was the number 205. Well?'

'Well, go on.'

'I didn't spot the inference myself, to begin with. Then I remembered Martin Morgenrot and his statement that he saw Eva going into your room.'

'Which I firmly dispute.'

'No more need to. I took a closer look at the passage leading to your apartment, and I'm fairly certain the boy mistook the door. Eva wasn't going into your apartment, No. 204, but into the one next door, i.e. No. 205.'

'Who lives there?'

'Nobody, by all accounts. It isn't officially let.'

'But I've sometimes heard noises coming from inside.

Running water, a door closing – nothing much else, and all very muffled. Those walls are pretty soundproof.'

'I only said, it isn't let. It may occasionally be occupied – after all, it's fully furnished.'

'Was Eva the only person to have a key?'

'There are or were three keys, I discovered. The letting agency instructed the porter to hand over two of them to Baroness von Wassermann-Westen several weeks ago. Only one of them was among Eva Morgenrot's effects. The other was held by the Baroness. When questioned about the possible existence of a third, she at first told me it was none of my business – a point of view to which she was legally entitled.'

'But you didn't give up, if I know you.'

'Of course not. When I pressed her, she disclaimed all knowledge of a third key or its whereabouts and suggested that it might have been mislaid. Before I could put the squeeze on her, Morgenrot senior intervened.'

'In person?'

'What do you think? He's no fool, that man. He merely fired off a mild but explicit complaint – aimed it pretty high, too. I imagine it contained references to lack of delicacy on the part of the police, gross interference in private affairs, persistent harassment of bereaved persons – that sort of thing. Anyway, Morgenrot managed to stampede a whole herd of top brass at headquarters, probably in one of the ministries as well. The result was an inquiry into my methods, and here I am. I'll probably stay this way until I retire, if I'm lucky.'

'Can't you do anything about it?'

'Not without Dr Bergner, not without you – not without a sizeable slice of luck. And that's just what I don't seem to be blessed with.'

'I may be able to help a little,' Wander said. 'I paid a call on Eva Morgenrot's mother. According to her story, which I find

126

convincing, Eva was due to inherit half the Morgenrot millions on her twenty-first birthday.'

'Say that again!' Kohl exclaimed incredulously.

'Eva's existence virtually halved the Morgenrot fortune. In less than two years' time she could have clamped down on her foster-father – and why shouldn't she have, under the circumstances? There are other implications, though. Eva would have been the prime beneficiary, not Morgenrot's son Martin. What's more, her survival would have robbed any prospective second wife of millions of marks. That suggests a motive or two, doesn't it?'

'And who, in your opinion, is likely to become Morgenrot's second wife?'

'The woman you suspect yourself. Morgenrot keeps a photograph on his desk – only one, in a heavy silver frame. It's a studio portrait of Baroness von Wassermann-Westen.'

Detective Chief Inspector Kohl tipped some more Guinness down his throat. It might have been lemonade. 'Damn you, Wander, you're a persuasive bastard. I don't feel as if I'm on leave at all, thanks to you, especially as I've seen a similar photo myself. Somewhere quite different, mind you, but also in a place of honour. I must brood about it, and brooding might easily lead to my doing something about it. The question is, what?'

INTERIM REPORT No. 6

BY THE MAN KNOWN AS JEROME

on the function of what is known as the public, the workings of powerful institutions, and the breakdowns to which both are subject.

No army in the world is perfect, of course, and each – depending on one's point of view – has its heroes and its villains, its promotion-seekers and its cannon-fodder, its martyrs and sentimental fools. Why should a German army be any different?

It is clear that Minister Feldmann had a pretty accurate idea of how to harass his opponents. His technique may vaguely have been modelled on the ousting of the first West German Minister of Defence, though circumstances naturally varied in many respects and different personalities were involved. Wander represented merely one card in the current poker-game, even if he was an ace. At least three and possibly five more informants were also involved in one way or another.

I was able to pinpoint at least two of them beyond doubt. One was a journalist who nursed and co-ordinated currents of patriotic opinion for a markedly Chauvinistic newspaper group, the other a former Gestapo official – with a clean personal record – who invested his stock of expert knowledge in return for a suitable fee.

Although Wander may be assumed to have known nothing definite about his fellow-contributors, it is probable that he guessed at their existence. From Feldmann's point of view – and still more from Krug's – he carried out his assignment in an exemplary fashion. Exactly what that would mean in the final analysis, I did not at first realize. Nor, of course, did Sandman, let alone Wander himself.

We allowed ourselves to be misled by the relative simplicity of the basic set-up. The operational jumping-off point was as follows: every army has to contend with problems and difficulties, but anything which cannot be suppressed or hushed up necessarily reaches the ears of the public. This is not a disaster in itself because the so-called public has a rotten memory and a big belly – which means, in practice, that people forget most things and swallow the rest. By tomorrow, the fine words of today can seem like ugly shadows of the day before yesterday. The expedient thing is to let them vanish into oblivion with maximum speed.

Feldmann's trick was to create constant, uninterrupted and, if possible, mounting public anxiety for a short period of time. This he did by combating people's readiness to forget quickly. He jolted their weary minds with electrifying doses of alarmist propaganda.

When Starfighters plunged to earth with monotonous regularity, when German deserters fled to Sweden, when millions of marks squandered on tanks resulted in dubious and laboriously ridiculed investigations, when a colonel was charged with grave corruption, in company with a senior government official and a member of parliament, people accepted these things as if they were occasional slips of a trivial nature. When soldiers were victimized, for example, the public soon came to regard it as more or less inevitable. Often, the facts were never published or played up by two or more rivals for personal reasons.

Systematic playing up was one of Feldmann's favourite PR tactics. Like Krug and one or two other political associates, he had long recognized the value of contact with influential journalists – an attitude which was usually reciprocated. The passing of inside information or advance news was rewarded by a concerted journalistic broadside or a speciously objective paean of praise.

At a so-called working lunch in the Hotel Rheinhof, Feldmann, Krug and five fellow-members of the Party got together with seven journalists carefully selected for their willingness to co-operate. This was the prelude.

For the first time, Feldmann gave vent to the slogan which he had personally coined for the forthcoming operation. It ran *'In profound and enduring concern for the Federal Army . . .'* Two of the journalists present informed me of this independently and their accounts tallied in detail.

Suddenly there came alarming but unconfirmed reports from abroad about the results, allegedly suppressed, of an opinion poll indicating that a third of the Federal Army already sympathized with the neo-Nazis, and the tide of national indignation ran high at this outrageous slander. While voicing criticism and concern, Feldmann leapt to the army's defence before the Minister of Defence could give tongue. It was Feldmann, not the Minister, who won the first round of this contest for the favour of the West German public. Nobody has yet proved that it was Feldmann himself who started the rumour only to win general approbation by scotching it.

Feldmann earned not only the approval of his Chancellor but also the patronage of the Minister of the Interior, who, being a skilled tactician himself, was evidently delighted and relieved that Feldmann had no designs on his own seat in the cabinet. The current Foreign Minister is also said to have breathed a sigh of relief and assured Feldmann of his support by telephone.

So everything got off to a promising start.

It never occurred to us that the private life of a man like Wander might be worth closer inspection. Hence the added embarrassment of our subsequent conclusion, namely, that the outcome of this campaign was not decided at the obvious level, not in one of the seats of power, but in someone's bed.

Chapter 7

As desired and instructed, General Keilhacke was busy playing the great and meritorious leader of men, ever on his toes and prepared to take a personal interest in the smallest detail. His current focus of interest was physical training.

The present gymnastic performance had been staged at the prompting of a big illustrated magazine which had, in turn, been prompted by Wander. A hundred pairs of buttocks presented themselves to Keilhacke's gaze. The General was regarding them with a cheerful smile and being photographed at the same time.

'Am I doing all right?' he asked Wander, who was in attendance.

'Try to look more businesslike,' Wander advised. 'Otherwise people may get the idea that you take an abnormal interest in the male posterior.'

'Kindly keep your filthy insinuations to yourself!' snapped Keilhacke.

'General,' Wander said, 'I'm simply trying to draw your attention to the fact that a man in your position has to reckon with the possibility of such insinuations at all times. It's one of my jobs to immunize you against them.'

Keilhacke nodded, appeased. He had recently been making a supreme effort to rise above himself. 'If questioned on the subject, I shall merely say "*Mens sana in corpore sano*," "creative vigour demands physical well-being" – or words to that effect. Weaklings, drunkards, cardiac sufferers, consump-

tives and men with other physical disabilities have often turned
into subversive scribblers.'

'I shouldn't put it quite like that, General – especially not to
journalists. A lot of them cherish secret literary ambitions, so
they might take it as a personal insult. You must try to avoid
that – writers are dangerously sensitive.'

'You make it all sound damned complicated,' Keilhacke
grumbled.

'It *is* complicated,' Wander replied. 'There's one golden rule,
though. Always try to give a positive impression. Concentrate
as far as possible on the things you're in favour of and draw a
veil over the things you oppose.'

'I'm a plain-spoken man,' Keilhacke declared. 'I've always
called a spade a spade.'

'Anyone who wants to be Inspector-General has also got to
be a diplomat.'

'Well, aren't I?' Keilhacke indicated the members of his
retinue, who had discreetly stationed themselves a few paces to
one side, where they could watch the General and events in the
gymnasium with due interest. Two of the party were military
chaplains, one Catholic and one Protestant.

'What about them?' the General demanded challengingly
'That sort of thing always makes a good impression these
days.'

'I wouldn't bank on it. People shy like nervous horses at the
"Onward, Christian Soldiers" attitude, however well camou-
flaged. It would be far better to imply that while the army
naturally tolerates the Church – meets it more than half-way,
in fact – it is not dependent on it.'

'The chaplains may fall out!' called the General, reacting
promptly.

Wander continued his lecture. 'A far more effective way of
earning the goodwill of the public at large is to demonstrate
absolute moral purity.'

'I'll make it my watchword on every possible occasion.'

The General was now strolling, with every appearance of professional interest, between rows of sweating half-naked male bodies. He did his best to look businesslike. The accompanying photographers winked appreciatively at Wander. Semi-nude torsos and a majestic-looking Federal German general made a saleable combination, particularly as Keilhacke was fortunate in possessing a martial profile.

'As it happens, General,' Wander pursued, 'a favourable opportunity to demonstrate moral purity presents itself in Coblenz. There's a major stationed there named Drau, universally known as "Dirty" Drau. I can supply you with chapter and verse on the subject. Drau talks and behaves with such vulgarity that he might be termed a threat to the army's image. You might think it advisable to get rid of him, preferably with the maximum of publicity.'

'I'll do that,' the General vowed. 'Any other suggestions?'

'There's an establishment under your command known as Hoepner Barracks – you inaugurated the place yourself.'

'Quite so. General Hoepner was a first-rate tank commander. Second only to Guderian, in my opinion.'

Wander smiled. 'General Hoepner was also one of the conspirators against Hitler.'

'I'm aware of that,' Keilhacke replied magnanimously. 'Men of honour, one and all – knew some of them well. The methods they used don't match my own idea of a soldier's duty, I grant you, but given the prevailing situation, given the unique and unrepeatable set of circumstances, there's no doubt that one can concede the existence of a certain what-d'ye-call-it – a certain degree of political necessity.' He stopped reciting and appealed for approval. 'Is that all right, Wander?'

'Yes, but in your position you must be prepared for all kinds of provocation. Remember that, General, especially if you receive a visit from an American journalist named Sandman in the next couple of days. He isn't easily hoodwinked.'

'I'm not hoodwinking anyone!' Keilhacke protested. 'All I'm doing is trying to instil a readiness to preserve the best German traditions. I know perfectly well the 20th of July conspiracy was a fiasco – it doesn't lend itself to our purposes. What about the wars of liberation, though? Surely we can get some mileage out of them?'

'It's been done – and in the so-called German Democratic Republic, what's more. Your fellow-generals in the East German army have already staked their claim to the mantles of Scharnhorst and Gneisenau. Do you want to be suspected of following in their wake?'

'Of course not!'

'In that case, what?' Wander demanded inexorably. 'Are you planning to return to the days of Frederick the Great, who used to thrash the subjects and soldiers he was reputed to love so dearly?'

General Keilhacke shook his head in bewilderment. 'What do you recommend?' he asked.

'A completely fresh start. A last attempt to make an entirely clean sweep.'

Dumbfounded, but not without a certain monumental grandeur, the General gazed into space.

The photographers plied their cameras rapturously, convinced they had discovered a new military genius. It was an understandable mistake considering the majestic way in which his countenance floated above the sea of straining buttocks.

'Very well,' Keilhacke declared, now grimly determined to appear grimly determined under any circumstances. 'From now on, no half-measures!'

'Always provided,' Wander said quietly, still in the deferential tones of an adviser, 'that you really have some conception of the possible consequences.'

*

'You're damned inquisitive, aren't you?' Maximilian Morgenrot was scuttling restlessly up and down his ornate old cage of an office. 'What are you so interested in? My conduct, my opinions, an offer of some kind?'

'I only came because you asked me to,' Wander replied, not sitting down. He glanced at Morgenrot's desk. The photograph in the silver frame was still there. 'I understood you to say that you wanted to hand over some papers.'

'There they are.' Morgenrot senior indicated a comparatively slim folder lying ready to hand. 'Only twenty pages or so, but stiff with facts and figures – pure dynamite. I said I'd deliver and I have. That's the way I operate.'

'I'll pass the stuff on to Herr Krug,' Wander said. He didn't move. 'Anything else?'

'As far as I can judge, you people have gone to work with a will.'

'The best is yet to come,' Wander promised, never taking his eyes off Morgenrot. 'You ought to view the future with optimism, judging by the way your shares are doing. Or are you worried about something?'

'Sit down,' Morgenrot said, almost fiercely. 'All that worries me at the moment is the sight of you hovering there.'

Wander sat down, not in front of the desk but in an armchair near the door. 'What else can I do to soothe your nerves?'

'You're doing a great job,' Morgenrot said, scampering across to the other side of the window. 'I appreciate that. Probably underestimated you.'

'If that's meant to be a compliment, save it. I'm only interested in tangible results.'

'You'll get them. I've enclosed a sheet of paper with a

summary of the details for Krug and Feldmann. It's intended for your own personal use. Regard it as a sort of bonus from me.'

'A bonus? What for?'

'Let's say I like you. I'll tell you why, later.' Maximilian Morgenrot skipped across to the door, rubbing his hands. 'It's to do with a senior civil servant in the Defence Ministry at Bonn, a man called Ewertz. The evidence I'm placing at your exclusive disposal proves that he's accepted at least two substantial bribes in recent years. The sums involved are twenty thousand and sixty-eight thousand marks respectively.'

'You say you have positive proof?'

'Down to the smallest detail. You only have to make use of it – and you will, if you're the man I think you are. Especially as Ewertz owes his job to a discreet nudge from the present Defence Minister. That gives you one more trump card.'

'And you're handing it over unconditionally?'

Morgenrot hurried over to the desk and, rodent-like, burrowed deep into his arm-chair. Drawing the silver-framed photograph mechanically towards him, he said in a mournful tone: 'If there's any need for me to explain what I really want, Wander, you aren't worth the money I propose to invest in you.'

'What sort of money?'

'Ten thousand marks.'

Wander concealed his surprise by nodding with extreme deliberation. 'You mean you want to speak to me about Eva?'

'What exactly happened to her?'

'All the indications are that she committed suicide,' Wander replied cautiously.

'Does anyone suspect otherwise?'

'Not officially.' Wander went on to describe the reactions of the police, Bergner's conjectures, and Barranski's findings. 'Not much chance of shaking them, I'd say.'

Morgenrot now looked more like an owl than a rodent. He

retracted his head until his chin was flush with his chest. 'That's all very well,' he said sharply. 'They always call it suicide when they can't find anyone who gave a helping hand. What happened beforehand, though? Who contributed to it?'

'Is that what you want from me?' Wander asked with a mixture of curiosity and uneasiness. 'A precise answer for the sum of ten thousand marks?'

'Exactly, Wander!' Morgenrot jumped up, stationed himself behind his high-backed chair and peered over the top. 'I want to know – with the maximum of accuracy – what really happened and who had a hand in it.'

'That won't bring Eva back to life.'

'Don't think you can wheedle me with a cliché like that,' said Morgenrot senior. 'Feelings of revenge are a dud investment – I don't indulge in them. I want to know the facts so that I can take precautions if necessary. If you know what people are capable of, you can anticipate their idiosyncrasies.'

'And steer them in the direction that suits you with the aid of incriminating evidence?'

'Exactly,' Morgenrot conceded. 'You're learning fast. With a little luck you should earn your ten thousand marks.'

'Even if the prime mover in Eva's suicide turns out to be someone in your immediate circle?'

'All the more so!' Morgenrot replied crisply. 'That would double the value of my investment.'

*

Dr Bergner looked aghast. 'You're asking me to do something completely unethical. I can't just stab a colleague in the back.'

'Which is precisely what you'd like to do,' said Wander. 'It's written all over your face.'

'You're reacting all wrong, Wander,' Chief Inspector Kohl said reprovingly. 'As for you, Dr Bergner, you're not thinking straight.'

137

Wander had ambushed Bergner outside the hospital and dragged him off to Mutter Jeschke's, where Kohl was waiting for them. The policeman had reserved the table in the far corner of the bar and told Mutter Jeschke to chill a couple of bottles of Chablis, harmless in appearance, spicy of bouquet, and guaranteed to dispel most inhibitions.

They all seemed to enjoy their wine. Kohl grew surprisingly loquacious, spoke of his work, chatted about unsolved cases, and then – quite abruptly – turned to the subject of criminals who murder by slow stages. This brought him to the subject of Dr Barranski.

'That sort of thing simply isn't done,' Bergner protested. 'What about you, Chief Inspector – would you put the finger on a colleague?'

'Of course,' Kohl replied calmly. 'I've done it before now, and always with a sense of conviction. How can a policeman with pretensions to honesty tolerate working with criminals?'

'It's different with doctors, of course,' Wander said provocatively. 'Every doctor, however good he is, produces the occasional corpse. That makes for solidarity.'

'Absolute nonsense!' snapped Bergner. 'The fact is, there are plenty of things in medical practice that can't be demonstrated with mathematical accuracy. Mutual trust is one of the cornerstones of the profession.'

Wander deliberately misunderstood him. 'See what I mean about solidarity? You're prepared to trust a man like Barranski.'

'I don't trust him, Herr Wander! I thought I'd made that abundantly clear already.'

'But you refuse to draw the inevitable conclusions.'

Detective Chief Inspector Kohl was thoroughly enjoying the confrontation. Everything was proceeding as he and Wander had planned. Wander showed signs of developing into a first-rate partner, but Kohl hoped he wouldn't overplay his hand.

'Even a man like Barranski is capable of acting in good faith,' Bergner said. 'You have to admit that.'

'God Almighty!' Wander exclaimed, feigning outrage. 'You don't really believe that yourself?'

'Let's be objective for a moment,' Kohl cut in. He judged the time ripe for intervention. 'According to my information, Dr Bergner, you entertain certain – well, certain misgivings about Barranski's professional methods. Are they just instinctive? If not, what caused them? Something you heard via the medical grape-vine? No? You know something definite, then?'

'Certainly I do. Unfortunately, knowledge and proof are two different things.'

'You don't have to tell me that.' Kohl sighed sympathetically. Then he asked, casually: 'Who gave you the low-down?'

'This is in the strictest confidence, of course . . .'

'Of course,' Kohl assured him brazenly. 'Who was it?'

'A girl I've known for years,' Bergner replied after a moment's hesitation. 'She's been working as Dr Barranski's receptionist for some time now.'

Wander had some difficulty in controlling his excitement, but Kohl laid a restraining hand on his arm. With immutable calm, he said: 'So your girl-friend confided in you. I need hardly inquire if the young lady is trustworthy.'

'I'd vouch for her any time.' Dr Bergner now had the bit firmly between his teeth. 'My suspicions were aroused by what she told me, but what could I do? Force my way into his consulting-rooms and confront him? Go through his records with her help?'

'Of course you couldn't,' Kohl said. 'We could, though. Not to beat about the bush, Dr Bergner, what we're primarily interested in is drugs. I have quite a hefty file on the subject back at the office, but virtually nothing of any practical value. Just suspicions, conjectures, allegations, guess-work – but not a single piece of evidence that would stand up in court. So far, that is.'

'And you expect me to produce some?'

'No,' Kohl replied. 'I wouldn't want to saddle you or your girl-friend with that. You two keep out of it and stay in the background as far as possible. All I need is one definite tip at the right moment. A date, a time and place, a specific name – any significant detail as long as it's accurate. The rest you can leave to us. Is it a deal?'

*

'I've nothing to tell you,' Sabine von Wassermann-Westen declared, staring past him. 'What's more, I'm not interested in anything you may be planning to tell me.'

'But you came,' Wander said.

'With extreme reluctance.' Her tone was condescending. 'You virtually bullied me into it by monopolizing my telephone.'

They had met at the Glocken Café in Cologne. Polished chromium elegance shimmered on all sides. Subdued lights were reflected in black lacquer tables. The customers, who seemed to be wearing cosmetic masks, might have stepped straight out of the pages of a glossy fashion magazine. They stared at Sabine's blood-red dress.

'At least you don't appear to be afflicted by any memories of the remote past,' she said. 'Personal ones, I mean.'

'On the contrary, I treasure them. It's a cosy feeling, like getting over a serious illness.'

'We all have to come to terms with ourselves,' she said indifferently. 'Me, I know pretty well what I want. I don't want anything from you and you'd do better to keep out of my affairs. It doesn't matter who . . .'

'. . . who suffers in the process,' Wander amplified.

'You're incorrigible,' she said, sounding almost bored. She ordered herself a large Scotch-on-the-rocks at Wander's expense. 'All this meddling in other people's business is more than just a nuisance – it's stupid.'

'All right, so I'm stupid.'

Sabine eyed him disapprovingly. 'Even you must have realized by now that there are a few basic rules in life. For instance, one man's gain is another man's loss. If two people sleep together, somebody always gets cheated. Anyone who loves generates hatred somewhere. You have to accept these things.'

'Just as you have to accept the widespread suspicion that you feather your own nest at other people's expense?'

'Still the same old flair for over-dramatization!' Sabine's eyes blinked lazily in the blue gloom of the café. She looked unimpressed. 'I can't tell you how it bores me, your stubborn self-righteousness, your narrow-minded sermons on morality . . .'

Wander leant towards her. 'What,' he asked in a low, insistent voice, 'did you do to Eva Morgenrot? In my opinion, you're responsible for what happened to her. For her death, in fact.'

'What would you know about it?' Sabine picked up her whisky-glass but put it back on the table untouched. 'I felt it would be a good thing if someone took an interest in her, that's all.'

'In her or the millions she was due to inherit?'

Sabine straightened up, displaying her figure to full advantage. The crimson silk of her dress clung effectively to the upper part of her body. She drew a deep breath, which heightened the effect.

'I'll forget that remark,' she said softly. 'I'm very generous in some respects and I've been so to you, though you may not know it. I was the one who got you this job.'

'Do you expect me to show my gratitude?'

'No, not that – I don't expect gratitude from anyone, just a willingness to pay debts when they fall due.'

'And what do you reckon a human life's worth?'

'You're on the wrong track again.' Sabine smiled her indulgent smile. 'Don't be a fool. You've got a job which not only pays well but seems to amuse you. Do you really want to lose it – and the perks that go with it?'

'I want to know why Eva Morgenrot had to die. Was it because of her inheritance? If so, who was to share it with you – the father or the son? Which was the lucky winner?'

'Don't say things like that,' she murmured almost inaudibly.

'What really happened to Eva Morgenrot? Who introduced her to drink? Did she take drugs? Who beat her up? Who had a date with her in Apartment 205?'

'Stop it!' Sabine's hands tightened convulsively. The skin of her neck, which was bare of make-up, looked pale grey.

'You systematically hounded Eva to death! You got her drunk, you gave her drugs – you eventually procured her for the man who holds the third key to No. 205. Who is it?'

'You don't know what you're saying!' Sabine's hands were trembling now.

'Did you set Martin Morgenrot on her, or was a hint to Sobottke enough? And why all the sweetness and light between Morgenrot junior and that playboy Frost? How much of that was your doing, and why? Was it just a means of hounding Eva – deliberately, because the pickings were so enormous?'

'You're a dirty, repulsive little snooper,' Sabine said in a low voice. 'You'll regret this.'

'Don't be too sure. It remains to be seen who'll do the regretting. Did you act by arrangement with or on instructions from Eva's foster-father, who keeps your picture on his desk? Or were you trying to protect someone who could have ruined you – someone you weren't in a position to destroy because you both knew too much about each other? If so, who was it?'

Sabine picked up her glass and dashed the contents into Wander's face. Then she rose and stalked off through a sea of staring faces, her rigid bearing and studied composure expressive of injured womanly dignity.

At least a dozen people witnessed the incident. All their accounts tallied, and all were prejudicial to Wander.

*

'He's expecting you,' Marlene Wiebke said, glancing at her watch. 'You're six minutes late.'

'That gives us the next nine minutes to ourselves.' Wander sat down on the chair in front of her desk. 'I'm sure I can afford to keep a cabinet minister waiting for a quarter of an hour.'

'Not Feldmann you can't,' she replied, reaching for the 'phone.

'Don't announce me yet,' he said. He laid his hand on hers so that the receiver was forced back on to its cradle. 'I'd like a little information first.'

'Why not?' she said, withdrawing her hand. 'Especially if it's the time of the next flight home.'

'Are you really so eager to get rid of me, Marlene?'

'Yes,' she said. Her tone was cooler than the look in her eyes. 'You know too much as it is – you even know my Christian name.'

'Not good enough,' he said, 'I'd appreciate a much more thorough talk with you some time.'

'What about?' she inquired sarcastically. 'Not about your circle of female acquaintances, surely?'

'It's dwindling day by day,' he said, trying to sound lighthearted. 'I'm not giving up yet, though, particularly as people seem to be so concerned about my welfare.'

'I'm glad you reminded me,' she said, swiftly and unerringly changing the subject. 'About Sobottke – Herr Krug asked me to give you the following message: he assigned him to you purely as a precautionary measure, and your objection is sustained. In other words, the matter's closed.'

'Exactly what does that mean, exactly?'

Marlene looked faintly amused. 'Do you want me to spell it out?'

'I presume that in this case "closed" means don't breathe another word about it, or certainly not in Feldmann's presence. Am I right?'

The girl gave an almost imperceptible nod. 'Anything else I can tell you?'

'Well, we could talk about keys, for example – keys to apartments. You should find it easy enough to enlighten me. From what I hear, this office exerts a direct influence on sundry building firms which own letting agencies. One of the latter issued Baroness von Wassermann-Westen with a number of keys – perhaps two, perhaps more. Who gave the order and who holds the third key?'

'No comment,' she replied curtly. 'That's no concern of mine.'

'Not even if it were very important to me?'

'Especially not then,' she said. 'When are you leaving? That's far more important. I don't want any more nocturnal visits from you, and it won't be long before you feel inclined to repeat the performance if you go on charging around here like a bull in a china-shop.'

Wander smiled. 'I wonder if you know how pretty you look – even if I do have to imagine you without the glasses and the smock and the prison haircut. Girls like you take a lot of earning, Marlene, but I'm a hard worker.'

She sighed. 'I know somebody who called you a hopeless case not so long ago. I'm afraid they were right.'

*

'Our campaign,' Konstantin Krug said, at a nod from Minister Feldmann, 'appears to be going more or less according to plan.'

'Which isn't surprising,' Wander retorted. 'The German mentality often reminds me of an instruction manual. You only have to open it at the right page.'

'Even so,' the Minister observed, 'we mustn't let ourselves be lulled into a false sense of security. One slip could result in a whole series of unpleasant repercussions.'

They had met, this time in Krug's office, for a routine check on the progress of their operations. Papers littered the table, but these were only reports from outsiders, newspaper cuttings, photostats, statistical material – no memoranda from Feldmann or Krug, no marginal notes in their handwriting, not even a set of initials. Even the file covers were devoid of clues to their department of origin.

Wander, who was forced to concede that these security measures were virtually foolproof, had adopted them himself. He never submitted anything in writing, merely attended each meeting, like Krug, armed with notes which he destroyed immediately afterwards. The Minister himself relied exclusively on his powers of total recall.

'A group of parliamentarians friendly to our cause,' reported Krug, 'are already taking a close interest in the Defence Commissioner's department.'

'Not the Defence Commissioner's department but the Defence Commissioner himself,' Wander amended gravely. 'And let's hope there's no repetition of the bungling that went on a few years back . . .'

Krug said: 'We must impress on the Defence Commissioner that he has to come down on one side of the fence or the other – and quickly.'

'We must try to convince him,' observed the Minister. 'That might be a better way of putting it.'

'The attempt will succeed this time,' Wander said. 'I can virtually guarantee it.'

'I won't inquire what methods you propose to employ,' the

Minister said suavely. 'I take it for granted that everything will be legal and above board.'

'Of course,' Wander assured him. 'It isn't too difficult to put the screws on a man of his type and still observe every legal nicety in the book.'

Even though Feldmann's face betrayed no emotion whatsoever, Krug noted a perceptible stiffening in his manner. He hastened to gloss over the point. 'Your speech to the Displaced Persons struck an extraordinarily effective note, Minister. Those well-rehearsed interviews with General Keilhacke also seem to have been effective. Other generals are showing signs of increased activity. A section of the press and one or two radio and television commentators are climbing on the band-wagon. Even the Chairman of the Defence Committee is beginning to manœuvre with marked caution.'

'He could be given a nudge,' Wander said. 'Shall I tell you how?'

The Minister raised an admonitory hand. 'Details of that sort would exceed the bounds of our present discussion,' he said, radiating confidence. 'I leave them entirely to you, Herr Wander. The overall picture is my first concern.'

'We now come to the Defence Minister and his Inspector-General,' Krug announced, with a thin smile of satisfaction. 'Those two seem to be adopting a policy of dignified restraint. In practice, this means either that they haven't grasped what's going on yet, or that they can't mount a counter-offensive.'

'Better arguments, better ideas and better men,' said the Minister, straight-faced, 'those are our only weapons. Everything must follow a strictly democratic course, needless to say.'

'The time has come to accelerate,' Krug said. 'Next week-end will be crucial. After that, the whole question can be aired in Parliament . . .'

'Unless the Chancellor steps in first, which I wouldn't completely rule out.' Feldmann pointed to the red folder lying in front of him. 'Morgenrot's information about grossly injudicious investments in the armaments industry is most alarming. If his figures are correct, sums totalling several hundred million marks have been squandered on the development and testing of new weapons.'

'If not thousands of millions,' put in Wander.

'Herr Wander,' Feldmann said, heavily confidential now, 'I realize that you have signed a pledge of secrecy. Please don't take it as a mark of suspicion, I beg you, but I must once more remind you of your strict and unqualified obligation not to divulge these figures. They may well be classified as top secret in due course.'

'Who actually decides these things?' inquired Wander.

'It's quite an automatic process, sometimes,' Krug interposed.

'It could conceivably be,' pursued the Minister, 'that the facts underlying this information have a bearing on national security. If any of them leaked out, it might be construed as treason. That being so, gentlemen, don't breathe a word to anyone until I've reported to the Chancellor. The national interest demands total secrecy.'

*

'Happy now?' Wander asked Corporal Fünfinger.

'Happy isn't the word,' Fünfinger assured him. He sounded positively grateful. 'I'm bloody well delighted.'

'Fine. Glad you enjoyed the show.'

'That General Keilhacke of yours really pulled out all the stops – in front of a big audience, too. I could hardly believe my eyes and ears. He charged into our barracks like a tank. Then they turned us out on parade and he fired off a speech that brought the tears to my eyes. Lovely stuff, it was – all about honour and human dignity – especially the army variety – morality, cleanliness, and so on. He wasn't going to put up with any filth in his command, so he asked us to help him clean the place up. Said it was our solemn duty. Well, that broke the ice. We told the old bastard what he wanted to hear, and two hours later Dirty Drau was as good as back in civvy street. How the hell did you manage it, Wander?'

'I happened to press the right button at the right time.'

They were sitting in a corner of the same bar as before. Champagne had been ordered because Fünfinger declared that he found it impossible to change his drinking habits, particularly in view of the happy occasion. He announced his intention of footing the whole bill and generously invited two off-duty tarts to drink their fill at his expense, provided they maintained a distance of at least ten feet. 'Not that you mightn't be needed later on,' he added.

'Well,' Wander said, 'I've kept my part of the bargain. Now it's your turn.'

'Is it?' Fünfinger grinned. 'What if I say I'm sorry but I can't deliver – you picked the wrong business partner? What would you do then?'

'Punch you on the nose,' Wander replied.

'Pity I can't give you that pleasure,' said the Corporal. 'I'm quite a useful boxer, divisional middle-weight champion. You wouldn't think so to look at me, would you? You wouldn't think I was a lot of things. For instance, my principles may be cock-eyed but I try to stick to them. I regret it sometimes, but not in this case.'

Fünfinger laboriously unbuttoned his tunic, reached into a capacious breast pocket, and pulled out a thick wad of papers secured by a rubber band. He tossed it down in front of Wander and said: 'Contents: one diary, three pornographic poems, five letters and eight addresses. Satisfied?'

Wander took the bundle, unfolded it and ran a cursory eye over the contents. His expression was sombre. Then, emulating

148

Fünfinger, he said: 'Satisfied isn't the word, but I can't say I'm ecstatic.'

'Nor me,' Fünfinger said. 'All the same, it's worth something to me to see that bastard Drau fall on his nose. Are you going to use the stuff?'

'Only indirectly – I hope that'll do the trick.'

'All the better,' said Fünfinger, and gave another grin. 'Would you be interested in some more of the same? Maybe I could offer you something else in return for another moral kit inspection. I really got a kick out of that last one.'

'No thanks,' Wander said hastily. 'You've given me quite enough dirt to go on with.' He shrugged. 'This was an exceptional case – an emergency, you might say.'

'I'm not talking about dirt,' Fünfinger said. 'There are plenty of other possibilities if you keep your eyes skinned.'

'How do you mean?'

'Well, you have to use a bit of imagination.' Corporal Fünfinger looked smug. 'I can be imaginative when I want to be. For instance, take that rocket that disappeared a while back, complete with magnetic warhead. Simply vanished, and what an uproar that caused! The whole country squirmed with embarrassment.'

'Yes, for a week or two, and the upshot was that they've trebled and quadrupled the security checks on that kind of hardware.'

'You may be a military expert, my friend,' said Corporal Fünfinger, 'but you aren't the practical type. It's true the stuff is surrounded by fences and check-points, one inside the other. So what? All you have to do is to get history to repeat itself. Another rocket or something equally valuable vanishes. Dead easy! You simply bury it. In a ditch, say. No one'll think of looking there. They'll search till they're blue in the face and kick up such a fuss the newspapers'll be bound to smell a rat. Well, what do you think?'

'Fünfinger,' said Wander, 'you're a perverted genius. Do it, this week if possible. We'll keep in constant touch from now on.'

*

'I believe I already had the pleasure of making your acquaintance,' the Chairman of the Defence Committee said politely. 'We met at the Baroness's, if I'm not mistaken.'

'You aren't mistaken,' Wander replied with equal politeness. 'But whether it was a pleasure I beg leave to doubt.'

The Chairman gave a smile of practised forbearance. 'In a job like mine you have to be prepared for anything – prejudice, interference, intrigue, even attempted blackmail. Not, of course, that I expect anything of the kind from you, Herr Wander, particularly as I was notified of your visit by my old and esteemed colleague Konstantin Krug. What exactly can I do for you?'

'Accept an invitation to dinner,' Wander replied, smiling. 'I can promise you at least one interesting topic of conversation.'

The Chairman had greeted Wander in a conference room assigned to him in the Parliament Building. The floor was carpeted in lime-green, dark-brown panelling sheathed the walls, and the ceiling and curtains were snow-white. The general effect was solid rather than sumptuous.

'Make yourself comfortable,' the Chairman urged, and indicated a black leather arm-chair.

Wander sat down and crossed his legs. 'From what I hear, you're one of the happy few who don't appear to have any political skeletons in the cupboard.'

'I am indeed.' The Chairman spoke with simple pride. 'A stroke of good fortune, you might say. The recent history of our country has left scarcely anyone without a stain on his character, but my record is clean.'

'Except for one minor blemish. Probably no more than a beauty-spot, of course.'

The Chairman's laugh conveyed total unconcern. 'I can guess what you're driving at. East German propaganda boosted the story artificially to begin with, but the whole myth was exploded on this side of the Iron Curtain.' He proffered a silver box of choice Havanas intended for special visitors. It was clear that he instinctively recognized Wander's importance.

'In 1944,' he continued, 'I was involved in a so-called treason trial. The accused man was sentenced to death in spite of my testimony. Unfortunately, the court records were destroyed.'

'Versions of your testimony vary considerably,' Wander said.

'Certainly they do – as I've already admitted. However, they can be proved to have been circulated by subversive elements, among them Communists, in the hope of thwarting my nomination to the chairmanship of the Defence Committee. Nobody takes them seriously today.'

'The name of the NCO who was sentenced to death was Kayser, wasn't it – Friedrich Johann Kayser?'

'Yes. And I did my utmost to testify in his favour. Kayser would tell you so himself if he could. Unfortunately, he's dead.'

'Are you sure?'

For the first time, a perceptible change came over the Chairman. His mouth opened and remained open for a full second. Then he said with an effort: 'What you are hinting at, Herr Wander, is quite impossible.'

'Just assume for a moment that this man is still alive – that he escaped execution at the eleventh hour. Further assume that he is prepared to resurrect the whole affair and give evidence that his conviction was attributable to your testimony alone.'

'You must be wrong!' the Chairman exclaimed, aghast now. 'It's a downright lie!'

'In your opinion, perhaps.'

'But why should the man make such a monstrous allegation --
if he really is still alive?'

'Well,' Wander said, 'perhaps he doesn't like the shape of
your nose. Perhaps his sense of fair play has only just come to
the surface. Alternatively, he may have his sights on a new and
rewarding job – in an arms factory, let's say – and won't be
appointed unless he gives a full and convincing account of his
past history. Are you prepared to risk that?'

'No, of course not.' The Chairman had gone pale. 'Not on
any account, but what can I do?'

Wander smiled. 'Meet me for dinner at eight this evening.'

*

Peter Sandman greeted Wander with exaggerated surprise.
'Beats me how you have the nerve to show your face round here.
You're one of the sharpest operators I've ever run into.'

'Is that what you asked me here to tell me?' Wander sat down
in the American journalist's office. 'I can do without such
compliments, especially from you.'

'You've been leading me by the nose, Karl, and that's my one
sensitive spot.'

'What the hell are you talking about?' Wander protested.
'There must be some kind of misunderstanding. Come on,
let's clear the air.'

'OK, let's do that.' Sandman reached for a file which obviously contained a sheaf of photographs. 'I can hardly wait to
see what sort of story you sell me this time, Wander.'

'Now listen, Peter – or Sandman, if that's the way you want
it.' Wander's bewilderment abruptly changed to anger. 'You
can accuse me of plenty and most of it may be true, but I do
draw the line at two things. In the first place I never hoodwink
anyone who genuinely tries to be helpful, and in the second
place I don't treat my friends like fools. Is that clear?'

'Sure, Karl.' The warmth had returned to Sandman's voice,

but he patted the file of photographs with mock severity. 'First, though, let's get this cleared up. Call me curious rather than suspicious, but I insist on a straight answer.'

'OK, Peter, fire away.'

Sandman opened a drawer in his desk and produced a bottle of whisky and two glasses. 'Let's have a drink first.' He filled the glasses, pushed one of them towards Wander, raised his own, and said: 'Let's also hope it's not the last.'

'You certainly pile on the suspense, Peter. I'm beginning to wonder if I've done something without knowing it.'

'It wouldn't be the first time. OK, you've told me plenty of times that all you're interested in is a radical reform of the West German army – not in helping Feldmann to become the next Minister of Defence.'

'You couldn't have put it better.'

'Well, I think Feldmann is the sort of man who'd sell the army to anyone who helps him to become Chancellor. In other words, he's forging a weapon with a view to using it as a bargaining counter – and you're abetting him.'

'I'm doing no such thing. All I know at present is that Feldmann is acting either on the Chancellor's instructions or with his blessing. I was given an assurance on that point and I believe it.'

'I don't. You see, it's my belief that the relations between you and Feldmann are of an unusually familiar, if not personal, nature. Your mutual connections go back a suspiciously long way.'

'That's absurd!'

'I can prove it,' said Sandman. Almost pedantically, he opened the file, removed a photograph and passed it to Wander. 'The Minister and his family – let's start with that. A little domestic idyll, neatly arranged with an eye to artistic composition. Frau Feldmann, a friendly self-effacing housewife type, two delightful children looking just like the kids next door, a guaranteed thoroughbred German shepherd-dog, and above them all, beaming gently like the sun, the Minister – a good, kind, God-fearing, family man.'

'Congratulations,' Wander said, unimpressed. 'Unfortunately, I don't know the Minister's family at all. I've never set eyes on his wife and children, let alone his German shepherd-dog, so the photo means nothing to me.'

'I'll grant you that,' Sandman replied. 'Just as I hope you'll credit me with a certain amount of professional experience. And experience tells me that Feldmann never poses for pictures unless there's something in it for him – as in this case, for instance.'

The photograph which he now put in front of Wander showed guests at a party of the kind popularly referred to as 'small and select'. A dozen men, mostly in tails and decorations, and half a dozen women dressed to kill. The gathering included two cabinet ministers, two ambassadors, a general, and others of the same social status. In the centre, Feldmann.

'The lady who was entertaining these glittering darlings of the illustrated magazines is in the left foreground,' Sandman said.

'It hadn't escaped me,' Wander said drily.

'And that's why I'm entitled to assume that you're very well aware of Baroness von Wassermann-Westen's role at this function.'

'Sorry, Peter, I can assure you you're barking up the wrong tree.'

'You can assure me of a lot of things, but not that. I'm pretty certain I know which way the wind is blowing. The Baroness and the Minister have been friendly – for want of a better word – for several years. In practice, that means he does her an occasional favour and she shows her gratitude by doing the same for him.'

'Could be,' Wander said thoughtfully. 'Sabine always did have an eye to the main chance.'

Sandman looked surprised. 'Do I have to spell it out for you?' he asked. 'They sleep together.'

'Really?' Wander looked equally surprised.

They stared at one another in silence. Then Sandman gave a shout of laughter.

'Man,' he said, 'you're one of the coolest poker-players I ever met. It's bluff, bluff, all the way with you, isn't it?'

He removed another photograph from his file and held it up triumphantly with the print facing Wander. 'I found this one while I was rummaging through some old papers which came into my hands via you almost ten years ago. The one-time scourge of the West German army, very much off duty.'

Then he flipped the photograph across the desk like a playing-card. Wander glanced at it briefly. It showed him in officer's uniform at a Press party in Munich, a cheerful-looking young man, smooth-skinned and slender as a boy. He was smiling at the girl by his side. Inevitably, it was Sabine.

'A real find, this picture – you'd admit that, wouldn't you?' Sandman saw Wander nod. 'And you'd also admit that I was justified in drawing certain conclusions from it?' Wander nodded again.

'Well, old pal, that's the last link in the chain, and the chain fits neatly around your neck. I've proved that the relations between you, the Baroness and Feldmann are far closer than might be supposed. That means it's an operation backed by capital investment of an exceptionally private nature. Would you deny that?'

Wander shook his head vigorously. 'Of course I admit I knew Sabine Wassermann, as she was then, but we split up. We didn't part on very good terms – maybe I'll tell you about it some day. I was glad to forget her. Never gave her another thought until I met her again here, once in person and the next time as a photograph on Maximilian Morgenrot's desk. Silver-framed. You ought to take a look at it some time.'

'I will,' Sandman said briskly. He sounded relieved. 'This throws an entirely different light on things.'

INTERIM REPORT No. 7

BY THE MAN KNOWN AS JEROME

on the danger of making firm rules and the improbability that everyone will observe them.

While the big show was getting under way – and very convincing it looked to the layman – my attention was slightly distracted by something one of my junior operatives brought in. This was a 'clarificatory statement' submitted by a police commissioner. It contained the following assurance: 'There is no substance in the rumour that a police officer under my command has been taken off a particular case.' This was an allusion to Kohl. The statement went on: 'Should such an impression have arisen, it can only be attributable to a redistribution of assignments necessitated by administrative technicalities.'

I did not find this particularly enlightening at the time when I read it, especially as I have a marked aversion to German officialese. It was a mistake to leave the matter there, of course. Equally little importance was attached to a report I received on a conversation with the Chairman of the Defence Committee. This had been recorded on tape 'at an advanced hour'. Among other things, it contained the following remarks: '. . . I was bound to regard the Baroness as a person of some social standing . . . especially as the Minister, who was one of her intimate circle . . . which helped to foster an atmosphere of mutual trust . . .' And so on.

The usual social chit-chat, or so I assumed. I did register the fact that Feldmann and Baroness von Wassermann-Westen appeared to be operating as a team, also that they were putting pressure on the Chairman of the Defence Committee – jointly, in all likelihood. But why not? To me, politics and business go hand in hand, and people like Wander are blissfully thin on the ground.

Material on that gentleman soon began to accumulate. I only thumbed through it because there was nothing essentially new to be learned from it. For all that, my picture of him took on sharper outlines.

It was obvious that we were dealing with an irresponsibly apolitical creature whose private emotions always took priority. I advised Sandman to write Wander off, but Sandman was adamant. He asserted that this growing pile of 'opinions' was largely an impertinence because those who gave them had the nerve to try and explain a human life in a couple of dozen lines.

One of these expert opinions came from a man named Unterpointner, one of Wander's former teachers and now an assistant headmaster. He wrote: '. . . one has to see everything in the proper context . . . he may have been a gifted boy in many respects, but he seemed to labour under some secret disability . . . obviously felt that he was never successful enough . . . very humble background . . . father a metal-worker or something similar . . . mother a chronic invalid . . . resented his origins, though he never admitted it . . .'

Wander had a marked weakness for literary-sounding clichés. Maybe he should have become a poet – he wrote all kinds of stuff. An ideal informant. He sometimes made observations like: 'The pillars of the existing establishment think their survival depends upon the breeding of as many moronic, credulous, complacent supporters as possible.' It's true, of course, but to get steamed up about it shows a deplorable lack of sophistication.

The same applies to this sort of pronouncement: 'Our only legacy from the past is total bankruptcy.'

Well, so what?

But that was Wander for you – he always had something of the mini-revolutionary about him. Not reprehensible in itself. Rulers of any intelligence have always tolerated court jesters. Professional buffoons are only dangerous when they come in packs, however small.

Unfortunately, this was the case here.

Chapter 8

'What,' the Defence Commissioner inquired politely, 'can I do for you?'

'Nothing,' Wander replied, sitting down.

He ran an appraising eye round the room. The usual senior executive's office with broadloom carpet and over-stuffed furniture.

'In that case,' said the Defence Commissioner with un-diminished courtesy, 'why are you here?'

'To bring you some reading matter.'

The current Defence Commissioner, former member of parliament, ex-officer of the army reserve, and a trained lawyer like his predecessors, had evidently come to terms with his job, which was not only difficult but rendered still more difficult at every turn. The light of patience shone in his weary eyes, and his face looked decoratively tired and masculine – in short, confidence-inspiring.

'What do you have to offer?' he inquired, regarding Wander with some benevolence.

'I'm acting as a postman, more or less.' Wander unzipped his briefcase and took out a bundle of papers, which he pushed across to the Defence Commissioner. 'These are only copies, but you'd recognize the originals easily enough. It shouldn't take you more than ten seconds to satisfy yourself of that.'

The Defence Commissioner picked up the papers – the diary, the poems, the letters and addresses. He flicked through them hurriedly, bit his lips and turned pale. It all reminded Wander irresistibly of a Hollywood film. He wouldn't have been surprised to hear an unseen orchestra break into the crashing discords of the disaster theme.

'What is your purpose in showing me these?' the Defence Commissioner asked. 'What do you want?'

'To bring you an invitation to an intimate little dinner. Tonight at eight, in the Hotel Rheinhof. Your host will be Herr Krug.'

*

'I'm a careful man – in my job, I have to be.' James Leinberger, a correspondent employed by several medium-sized daily papers, spoke with total conviction. 'Nobody puts anything over on me – I know this business backwards.'

'I gave you a sort of reference on the telephone – Herr Krug.' Wander opened the drinks cupboard in his apartment. 'Did you get in touch with him?'

'Certainly I did.' James Leinberger, real name Jakob, was a pale, narrow-shouldered man who seemed to find any form of exertion taxing in the extreme. He now propelled himself in the direction of the liquor cabinet and deftly selected the most expensive brand. 'What are you offering me, apart from a drink?'

Wander handed him a sheet of paper bearing a typewritten list of particulars about Ewertz, the senior civil servant from the Defence Ministry. Subject: bribery. Sums received: twenty thousand and sixty-eight thousand marks. Details supplied included names of banks and account numbers.

Leinberger absorbed the information without any change of expression. 'Usable stuff,' he said eventually, 'if you can make it stick.'

'You can inquire at the Morgenrot Works in Essen. Speak to the accountant whose name appears at the bottom of the sheet.'

Leinberger looked faintly amused. 'And he'll confirm all this muck?'

'Not directly, of course, but he's prepared for questions. When you 'phone him he'll start by refusing to make any statement at all. That's the usual ploy. After that, all you need to do is ask him if he's in a position to deny the accuracy of your information. He won't say anything to begin with, then he'll reply in the negative – hesitantly. You can take that as confirmation.'

'And I'll get it in writing too, if I want?'

'That's been arranged,' Wander said.

'A prize piece of dirty work,' Leinberger commented. 'Vintage Krug – I mean that as a compliment, of course. What's it going to cost?'

'Nothing.'

'I don't like taking something for nothing.' Leinberger looked suspicious. 'It violates my principles, not to mention current business practice. What information do you want in return?'

Wander glanced at the whisky-bottle, which was already down by a third, and said cautiously: 'I'd appreciate something on Minister Feldmann, preferably something to do with his private life.'

'You're welcome,' Leinberger replied with alacrity. 'I don't know much, but I do have one or two nice little titbits. Does the name Erika Ritter mean anything to you?'

'No.'

'Think yourself lucky.' Leinberger stowed the sheet of paper with the details about Ewertz in his pocket-book and pulled the whisky-bottle closer. 'She did have her points, though, I must admit.'

'Any connection with Feldmann?'

Leinberger's pallid face creased into a broad grin. 'It didn't matter where you were in her cosy little love-nest – standing, sitting or lying – you could see him everywhere you looked. HIM, spelt out in bold caps. There was a gala photograph of him on her bedside table, bathed in a warm pink glow. HIM as the future statesman and prospective father of his country. And there, scrawled across his paunch in his own inimitable hand, were the words: *To Erika Ritter, my ever-faithful assistant, in appreciation of her exemplary devotion to duty.*'

Wander attentively refilled his visitor's glass. Leinberger held it up to the light and smiled. 'She warmed Feldmann's heart by her exemplary devotion to duty for about a year. Then he got rid of her in the approved fashion. Kicked her upstairs into a better-paid job.'

'So the relationship paid off from her point of view.'

'Not only that – she genuinely enjoyed it. Found it hard to get him out of her system. I suddenly realized that during one of her more athletic performances. The thing was, she used to bite when she really got going – sank her teeth into anything within reach.'

'But you were ready for her, I suppose.'

'Not always,' Leinberger replied. 'I generally managed to shove a pillow between us, but one day I was forced to give her a couple of slaps which made her teeth rattle.'

'And that was the end of it.'

'Wrong – that's when it really started. She was so delighted she actually wept for joy – moaned with ecstasy and told me I was just like HIM.'

*

'I have to speak to our employer for a moment,' Wander said.

Marlene Wiebke shook her head. 'Herr Krug is engaged – he's not seeing anyone.'

'But I've got something very important to discuss with him. It's urgent.'

She eyed him appraisingly. 'Only one thing qualifies for an urgent rating, and that's your departure.'

'Why not let well alone? Unless, of course, you're planning to come with me.'

'Don't you ever tire of playing the clown? You come into a very different category.'

'You've seen through me, just like my friend Peter Sandman and who knows who else. You're right. I'm not a clown, I'm a sort of vulture. All I do is hire out my brain for the sake of my belly, and I deposited the last remnants of my integrity in the left luggage office at Cologne airport. Never mind, that shouldn't deter you from telling Herr Krug I'm here.'

'You have your job and I have mine,' she replied, matter-of-fact as ever. 'One of my duties is to fend off unwanted visitors, and I can't see your name anywhere in the appointments book. I'm afraid you can't see him.'

'Not even if I have an important telegram to discuss with him? Here, take a look.'

He held it out. She hesitated and then made it clear that she had no intention of taking it. He laid it on her desk and pushed it towards her. She pretended to ignore it, but her sharp eyes took in the contents at a glance. It read:

EGG LAID AS ARRANGED STOP DOING NICELY BUT NEEDS HATCHING STOP YOUR MOVE NOW STOP
REGARDS FÜNFINGER

'What's that supposed to mean?' Marlene demanded. 'It sounds just as pointless as most of the stuff you spend your time on round here.'

He chuckled. 'I thought you didn't know anything about it.'

'Of course I don't,' she retorted fiercely. 'I'm not paid to pry into other people's affairs – I leave that to professional meddlers like you. However, I'll tell Herr Krug you want to speak to him urgently.'

Konstantin Krug emerged from his inner sanctum before Wander had reached the door. He even extended his hand, but the smile imprinted on the front of his bullet-head was thin and mirthless.

'You have something important for me?' he inquired, when the door had closed behind them.

'Two or three days ago,' Wander replied, 'a packing-case disappeared from an army depot in the Coblenz area.'

Krug looked incredulous. 'And that's why you insisted on speaking to me? Is that the only reason?'

'Reason enough. The depot I refer to is a top security establishment, and the missing crate contains three warheads for short-range rockets with a magnetic guidance system. A secret project of the first order, freshly imported from the States.'

'And this happened two or three days ago?' Krug asked, pricking up his ears.

'Certainly. It comes just when the Ministry of Defence is under fire from all sides – just before the final assault. What's more, the public haven't been informed.'

'Who's keeping it dark?'

'The officer in charge, on instructions from the Ministry of Defence. The boys from the Ministry didn't take long to see what an outcry there'd be, so they gave it the full treatment – declared the incident taboo and imposed a complete security black-out. The area has been barred to unauthorized persons, which means that any personnel who may have even half an idea of the truth are effectively isolated. Patrols have been stepped up, extra sentries and check-points installed. They've even been using officers of field rank to seal the place off.'

'And nobody has caught on yet?'

'One or two newspapermen already suspect there's something afoot, but nobody'll tell them anything. They don't have access to detailed information and they can't go far on guess-work.

Besides, they've been systematically warned off – reminded of their liability to prosecution under the Official Secrets Act and so on. For every journalist there's at least one agent from the Constitutional Protection Office. The place is lousy with little men in grey raincoats.'

'How do you happen to be so well informed?'

'Our rules have paid off so far, Herr Krug – I'm sure you wouldn't want to alter them at this stage. The information is all that matters. How I obtained it is immaterial. Just to set your mind at rest, though, it's all first-hand stuff – straight from the horse's mouth, so to speak.'

Konstantin Krug picked up the telephone. 'Get me the Minister,' he said.

*

Minister Feldmann received Wander in private – 'between appointments', as he put it. The meeting-place was a house in Cologne which Wander already knew. Baroness von Wassermann-Westen lived there.

Sabine was nowhere to be seen. Feldmann, comfortably attired in a light linen house-jacket, was sitting in majestic solitude in the big drawing-room. He beckoned Wander towards him and indicated a trolley laden with bottles, glasses, and an ice-bucket. 'Help yourself to anything you fancy, but go easy on the vodka. I shall be needing some of that for my next appointment.'

The Minister's eyes twinkled as if he had just conferred a distinction on Wander by alluding to something highly confidential. Then he said soberly: 'Krug gave me some indication of your news – a remarkable story, if it's accurate. Please fill me in on the details.'

Wander, sitting where he had sat with Sabine a few days earlier, told his story for the second time. He used almost the same carefully rehearsed approach as he had with Krug.

Feldmann listened to him with great attention, the faintly benevolent smile on his face growing broader all the time.

'A really remarkable story,' he said again, when Wander had completed his report. 'You realize, of course, that there's a big fly in the ointment from our point of view?'

Wander nodded. 'Of course. The Defence Ministry people have dug in behind the Official Secrets Act. Whether they're justified is doubtful, but we can't afford to dismiss the possibility – not at the moment. Our hands are tied in the same way as those of the worthy General Keilhacke and his associates. It's a great pity, considering the nature of the information.'

'Wouldn't it be possible to find a newspaperman to leak the story?' Feldmann inquired cautiously. 'You know what journalists are – what one knows the rest know within twenty-four hours at most.'

'As things stand, no reporter could risk airing it without landing himself in gaol – no German reporter, that is.'

'Do you have someone else in mind, Wander?'

'An American correspondent.'

'Who, exactly?'

'Sandman of USP.'

'Do you know him well?'

'He's a friend of mine.'

The Minister took his time. He picked up a glass and filled it with mineral water.

'Very well,' he said eventually. 'Pass your information to Sandman and make it clear that you are the sole source. Don't encourage him to draw premature conclusions of any kind.'

'Right.' Wander's hand reached almost instinctively for the vodka bottle. He poured himself half a tumbler and drank some. Then he said: 'This isn't the first time I've been here.'

'I know,' the Minister replied amiably.

Wander studied the contents of his glass. 'Charming house,'

he said. 'Attractively decorated – very expensively too, I imagine.'

'Your supposition is correct,' the Minister said. He might almost have been expecting the conversation to take this turn. Certainly, he showed no signs of resentment.

'In my position,' he continued, 'a man sometimes has, quite deliberately, to evade the public eye. There are things which do not lend themselves either to the office or the family circle – highly confidential discussions, for example. One sometimes has to confer with a leading industrialist or a fellow-politician who happens to be temporarily on the other side, or with embassy officials from countries which are not – or not yet – allied with us. For that one needs friends. Friends like Baroness von Wassermann-Westen, for instance.'

'I'm already aware of your friendship with her.'

'In every detail, no doubt.' Feldmann spoke as if he were discussing qualitative variations in the German automobile industry. 'You must have gathered that a certain degree of intimacy exists between me and the lady of the house. What is more, the inferences habitually made in social circles are justified – or, rather, were so until a few weeks ago.'

'Any further contentions to that effect are out-of-date, you mean?'

'You might put it that way,' Feldmann replied musingly. He gave Wander a brief sidelong glance. 'My dear Wander, I've reached the age when almost every man is susceptible to temptation if a favourable opportunity presents itself. I am subjected to a host of such temptations – not, of course, that I can claim personal credit for that. In addition, I have a devoted wife and two exceptionally promising children. I'm entitled to feel contented.'

'But you're not?'

'I wasn't, let's say, because I met the Baroness, whom you know.'

'I only know her very slightly,' Wander said. 'Besides, who really knows anyone?'

The Minister accepted this statement with amiable serenity. 'The friendship between Sabine and me,' he said deliberately, 'has always seemed like a gift from the gods – at least to me – but there was no future in it for either of us from the start. I could never entirely sever relations with my family. You would understand that only too well, my dear Wander, if you had met my wife and children. Perhaps we should remedy that deficiency some time.'

'It would be a pleasure.'

'We'll arrange it,' promised Feldmann. 'At all events, the Baroness and I are just good friends, nothing more. She intends to marry soon. Someone from the world of industry, I believe.'

Wander smiled. 'I'll save my congratulations until the happy day.'

*

'Where the hell have you been?' Kohl demanded indignantly. 'I've wasted almost two hours waiting for you.'

'You can afford to,' Wander said. 'You're on leave, remember?'

'Only till tomorrow. Then I turn back into a regular member of the snoopers' trade union.' Kohl looked fidgety, almost nervous. 'That means today is my last chance to nail Barranski. Bergner turned up trumps, you see. That's to say, his girl-friend did. Now it's your turn.'

Wander tried to brush past the policeman, who was blocking the entrance to his apartment house. 'Give me a chance, Kohl, I'm dead beat.'

'Save it,' Kohl said drily. 'A promise is a promise. Come on, we have to drive to Cologne right away.'

Wander tried a final protest. 'But I've just come from there.'

168

'Fine, then you can drive back with your eyes shut.' Kohl grinned at his partner expectantly. 'Besides, I've brought you something which may make you feel better.' He pulled a flat object the size of a man's palm from his coat pocket. It was wrapped in a piece of grey linen. 'A sort of present from me.'

'What have you dreamed up for me this time?' Wander demanded suspiciously.

'A gun. In mint condition – never been fired. A Walter 7.65 with six rounds in the magazine. You know how to handle these things – they tell me you were a good shot in the army, so you're unlikely to score a bull's-eye when a couple of warning shots would be more to the point.'

'What makes you think I might need it, Kohl?'

'Quite frankly, I've no idea. You never can tell, that's all. Besides, I'm satisfied you won't misuse it, and I've had my doubts about your safety for several days now.' He held the gun out.

Wander pocketed it and they climbed into his rented car, he grumbling and Kohl swearing amiably. The policeman had ample time to enlighten him thoroughly during the drive to Cologne.

'The most essential thing is to have a witness with good eye-sight and the power of speech. That's rule number one. A story corroborated by two parties can't easily be shaken by a third. You're going to be my witness and I'm going to be yours.'

'You mean to say I was the only fool you could find?'

'Steady on, man. This is a question of mutual trust.'

Kohl proceeded to explain his plan. Wander slowed down when he heard the details, almost as if he was afraid of swerving off the road. He shot a wondering glance at the burly man beside him and wagged his head.

'Your methods would do credit to a gangster, Kohl. And I always thought you were a policeman.'

'Plenty of policemen are frustrated gangsters, and vice versa.

They all have one thing in common if they're above average – they know their trade. What's more, their aims may be different but their methods often coincide.'

'Why the hell did I have to run into you in the first place?' Wander complained.

Chuckling, Kohl disclosed some more details of his self-imposed holiday assignment. Armed with an introduction from Dr Bergner, he had made friends with Barranski's receptionist. He was now acquainted with various names and times, with certain drugs prescribed by her employer and the way in which they were passed on. The prices charged could be left to Wander's imagination.

'And this evening, at nine o'clock sharp, it's the turn of a society lady to receive special treatment from Dr Barranski – the wife of a South American diplomat. So step on it, or we'll be late for the show.'

They were in position ten minutes before the appointed time, standing outside a building in a side street near the cathedral. Dr Barranski had his consulting rooms on the first floor. There was little traffic, and only a few people were sauntering through the quiet old quarter, mostly in pairs. The street lamps blinked sleepily.

Wander took up his post in the brightly lit entrance hall, as arranged, while Kohl loitered near the door. They waited. Then the lift purred down the shaft and came to a gentle stop. The door opened and a woman emerged, a tall bony creature in a grey suit. Kohl gave Wander a nod.

Wander approached the woman, almost bumped into her, said a loud 'Pardon, madame!', and reached for her handbag. Startled and disconcerted, she released her grip on it. She stared at him, clearly surprised to find herself looking into a comparatively innocuous face, then mechanically opened her mouth to scream. Wander, who had glanced into the handbag by this time, nodded to Kohl.

The policeman hurried over to them. 'Is something wrong, madame?' he inquired.

'This man assaulted me!' she gasped.

'Not at all, madame.' Kohl made a dismissive gesture. 'You weren't feeling well – a momentary attack of faintness, perhaps – and this gentleman came to your aid. I saw the whole incident quite clearly. I'm from the CID, by the way. Would you mind telling me what this small packet in your handbag contains?'

'That is no concern of yours!' the woman said fiercely, a note of hysteria creeping into her voice.

'Morphia,' declared Kohl, who had been expecting that or something similar. In an official tone perfected by long years of practice, he asked: 'May I ask where you obtained this?'

'That's my business!' She hissed the words like a cornered snake.

'Not now it isn't,' retorted Kohl. 'Unless, of course, you have a prescription for this quantity of morphia. You haven't? In that case you acquired it in contravention of the Dangerous Drugs Act. Well, I'm at liberty to inform you that there may not, in certain circumstances, be any necessity to file charges against you. Provided you give us your voluntary and wholehearted co-operation from now on – provided, in fact, that you name the supplier of this morphia . . .'

'Never!' she exclaimed, shaking her head.

'I don't think you realize the gravity of your position,' Kohl said. 'This packet will no doubt yield fingerprints, some of yours and some of Barranski's. If you admit here and now that it was Barranski who passed it to you – all right, we'll hold him solely responsible. If you don't, the natural inference will be that you appropriated it – stole it, in fact. I don't have to tell you what that would mean. I should be forced to arrest you on the spot. Well?'

The woman stared wildly round her like an animal at bay.

Wander could hardly bear the spectacle but Kohl seemed to be enjoying it. It meant that he had cornered Barranski, and that was his sole concern.

'You're right,' she said in a flat voice. 'Dr Barranski gave it to me.'

'That's that, then,' the policeman said. 'We seem to have pulled it off.'

*

'You really do seem to have pulled it off.' There was no admiration in Sandman's voice. 'I'd never have believed it of you, Karl – I thought you were above that kind of thing.'

'Sorry to have to disillusion you, Peter, but once I was on the merry-go-round I couldn't get off.'

'You didn't want to, either – right?'

'Could be.' Wander had agreed to dine with Sandman at a hillside restaurant overlooking the Rhine. He accompanied him from the car park in silence. 'That's human nature, though. I was tempted by a lot of things – the fat fee and the thrill of the chase, for a start. Nearly all of us are prepared to take a gamble when the opportunity presents itself. Anything I've left out?'

'Yes, one trifling detail, but we'll talk about it later.'

'I can see I'm in for a cosy evening.'

The proprietor of the small inn hurried over to them – he had obviously known Sandman for a considerable time – and spoke in a low, confidential tone which suggested that no other customer was privileged to hear what he had to impart. 'Your favourite claret, sir, the Château Coufran, has already been brought to room temperature. The sucking-pig will be ready in about thirty minutes. I also have a plentiful supply of ice-cream specially imported from Higgins of New York.'

'Followed by champagne – the best you have,' said Sandman. 'My friend is paying – he can afford to. First, though, the usual. Out on the terrace, of course.'

172

Sandman's 'usual' was Black Forest Himbeergeist, a rasp-berry-flavoured, hundred-per-cent-proof spirit which he considered peculiarly suited to the climate – and it looked like a long hard winter. The glasses stood in front of them on the balustrade. Beneath them, the Rhine flowed sluggishly through the night.

'My favourite spot,' Sandman announced with a sweep of the arm.

'I can understand why,' Wander said. 'Up here you get the feeling you could spit in anyone's eye and get away with it. What's the point, though? Either they wouldn't notice or they'd think it was an act of God.'

'You don't look exactly overjoyed with life, Karl. I should have thought you had every reason to be.' Sandman gazed down at the garlands of light which now illuminated the city. 'What about this hatchet-job you've helped organize? At least that seems to be going well.'

Wander nodded. 'Like clockwork. The Defence Commissioner has just issued a statement on the subject of alarming abuses in high places. The Chairman of the Defence Committee has found it necessary to present the Chancellor with a list of grossly ill-advised investments in industrial development programmes. The President has summoned the Defence Minister for an interview – not a friendly little chat, either. Meanwhile, meetings are already taking place between the top brass of the government party, the chairmen of their regional associations, and the members of the parliamentary party. Apparently, they're to hear a report from Minister Feldmann.'

'Well, then, give yourself a well-deserved pat on the back.' Sandman raised his glass and drained it. 'Landlord!' he called over his shoulder. 'The same again, for health reasons!'

Wander glanced at him. 'Don't tell me you've lost your appetite.'

'You obviously don't know me,' the American said. 'As for

me, I know you a lot better than you give me credit for. I'm pretty well acquainted with your country, Karl. When I first turned up here you were still at school and I was a teen-ager in uniform – not a care in the world and flushed with victory. However, it didn't take even me long to realize that we'd marched into the biggest ruin the world has ever seen. And what is it now?'

'Nothing,' said Wander. 'An agglomeration of concrete, glass, sheet metal, chemicals and money. The heart of Europe – that's what a few megalomaniacs think. I'd prefer to describe it as Europe's gilded arsehole.'

'I know, you're one of the people who are appalled by the way your country has developed. Just because it's your country and you'd like it to look different.'

'The whole thing nauseates me,' Wander said fiercely. 'Everything – what happens here and what doesn't happen, and what is allowed to happen.'

'Poor old Uncle Sam,' Sandman said. 'As if he isn't un-popular enough already! Just because he tried to be helpful but didn't know the best way to go about it, people will go on blaming him for everything in general and your favourite bunch of Germans in particular.'

'Who else would you suggest?'

'Our ambassador would call your megalomaniacs a purely German concern. OK, I grant you the Americans helped put the country on its feet again – pretty effectively, too – but how were we to know what it would develop into?'

'Couldn't you guess? Couldn't you really – not after all the things that had happened a few years earlier? Wasn't the blood-stained record of the Thousand-Year Reich enough of a lesson? What about the five or six million dead Jews? Were they just a distressing but inevitable by-product – dust between the mill-stones of history or something? Was it all supposed to be forgotten as quickly as possible, with America's help?'

'So that's it,' Sandman said quietly. 'You hate this country –
I half suspected it.'

Wander shrugged. 'Perhaps I do, but I only hate this
Germany because I love my own.'

'Your Germany never existed.'

'But it could have. All the opportunities were there, all the
signs were right. We were at rock bottom, the perfect place to
make a really fresh start. We had people who had proved their
worth in times of trial and survived. What's more, we had
countless young people who had never voted for Hitler, who
had been dragged into the war by their parents' generation
and realized the extent to which they had been betrayed. We
had a host of people who could have helped us to start from
scratch.'

'Is that why you joined the Federal Army, Karl?'

'I don't know. I only know I'm better informed now than I
was then. I was barely twenty at the time. I suppose I wanted to
be able to believe in something, become committed to something – that's the way I am. Maybe I should have become a male
nurse or a road-sweeper, who knows? Instead, I became an
officer. That was when I realized how appallingly little the basic
set-up had changed or was likely to change – the same old
uniformed has-beens, the same old barrack-square martinets,
technically obsolete and mentally retarded. Some of them were
still living in the Third Reich, others in the days of Frederick the Great. And an outfit like that dares to claim that
it's equipped to defend the rights of man? Don't make me
laugh!'

'These theories of yours, Karl – are they really enough? Are
they a sufficient motive for helping to give the West German
army a face-lift?'

'Good enough for me.'

'In that case, God help you if it turns out that you're not
heading for a fresh start – that all you've done is play errand-

boy for a set of ruthless, immoral, self-seeking bastards. What are you going to do then?'

※

'We're going to take care of you,' announced Martin Morgenrot. 'Permanently.'

Wander had emerged from the inn alone. Sandman had stayed behind, saying he had an appointment with a man named Jerome. The night was starless, damp and cold, the carpark dimly illuminated by a neighbouring streetlamp.

Morgenrot junior barred his path. There was a metallic object in his right hand, presumably a jack-handle. He moved forward like an automaton.

Behind him, Wander made out the figure of Felix Frost, once the self-styled fiancé of Eva Morgenrot. He was still smiling, as far as Wander could see. His voice, when he spoke, sounded positively benevolent.

'This is your last chance, you know.'

'To do what?' Wander asked, retreating step by step.

'To make a confession,' Frost replied. 'In writing, preferably.'

'I've nothing to confess.'

'Why waste time talking?' Martin Morgenrot said. 'He obviously doesn't realize what he's done. We'd better let him in on it.'

'He's no fool,' Frost said. 'Perhaps he's just slow on the uptake.'

Still retreating cautiously, Wander looked round in search of help. They might have had the world to themselves. A radio was blaring somewhere in the distance and a car swept past on one of the lower roads, but there was no other sign of life. He said: 'I honestly don't know what you want.'

'Of course you don't,' sneered Morgenrot junior. 'Innocence personified, that's you. You put the fear of God into Eva, set the

176

old man against me, he tries to blackmail Sabine and land me in gaol – and you don't know a thing about it!'

'What if we let you off the confession, Herr Wander?' Frost asked, hanging back. 'We might reconsider if you just hand over the document you took from Eva.'

'What document?' Wander was relieved to feel his back make contact with the car. The near-side window was open, which meant that the glove compartment was within reach. The automatic supplied by Kohl lay inside. 'You two must be out of your minds!' he shouted belligerently.

Felix Frost recoiled but Martin Morgenrot resumed his advance. 'Let's knock some sense into him!'

'Better not try anything,' Wander said crisply. He had managed to reach the automatic. His fingers closed on it tightly and he pulled it out. 'I don't know what you're after but you've come to the wrong address. There's no truth in any of your suspicions. Somebody talked you into this and I can guess who. Added to that, you're probably trying to double-cross each other at my expense.'

'That's enough!' the boy roared. 'I'll finish you for that!'

Felix Frost hurriedly retreated farther into the darkness. 'Look out!' he called. 'He's got a gun!'

Wander flicked the safety-catch off and pointed the automatic in their direction. 'I'm a pretty accurate shot – anyone care to try me? If so, what'll it be?' He focused his attention on Martin Morgenrot. 'Perhaps you'd like me to ventilate your shoes or shoot that cosh out of your hand? I can think of plenty of ways to put you out of action.'

Frost appeared to have vanished. Morgenrot junior lowered the jack-handle. His face twisted as if he were suffering from stomach-cramps. Then, like a stone from a catapult, he launched himself forwards. A shot rang out and a tiny fountain of dirt and pebbles erupted at his feet. It stopped him in his tracks.

'Will that do,' Wander said harshly, 'or would you like to

have another try? I could aim a bit higher next time, but I hope you'll save me the trouble. Just remember one thing: not everyone lives the sort of life your sordid imagination thrives on.'

Wander climbed into his rented car and drove off with a faint smile of relief. It soothed him to have sensed fear in an opponent. Leisurely, he drove down the winding road that led back to Bonn.

Two cars appeared in his rear-view mirror, following him with headlights blazing. The first was a squat, road-hugging Mercedes with dark paintwork, one of the older 220 SEs, with Martin Morgenrot at the wheel. Behind it came the snow-white Jaguar belonging to Felix Frost.

They drove that way for miles, sedately keeping their distance, headlights undipped. Few people gave them a second glance because it was late and the streets were almost deserted. If Wander put on speed the cars behind him promptly accelerated; if he slowed, they followed suit. It was like being stalked by two beasts of prey.

Wander forced himself to remain calm during the twenty minutes that followed. Occasionally a horn blared behind him and he pulled over to the right, but nobody overtook him.

He stepped hard on the accelerator but the thoroughbreds behind him were not to be shaken off. He took the Rhine Bridge at fifty, but the Mercedes driven by Martin Morgenrot overhauled him with contemptuous ease. For a fraction of a second, Wander glimpsed the grim smile on the boy's face.

Then, when he was exactly level with Wander, Martin Morgenrot wrenched his wheel to the right. His Juggernaut of a car smashed into the frail bodywork of Wander's, crushed it, catapulted it sideways across the narrow walkway for pedestrians and into the railings. The railings snapped like match-sticks and the shattered remains of Wander's car vanished into the gaping void.

Wander felt like the hub of a Catherine-wheel. A wave of sound threatened to burst his ear-drums, lights flashed confusedly before his eyes, invisible forces seemed to pound his body with the ruthless insistence of piston-strokes.

Half-dazed, he pushed open the door and stumbled out on to the asphalt, where he tried to crawl sideways. His car dropped away, slowly and noiselessly at first, then hit the water with a dull splash.

When he recovered consciousness he found himself looking, from ground-level, into a long line of headlights. He was ringed by people who seemed to be bending over him with expressionless faces, policemen among them. One man, presumably a doctor, was running his hands over him. A woman peered into his bleeding, dirt-encrusted face with horrified fascination. A vague murmur of voices engulfed him.

Closing his eyes, he heard a voice he knew and tried to make out what it was saying. 'It was all his fault,' the voice said. 'He was holding up the traffic out of sheer cussedness – I can swear to it. He was blocking the whole lane, and when the car in front of me – the Mercedes – tried to overtake him, he accelerated. Started swerving too – must have been drunk or crazy. He caused the crash deliberately.'

The convenient witness was Felix Frost.

*

'Let me out of here,' Wander said, sitting up. 'There's something I have to do, urgently.'

'Haven't you had enough?' Dr Bergner shook his head. 'You ought to try and sleep now.'

'But I can't. I think I've worked out the answer to a sum and I want to check it.'

'Tomorrow,' Bergner said, 'at the earliest.'

'Right now,' Wander retorted, and climbed to his feet. He was in one of the hospital examination rooms. His first words on being brought into Casualty had been a request for Dr Bergner, who now stood beside him, motionless and alert. 'You see, Doctor? I'm quite capable of standing on my own two feet.'

'You might have ended up in the morgue,' Bergner said.

'But I came to you instead, and your diagnosis was as follows: slight concussion, a few bruises, a grazed face and leg, nothing more. Correct?'

'Correct,' Bergner replied, never taking his eyes off him. 'However, that's enough to keep you in here for a couple of days.'

'Another hour and I may be too late.'

'You have a slight temperature.'

'And the constitution of an ox.'

'But not the brains of one. Why not stay here a few days? It's no problem for me to keep people at bay – the police, for instance, who have a lot of awkward questions to ask you about the accident, or the man who saved your life. He's already called several times to ask how you're doing.'

'The man who saved my life?' Wander raised his eyebrows. 'Who would that be?'

'Martin Morgenrot.' Bergner had gone to the wash-basin and was watching Wander in the glass. 'He says he hauled you out of your car at the last minute, just as it was going over the edge. You were unconscious at the time.'

'Let me out of here, Doctor!' Wander did his best to stand straight and look calm, but his fists were clenched.

'What if I refuse, for perfectly valid medical reasons?'

'There are equally valid reasons for letting me go. I know you could keep me here with a good conscience, Doctor, but you won't.'

'Oh? Why not?'

'Because I'm asking you not to – as a friend, if you like. Remember I said something about having worked out a sum? Well, here it is: when four people could have committed a crime and two of them suspect a third, and the third knows he's innocent, it must have been the fourth. I've got to have a long talk with the lady in question before someone beats me to it.'

'I hope you haven't got your figures wrong. I also hope you never regret having asked a favour of me, but I won't stand in your way. After all, friendly impulses apart, I'm indebted to you.'

'Thank you, Doctor.'

'It's pretty late – just after one a.m. I'll give you another shot and a few bits and pieces to take with you. One thing, though. I don't think your condition will deteriorate but you must inform me at once if it does. You're a tough nut. Your reactions seem to be back to normal. At least, I don't notice any weakening of your aggressive urge.'

'No danger of that. It's rising steadily.'

'I can't imagine why.' Bergner broke the end off an ampoule and prepared a syringe. 'Perhaps I should tell you what I gathered about your crash from listening to the police. You're considered solely responsible. Two witnesses confirm that, and their stories tally – Martin Morgenrot and Felix Frost. The blood-test showed a reading of 1.1 per thousand. The police looked for your driver's licence but failed to find any papers on you whatsoever.'

'Good work but not good enough,' Wander growled. He rolled up his right sleeve. 'Be quick, I'm in a hurry. And just in case my so-called rescuer calls, tell him not to worry. I'm as good as done for.'

INTERIM REPORT No. 8

BY THE MAN KNOWN AS JEROME

on the ever-present possibility of disastrous misunderstandings and their negation by means of would-be realistic thinking.

I didn't realize until later what a boon Corporal Fünfinger was to our friend Wander, at least to begin with. The fact is, Fünfinger had an ability to see through the manœuvres employed by the Machiavellis of his time. What's more, he happily accepted them as a personal challenge. If there had to be puppets, he wanted to see them dance. After all, who ever took notice of a humble corporal in the thick of a ministerial battle?

Fünfinger's other side did not become apparent until later – too late, in fact. The moral campaigner who had gone into action with such cheerful abandon soon turned out to be a sort of social worker in uniform, a champion of widows and orphans. Wander never guessed the truth because Fünfinger opened his campaign so flamboyantly. He spouted a bewildering assortment of details and liked citing facts and figures. And figures nearly always carry conviction because nobody enjoys checking them.

For example: the maintenance of the West German armed forces absorbs billions of D Marks; their unreliable aircraft, injudicious building projects, ill-constructed tanks and irresponsible arms deals make them the biggest and most expensive junkyard in Europe.

But who gets worked up about that kind of thing? Pig-headed pacifists, professional protesters and unsuccessful writers – in short, poor deluded fools. Their vocabulary is familiar enough. Practical politicians have long since discovered that the best and most effective plan is to ignore them as completely as possible.

'War on waste!' is one of their battle-cries – allegedly waste at the expense of the young, the poor, the sick, the old. Each

Starfighter that crashes, they argue, costs the equivalent of half a high school, four primary schools or fifteen to twenty nursery schools.

But does any normal human being subscribe to that form of arithmetic?

Fünfinger did, and Wander followed his example. Between them, these starry-eyed conspirators smashed quite a lot of neo-nationalist china. Wander went at it with a will. He wanted to see Germany – his Germany – burst into flower. Any tender shoots he stepped on in the process were dismissed as weeds. Fünfinger, on the other hand, seemed to be more of a frustrated clergyman. He was once heard to say that he aspired to a really worthwhile existence – or something like that.

Imagine aspiring to that in the army, let alone in a country where his colleagues in uniform had been persuaded that they were arms-bearers to the nation, a select body of men invested with special distinction, servants of the people but aware of their collective responsibility towards Europe, custodians of Western civilization, defenders of the free world – indeed, of freedom in general – etcetera! It's an old story.

Admittedly, the Germans don't have it easy in this respect, but they also enjoy making it hard on themselves. They need only have given the matter a little hard thought, and they could easily have written finis to what had gone before.

But that was precisely what the Germans couldn't bring themselves to do. The ballast they refused to jettison included not only Hitler's officers but also their so-called *esprit de corps*, their know-how and experience – in other words, their bigotry, blind obedience and incorrigible inability to learn.

Very few Germans blushed at the re-emergence of these people. Why should they have? That was the way they were and that was the way to use them – practical politicians in various parts of the Western world accepted their reappearance with few qualms. Not many of them welcomed it, but they took it in their stride. They allowed the dregs of Germany to retain the so-called sense of tradition which inspired them with such pride. What a feast for Wander and company!

Like quite a few other people, Wander allowed himself to be panicked by this updated version of the Nazi 'spirit' and the embarrassing growth of neo-Nazism. One of the results was that he went off at half-cock. Frustrated poets shouldn't dabble in politics. They're too pathetically naïve to do anything but harm.

Chapter 9

'Ten to one you were expecting me,' Detective Chief Inspector Kohl said, when Wander had opened the door to him. 'I'll bet you hoped it was me and not someone else.'

'I'm still asleep,' Wander replied, yawning. He stepped aside and let the policeman in. 'I feel as if I'd been systematically dismantled and then reassembled.'

'You look like it too,' Kohl said. 'Had an exhausting night?'

'One damn thing after another. First I was hauled over the coals by someone who calls himself a friend of mine, then I was temporarily immobilized by a fake accident. Did you hear about it?'

The policeman nodded. 'But that's not why I'm here.'

'What is it, then?'

Kohl had stationed himself near the window, with his back to it. It was second nature to him to stand where he could see as much as possible. Wander, wrapped in a bathrobe, sat on the edge of his bed trying to concentrate. He looked battered and bleary-eyed. Meditatively, Kohl fingered the angular ribs of the radiator behind him.

'Not bad,' Kohl said, surveying the décor. 'Every modern convenience – parquet flooring to slip on and Persian rugs to trip over. Do you always stay in high-class pads like this?'

'I know you couldn't, not on your lousy pay.' Wander yawned again, gingerly fingering the plasters on his face and head. 'I'm staying here for free, but I don't know for how much longer.'

'You could be leaving today,' Kohl drawled.

'I could be,' Wander conceded. Then the policeman's remark sank in. 'What was that, Kohl, polite conversation or a hint?'

'I don't know yet,' Kohl said, watching him intently. 'I don't know much about anything – you, for instance. All that stuff you've fed me recently could just have been a smoke-screen. I don't like people trying to fool me, Wander. I'm a policeman, not a social worker.'

Wander was gradually waking up. 'Bar-room repartee doesn't appeal to me at this hour. Well, what do you want?'

'Where were you last night?'

'Are you interrogating me?'

'Not yet. Call it a private inquiry.'

'Has something happened, Kohl? Something must have happened – I can see it on your face.'

'Either you know already, Wander, in which case I've no need to tell you, or you don't know, in which case you'll find out in due course.' Now it was the policeman's turn to look tired and beaten. 'I want you to tell me how you spent last night.'

'Talking, boozing, and making inspired guesses. The car crash was a bonus.'

'Be precise, please. It's important.'

'All right. I met Peter Sandman at about eight o'clock and we drove out to a small restaurant. I left him shortly after eleven. About twenty minutes later I had this accident – or, rather, somebody staged it at my expense.'

'Just confine yourself to details that can be corroborated.'

'I'll try to. I was taken by ambulance to the local hospital a few minutes after midnight. There I was treated by Dr Bergner. He discharged me at my request shortly before two a.m.'

'Not later?'

'Is that important? Why?'

'When did you get back here?'

'Maybe three a.m., maybe later.'

'It wouldn't take longer than fifteen or twenty minutes to walk from the hospital to Koblenzer Strasse,' said Kohl. 'Why did it take you over an hour?'

'I stopped for a rest by the cemetery between Dietzstrasse and Herzstrasse. Actually, collapsed is a more accurate description. I leant against some railings and slid to the ground. I was all in.'

'Any witnesses?'

'What's the matter – am I suspected of something I don't know about?'

'Of course not. I'm merely giving you a friendly tip. It's probably the first and last piece of advice I'll be able to give you on the subject.'

'What's eating you, Kohl?' Wander protested uneasily. 'What the hell are you driving at?'

'Sabine von Wassermann-Westen died between two and three o'clock this morning,' Kohl replied, 'here in this building, right next door in Apartment 205. She probably died as a result of striking her head on a radiator. Accidental death hasn't been ruled out, if that's any comfort.'

Wander stared at the policeman incredulously. He found himself looking into a grim, uncommunicative face. A strange feeling stole over him. It was like being in a cold, cramped, airless room.

'Well, go on,' he said. 'What if her death wasn't accidental?'

'Murder or manslaughter, you mean? Quite possible – probable, in fact, but it isn't going to be easy to prove. There's at least one murderer to every murder, but we don't have any definite suspect at this stage of the investigation.'

'Which doesn't mean you haven't evolved some theories on the subject.'

'A new one pops into my head every two minutes,' Kohl said. 'At any rate, I must ask you not to leave town for the next few days. Not even temporarily.'

'Is that an official request?'

'I'm not in a position to make one yet – I don't have to tell you that. Let's assume that I can't dispense with your invaluable assistance. I'm asking you to co-operate. Does the idea alarm you?'

*

'Only a few hours to go,' Marlene Wiebke called to Wander as he entered the outer office. 'There's a plane leaving Cologne for Munich at 6.0 p.m. – the last flight today with seats still available. Shall I book you one?'

'No thanks. Not now things are beginning to look really interesting.' Wander did his best to sound light-hearted, but the effect on Marlene was nil.

'How much more will it take to convince you you've caught the wrong boat?'

'I may have caught the wrong boat but I seem to be getting places.' He smiled painfully.

'What happened to you?' Marlene asked. 'Were you beaten up or run over, or both?'

'Why do you stay mixed up in this racket?' he demanded. 'Is it out of love and devotion for Herr Krug?'

'I don't love Herr Krug and I'm not devoted to him – I just work for him. Loyally, too, if you've any idea what that means.'

'Not a clue.' Wander started to flick through the papers on her desk.

'Leave them alone!' Marlene said sharply. 'This isn't a book-stall. Besides, you're suspended until further notice.'

'What do you mean?'

'What I say. You've been put on ice.'

'Just me or the whole operation? What's the big idea?'

'Simply that you're temporarily suspended from duty. That's what I was to tell you – very politely, too, Herr Krug said.'

'He's trying to head me off!'

Marlene eyed him with concern. 'Herr Krug never even hinted at such a thing. He simply instructed me to tell you that you can take it easy for the time being – the operation is going according to plan and it seems advisable to let things take their course without further assistance.'

'I must speak to him at once.'

'He won't see anyone, not at present. He's in conference and he doesn't want to be disturbed on any account.'

'He needn't think he can get away with that. I'm not the sort of person who can be switched on and off like a light. You'd better make that clear to him.'

She shook her head. 'You must be suffering from concussion.'

'Tell him I insist on an immediate interview,' Wander said stubbornly. 'If he refuses – and kindly tell him this verbatim – he'll have to take the consequences.'

'Nobody insists on anything with Herr Krug,' she said. 'You don't know him.'

'The reverse applies too, evidently. High time we changed that.'

'Why don't you leave?' she pleaded. 'Krug has no objection, and he's your employer. Besides, there's a signed cheque waiting for you on Krug's instructions – three times your agreed monthly salary. What more do you want?'

'A chat with Krug and a chance to cry myself to sleep in your arms. Joking apart, though, I'm not allowed to leave town. It's the CID – they can't face life without me.'

'Karl,' she said, 'did you have anything to do with that woman's death?'

'No. Maybe I ought to apologize for the fact. I don't have any talent for overt violence, I'm afraid. All my crimes are mental ones.'

*

'I have to draw your attention to the following point,' Detective Chief Inspector Kohl said sternly. 'Anything you say may be taken down and used in evidence against you.'

'Do you mind!' Wander protested. 'That sounds like an official caution.'

'It is, but it's designed to protect anyone who has to submit to questioning. And since we live in a country which acknowledges the rule of law – kindly take that grin off your face, Herr Wander – the Ministry of Justice has suggested that the phrase should be used for precautionary purposes, even when there is only a very remote possibility that the person interrogated may be suspected of or charged with the offence in question.'

'If that is so,' Wander replied firmly, 'I decline to make any statement at all.'

'But you don't know yet what you're supposed to make a statement about.'

'I couldn't care less. There's no legal obligation on me to talk to the police without being charged – nor to the public prosecutor either, for that matter. As far as I'm concerned, this interview's at an end.'

Kohl walked across to the barred window. The detective whose job it was to keep a record of the interrogation sat crouched over his shorthand pad looking slightly stupefied. Kohl turned to him.

'Get me some cigarettes.'

The man got the message: his presence was superfluous. He hurried out. There was something weird about the conversation he had just heard. Wander was something new in his experience and he wondered if Kohl would manage to crack his shell. On the other hand, who if not Kohl?

'Congratulations,' grunted the detective chief inspector. 'So you're trying to outsmart me – me!'

'Why are you so obsessed with the idea of taking me apart?'

'Because there's something odd about you. I've thought so ever since we met.'

'Then you're not very perceptive.'

'Listen, Wander,' Kohl said, pulling up a chair. 'You've

190

made a lot of trouble for me but you've also given me a helping hand occasionally. I don't dislike you and it's possible you've taken advantage of the fact. Well, that's your doubtful privilege.'

'Stop talking in riddles, Kohl. You're in a fix of some kind, aren't you? What you're probably wondering is two things: first, who got me into this, and, second, who can get me out of it. Am I right?'

'Perfectly right.'

'In that case, why try to cook up some connection between me and Sabine Wassermann's death?'

'Cook up? That's rich! You're the obvious suspect – and the only one.'

Wander screwed up his eyes as if the light were dazzling him. 'You might have spared me that,' he said. 'After all, you're a man of instinct.'

'Precisely, Wander, and my instinct tells me you play a good game of poker. You're not unfair at heart, though – in fact you're a good sport.'

'You can cut out the last bit – it's been deleted from my dictionary. But do go on.'

'Well, to begin with there's your alibi. It's so shaky it's almost non-existent.'

'Come off it!' Wander said, with a belligerence born of uneasiness. 'You might just as well suspect anyone in Bonn who can't prove exactly where he was between two and three o'clock this morning.'

'What made you pick that particular time?'

'You're slipping, Kohl – you mentioned it yourself earlier today, presumably while you were still using your instinct. You should have stayed with it.'

'Not so fast. You aren't just one of a number, my friend. You not only lived within spitting-distance of the dead woman – you knew her exceedingly well and you recently tried to assault her in a restaurant.'

'Who gave you that story?' Wander had jumped to his feet.

'I know about it, Wander, that's good enough. There are almost a dozen witnesses in Cologne who saw the woman chuck her drink in your face, and they all agree she was provoked beyond endurance.'

'I simply told her what I thought of her. That was as far as it went, though. Murder isn't in my repertoire.'

'What say we compromise and call it manslaughter?'

'Sorry, Kohl, you're not going to nail me that or any other way.'

'Hang on, I haven't finished yet. You wouldn't deny that you hated the woman . . .'

'Despised would be more accurate.'

'Just as passionately as you once loved her, I presume.'

'Sabine wasn't the sort of woman you love. She was more like a virus.'

'Anyway, you had an affair with her.'

'That was ten years ago. Stop trying to play hide-and-seek with me, Kohl! I suppose you're only doing it to avoid burning your fingers on something else. All right, what about those two night-birds Morgenrot and Frost? Would you put anything past that pair?'

'I hadn't overlooked them,' Kohl said. 'However, they were both in Cologne at the time in question.'

'They can confirm each other's story, too, I've no doubt.'

'They even have witnesses.'

'Which only proves that money talks.'

'Quite possibly,' Kohl replied wearily. 'But it'll take some time to soften their witnesses up, and until then I'm sticking to you and the information I've been given about you, it doesn't matter who by. My reasons are simple but cogent. You'll defend yourself, Wander, you're bound to, and the best way you can do that is by helping me find the guilty party or parties.'

'What are you doing, Kohl – trying to turn me into a pet

retriever? What about inviting me to co-operate with you on the old basis – a partnership basis.'

Kohl drew a deep breath, closed his eyes and opened them again. 'All right,' he said, loudly and deliberately. 'Will you?'

'It's a deal,' Wander replied. 'On condition you give me the answer to one question.'

'I thought we'd finished haggling.'

'I have to ask this question for personal reasons which are extremely important to me. You can answer it in one of three ways, with yes, with no, or with silence. No quibbling, no qualifications of any kind – just that. Here it is: did you get the details of my one-time affair with Sabine Wassermann from Peter Sandman?'

'Is that all?' Kohl looked perceptibly relieved. 'The answer to your question is no.'

'Good. Then what's the next act on the programme?'

'First I have to cover myself – and stop smirking like that, Wander, it irritates me. I shall draft a memo to the effect that you've declined – quite legitimately – to submit to interrogation. I shall also draft another memo listing the information on you that's been brought to my attention. That can't be avoided, but I'll append one or two critical comments and reservations of my own.'

'Thanks a million!' Wander said sarcastically. 'If the judge takes extenuating circumstances into account I'll remember you in my prayers. What about those names I gave you?'

'A very tricky point. I know them already, but to get at them I need tangible evidence – the sort that would carry weight in court. Can you provide me with any?'

'Not yet.'

'There you are, then. What do you suppose would happen if the name of one of those so-called VIPs suddenly turned up in a report of mine? They'd take me off the case in two minutes flat, that's what.'

'We must avoid that,' Wander said. 'The question is, how?'

'The essential thing is to give me your wholehearted co-operation. I'm banking on it.'

'My dear Kohl,' Wander said, 'you seem to be doing more than trusting me – you're putting yourself in my hands. Why be so foolhardy?'

'Well,' Kohl replied, 'you could have blackmailed me after our joint intervention in the Barranski case, and that would probably have finished me. You didn't try it once, though, not even by implication.'

'I may not be a model pupil,' Wander said with a friendly smile, 'but I'm learning something new every day. Looks as if my survival depends on it.'

*

The same day, Wander received a visit from Corporal Fünfinger. The Corporal, who was on what he described as a pleasure-trip, demanded a bottle of champagne.

'What brings you here?' Wander inquired. 'If you've come for a laugh at my expense, carry on. I'm beginning to feel like a regular clown.'

Fünfinger settled his thick-set body more comfortably in the arm-chair. 'You're all right,' he said. 'The fact is, I came to make you another offer – very attractive, too.'

'I'm afraid all my requirements are met.'

'In that case you might like to put a couple of items in stock.'

'You overestimate me, Corporal. I'm not the man you take me for.'

'No reason why you shouldn't sit back and take it easy, I grant you,' said Fünfinger, 'not now our little show is running so smoothly.'

'You really get that impression?'

Fünfinger raised his glass and gave Wander an optimistic wink. 'Things are moving at last, I tell you. You can notice the effect, even on the most stubborn parade-ground hacks. Some of them are getting worried about their jobs, which means it's dawned on them that they're paid to do something constructive.'

'They're just scared, temporarily.'

'That's why we must keep up the good work, Herr Wander. I'm not alone, you know. There are plenty of youngsters who've got the itch, officers included. They'd like a chance to criticize or at least discuss the situation, but just try discussing things with generals! All those uniformed zombies want is to carry on dozing undisturbed. As long as the arms and equipment are properly taken care of, everything else can go to hell. They dream about stripes and epaulettes, orders and decorations, wire-pulling and promotion – that's their idea of heaven on earth.'

'I know,' Wander said. 'Death or glory . . . Even after two disastrous defeats, they're still not ready to stuff that muck where it belongs, which is up the arsehole of history.'

'Exactly. They've got to learn the hard way or they'll never learn at all. You're teaching them, Herr Wander, and I want to help.'

'You don't feel it's pointless?'

'I'll tell you what's pointless about this job – ceremonial parades, brass bands, chaplains making the sign of the Cross over tanks, flag-wagging, all the crap about discipline and obedience, nuclear sabre-rattling and officers' mess jargon. You're against that sort of thing, Herr Wander. That's why I'm on your side.'

Wander shook his head wearily. 'It doesn't matter what I do, people are always making new demands on me – expecting things of me. You're one of the worst offenders, Corporal. You don't ask for payment, you simply offer your services as a partner in crime. Do you think that's fair, with the world the way it is?'

'Don't tell me you're going soft on me!' Fünfinger exclaimed.

'I thought you were the new broom type, the sort who doesn't mind peeing on the grass if necessary, even when it says *keep off*.'

'Stop inventing parts for me, Fünfinger. I'm a typical German at heart, or what passes for one. That means I'm one of the people who call a halt to revolution when the traffic lights turn red. I may have started out as a reformer, but it could be that I want to cash in now. Hadn't that occurred to you?'

'Then let me in on the deal.'

'Even if it doesn't show an immediate profit?'

'The fun's enough for me.'

'Well, what can you offer me this time?'

'Plenty,' Fünfinger assured him. 'For instance, we could make some more special equipment vanish – complete guidance devices as well as warheads. Top secret papers, too. What would you say to the sudden disappearance of an armoured vehicle – latest model?'

*

'I suppose you're entitled to congratulate yourself,' Peter Sandman said coldly. 'You actually managed to deceive me, and I've always been considered an expert on local intrigue.'

'You can accuse me of anything you like.' Wander spat the words out as if they nauseated him. 'Why shouldn't you be right? I'm a fool, a liar, a schemer – maybe a lot of other things. I may even be indirectly guilty of murder.'

'Stop dramatizing yourself.' Sandman looked annoyed. 'The fact that you pulled the wool over my eyes is enough for me.'

'When was that?'

Sandman had asked Wander to meet him at a wine-bar near Römerstrasse in Bad Godesberg, a stone's throw from the Rhine. He said:

'Would you deny that things have taken the very turn you told me was out of the question?'

'I'm sorry, Peter, but I'm beginning to wonder just what I really have achieved round here – some of it without my knowledge or intention. What is it this time?'

'I mean Feldmann, of course! He's got the Defence Ministry in his sights and you've helped to sell him the army you love so much – him, of all people!' Sandman brought the flat of his hand down on the heavy oak table-top with a noise like a pistol-shot, but he was the one it startled most. He looked nervous and irritable. 'Can't you see what's going on or is it just that you don't like watching any more?'

Wander shrugged. 'Maybe I'm just tired. I feel as if I was being batted to and fro like a tennis-ball. As far as Feldmann's concerned, I still think he's acting as front man for the Chancellor himself.'

'You might be right, but the Feldmanns of this world don't surrender the lead once they've got it, whoever they owe their position to. I suspected that, Karl, but you talked me out of the idea. You should have known better. Nobody had his ear closer to the ground than you did.'

'Too close, perhaps.' Wander's tone was apologetic. 'Seems I stumbled over a lot of things without recognizing them. Do you really think Feldmann wants the Defence Ministry for himself?'

'It's practically in his pocket,' Sandman replied. 'Feldmann's supporters – you not least among them, Karl – have all made their contributions. Krug did a particularly good job whipping his parliamentary group into action, even if they didn't all co-operate. Covering fire is pouring in from all sides. Most people think Feldmann is playing their game, and they all want to join in – advocates of increased military preparedness, veterans' associations, freedom-loving men from the world of politics, scientists and artists, members of the so-called Opposition. I know they couldn't be expected to be clair-voyant, but it shouldn't have taken them long to see which way the wind was blowing. Anyone who gets involved with a man like Feldmann ought to take out insurance – and that includes you.'

'I trusted him,' Wander said quietly.

'You damn fool.' Sandman spoke without rancour. 'And to think I'm a friend of yours!'

The two men burst out laughing simultaneously. They both shook their heads, each tickled by a sense of his own stupidity.

'What a series of unfortunate coincidences!' Sandman said, still chuckling. 'Krug had to pick on you, the Chancellor trusted a man like Feldmann, and the present Defence Minister pursues a policy of dignified restraint. I know generals use each other for target-practice when there's promotion in the air, but that's kid's stuff compared to this political bloodbath.'

'Not Feldmann,' Wander said to himself. He was no longer smiling. 'Feldmann mustn't become Minister of Defence – his record isn't clean enough. I know that now. It's my conviction that politics should be restricted to men who are morally irreproachable.'

'That's all I needed to hear!' Sandman exclaimed in mock horror. 'Have you always suffered from attacks of high moral tone? That would explain a lot.'

'An unscrupulous man – a man without a genuine sense of responsibility – should never be allowed to wield power over other men.'

'Marvellous! Shall I tell you what the new set-up will really look like? The next Inspector-General's name will be Keilhacke, Krug will take over the chairmanship of the Defence Committee, and Feldmann will become titular commander-in-chief of the West German army.'

'That,' Wander said, very gravely, 'must not be allowed to happen.'

'How are you going to stop it? Feldmann can't turn back now. Here's what he told the parliamentary party today: "I have never thrust myself forward, but if I am called upon I shall not evade my duty." Who's to stop him now – you?'

*

Wander opened the door of his apartment to reveal a glum-faced Detective Chief Inspector Kohl.

'There you are at last. You look depressed.'

'They've made me police chief of Neuberg. Never heard of it? Neither have I, but they say it's a nice little town with a big future, a bit off the beaten track but brimming with potential. About ten thousand inhabitants, one hospital, three churches, thirty local associations and over forty bars. It'll be a grand life.'

Wander looked puzzled. 'How did you land the job?'

'I owe it all to you, no doubt, but don't expect an illuminated address of thanks. I came to say goodbye, possibly for good.'

'Does that mean you're running out on me?'

'That's irrelevant. I didn't pay enough attention to the rules of the game and I'm reaping the consequences. I wasn't able or willing to supply the information requested of me – information about you, Wander. Someone else will do it instead. That's what I wanted to warn you about.'

'Not so fast. Couldn't you really find anything that would point to the man responsible for Sabine Wassermann's death – or Eva Morgenrot's, for that matter?'

'Not a thing. Not a single definite indication. No basis for a charge that would stick. No promising clues at all, with the exception of those that lead directly to you.'

'But it's a false trail – you know that.'

'I don't know, Wander, I simply assume it. Maybe we'll meet again some time – in front of an assize court, with you in the dock. When that day comes I'll have to testify to what I know, and my evidence will tell against you.'

'Only against me?' Wander demanded with a tremor in his voice. 'Nobody else?'

'Who do you suggest?' The policeman stared at him mournfully. 'I didn't ignore your tips, direct and indirect. I even followed them up.'

'Without any success at all?' Wander looked dismayed and resentful. 'Don't give me that, Kohl! There was substance to what I told you.'

'My inquiries,' the policeman replied with patient resignation, 'have so far failed to yield any worthwhile results. I've drawn a blank with you, with young Morgenrot and his pal Frost – even with that girl-friend of yours, Marlene Wiebke . . .'

'She has nothing to do with it!' snapped Wander. 'Besides, she isn't my girl-friend. I'd like to make that clear.'

'With regret, no doubt. Be that as it may, I don't think I've missed a single person who had or could have had any connection with the dead woman. I even took Feldmann and Krug into account – wasn't careful enough either, from the look of it, or I wouldn't have been posted to Neuberg. Anyway, Krug was in conference with members of his party at the time in question. They all confirm that.'

'And Feldmann?'

'You must be joking!' Kohl wagged his head indignantly. 'You honestly expect me to haul in a cabinet minister for questioning? In the first place, both he and Krug enjoy parliamentary immunity. Secondly, we're bound by a set of directives which request the lesser lights of the CID – me, for instance – to proceed with the utmost discretion in certain cases, e.g. when even the vaguest suspicion attaches to a member of the government, the diplomatic corps, Parliament, or the Ministry of Defence. That includes straightforward traffic infringements. In such cases we have to report the matter immediately to higher authority, so that – as official phraseology so neatly puts it – we can be assured of the fullest backing. In other words, the hot potato is passed directly to a department which specializes in these things.'

'But you don't always obey directives, not if I know you.'

'I do my best,' Kohl said thoughtfully. 'It doesn't amount to much, most of the time. As a matter of fact, Feldmann states that he was working at his office all that night and even slept there. I can't shake his story. I didn't have enough time to work on it before I was kicked upstairs to Neuberg. What more do you expect?'

'One last piece of information. Who supplied you with the details of my former relationship with Sabine Wassermann?'

'Krug, of course. His files are remarkably comprehensive. They contain a mass of information about your affair with her – more than enough to make a lot of trouble for you.'

'But that can only mean one thing,' Wander exclaimed. 'Krug gambled on his inside information from the start.'

'Quite conceivably. It could be that he never regarded you as anything more than a tool, a reliable item on his balance sheet – if he was ever forced to submit one.'

'A disposable handkerchief, you mean. Something you blow your nose on and consign to the trash-can.'

'Why not face facts?' Kohl demanded harshly. 'You've no choice, have you?'

INTERIM REPORT No. 9

BY THE MAN KNOWN AS JEROME

on the dangerous stupidity of always expecting people to think rationally and the advisability of being prepared for uncontrollable reactions.

It isn't that we underrate the significance of private relationships in our business – it's just that, in practice, they seldom turn out to be of more than secondary importance. When it comes to power politics, public influence or financial gain, the question of who sleeps with whom carries little weight.

201

One of the most widespread errors in our profession is to overestimate the importance of bedroom conversations. They may occupy a useful place in spy stories but they don't have much currency to the professional agent. Not that a knowledge of certain intimate details, e.g. homosexuality, may not sometimes lend itself to effective exploitation, mainly as a supplementary form of pressure.

The subject referred to as 'Feldmann's private life' was quite familiar to my department, and had been for years. Nobody could have called Feldmann's tastes exceptional – in fact, he might justifiably have been congratulated on his discretion and restraint. Other men are far less fastidious.

Feldmann cultivated his image carefully, so much so that even the women's magazines developed a soft spot for him. Although his affair with Sabine von Wassermann-Westen did not entirely escape notice, he did more or less succeed in representing it as a close but Platonic friendship.

The Baroness was either shrewd or cunning enough not to exploit her relationship with him publicly. She even avoided hinting at it, not that well-informed circles failed to realize what was going on. The fruits of her discretion were a house in Cologne, a substantial bank balance, and various influential and profitable business contacts. She feathered her nest in the cosiest possible way without costing Feldmann the price of a packet of cigarettes.

The Baroness seemed to lose some of her drive during the last few months. It may be that she had also lost some of her reputation for drive in a more intimate sphere of operations. It was evident, however, that she arranged for the recruitment of surrogates, and one of them – presumably – was Eva Morgenrot.

Even Feldmann failed to realize the way the wind was blowing. There is little doubt that his overriding concern was to avoid any investment of personal feeling, refrain from making unnecessary promises, and nip any potentially embarrassing developments in the bud. He did not, of course, spare Wander a moment's thought.

Some features of this set-up gave Sandman particular food for thought – me too, at first. For instance, was it an isolated lapse, Feldmann's involvement with a girl as unstable, highly-strung and impressionable as Eva Morgenrot? After all, she was the daughter of an influential man whose co-operation was essential to the success of his campaign, a backer who must not be alienated at any cost. A strange and extremely injudicious thing to do – not what one would have expected of Feldmann.

I eventually hit upon the only possible answer, and with it the key to a number of thorny problems. The Baroness's diary, a calculated and not unsubtle apologia for her actions, was a big help to me in this respect.

It turned out that Feldmann was genuinely ignorant of Eva Morgenrot's precise identity at their first meeting. He probably thought she was just one of many, and failed to discover the truth until later. Pressure may have been brought to bear on him as a result, though only indirectly.

But the most important conclusion from my point of view was as follows.

The anti-Defence Ministry campaign may well have been Feldmann's idea but the inspiration probably came from Krug, and Krug was far-sighted enough to work in harness with Morgenrot senior and Sabine von Wassermann-Westen. This unholy alliance held the real key to all subsequent developments.

It was hardly surprising, then, that – as Sandman reported – Wander's suspicions were automatically aroused by Morgenrot senior's curiously obliging attitude. He did not, of course, realize what a marriage of convenience he had stumbled upon.

Having finally identified this basic set-up, I instituted a number of inquiries. Their outcome was not particularly surprising: Feldmann and the Baroness had maintained a close and unbroken relationship for some years, but active business links had developed between her and Konstantin Krug in the meantime.

Once the Baroness had come into Morgenrot senior's orbit – or he into hers, perhaps because Krug had engineered it – the seal was set on a promising partnership and the million-dollar project could get under way.

The idea of using Karl Wander as a pawn was probably the Baroness's personal brainwave. She regarded him, quite understandably, as a handy fall-guy, an idealistic emptier of political garbage-cans but also, if necessary, a useful scapegoat.

Manipulators of this kind inevitably make mistakes, but in Wander they had come up with a man who seemed to be lacking in any ability to discriminate between expediency and legality, reality and fantasy, psychological theory and every-day practice.

In this world, nothing can be more disastrous.

Chapter 10

'You've no idea what pleasure it gives me to see you, Herr Wander.' Maximilian Morgenrot rubbed his hands. 'I've toyed with the idea of asking you to call, but you might conceivably have taken it as an invitation to cash in.'

'On what?' Wander asked. His eyes roamed the managing director's desk in vain for the silver-framed photograph of Sabine. It was no longer there. 'Am I really supposed to have done something of value to you?'

'You've been most helpful. Take our joint venture, for instance. It's progressing splendidly, wouldn't you say? An impressive piece of work, that campaign of yours – or rather, the campaign launched by Krug and his associates – but its only result has been to shake the Defence Minister up. My material will give him the coup de grâce.'

'I suppose you invested a lot of money in the project.'

'As one partner in crime to another – nothing. I was already in possession of the requisite information when you turned up with your offer. After that I negotiated with Feldmann for payment on every document. I also extracted certain future guarantees from him.'

'And what does my commission amount to?'

Morgenrot senior laughed ghoulishly. 'You should always fix these things in advance, my dear fellow. You may be a pretty smart customer, but I could still teach you a thing or two.'

'I'm afraid you could.' Morgenrot was tacking to and fro with such rapidity that Wander found it hard to focus on him. 'Why did you invite me to call again?'

'Why ask when you must know the answer? You're no doubt aware that I'd appreciate some detailed information about one or two recent events – in confidence, of course.'

'The deaths of your step-daughter and Baroness von Wassermann-Westen, you mean? What sort of information had you in mind?'

'Anything that occurs to you. I'd also be interested in any theories you've formed, perhaps only as confirmation of what I already know or suspect myself.'

'You recently offered me ten thousand marks,' Wander said,

'The offer still stands,' Morgenrot assured him. 'In the first place, I've already made a small fortune and stand to make a far bigger one in the near future, thanks indirectly to you. Secondly, I'd like to put you under an obligation. Men of your talents shouldn't lightly be left to one's competitors.'

'But your fee will only commit me to give you all the information I have here and now, nothing more. Agreed?' Morgenrot nodded expectantly. 'Then write your cheque and put it on the desk where I can see it.'

Morgenrot senior complied. He swiftly scrawled some words and figures on an oblong slip of pale blue paper, appended his name with a flourish, and handed the finished product to Wander. Wander glanced at it and nodded.

'Well,' Morgenrot said eagerly, 'who was responsible for Eva's death?'

'You, in all probability. However, since you're only interested in the final stage of the proceedings, I'll confine myself to that. It may have been your son Martin. Does that surprise you?'

'Why should it, my dear fellow? It's what I expected.' It sounded as if he had meant to say 'hoped'. He went on coolly: 'The relationship between those two was bound to blow up sooner or later. If Eva had been a little more far-sighted she'd have given in to him and acquired a devoted slave for herself.'

206

'So it was her own fault if she was beaten up by your son, possibly with the help of Sobottke and very probably under the supervision of your friend Sabine. Felix Frost may also have had a share in it, indirectly.'

'And your own share, Wander?'

'I wasn't aware I had one. I'll swear on this cheque if you like.' Wander derived no pleasure from his attempt at a joke. 'I really don't know how far I influenced the course of events. I think I just wanted to help, but even help can turn out to be dangerous interference, especially in the case of someone like Eva. She struck me as emotionally disturbed.'

Maximilian Morgenrot was hovering behind his desk now. In an almost toneless voice, he said: 'You must have scared her – sent her into a panic. How? What did you know about her? Did you ask her for a certain document – threaten her in any way?'

'Why should I have? I suppose Sabine sold you that story – your son and Frost seem to be pursuing a similar train of thought. Was Eva in possession of dangerous information of some kind?'

Morgenrot jumped up and scuttled to the farthest corner of his office as though fleeing from some nameless horror. From there he cried with suppressed triumph: 'So you don't know a thing – not a thing! You aren't worth those ten thousand marks but you're welcome to them all the same.'

'As a sort of tip, I suppose, Eva's death saves you from halving your estate and automatically doubles what Martin stands to inherit. Sabine knew that, but did you know that it was Sabine who launched Eva on a short-term and pretty sordid affair with Feldmann?'

Morgenrot turned away and stared up at the tapestry-covered wall. 'If that's true, he'll pay for it.'

'You intend to make capital out of it yourself?'

'What alternative do I have?' Morgenrot abandoned the

tapestry, which depicted a reclining goddess of ample proportions. 'Don't expect me to cry over spilt milk.'

'Does Sabine come under that heading too? The last time I was here I saw her photograph on your desk, complete with silver frame.'

'Well?' Morgenrot now appeared to be examining his windows for traces of dust. 'She's a fine-looking woman – pardon me, was a fine-looking woman. I'm sure you'll confirm that from personal experience. How do I know? Because Sabine told me. She was shrewd enough to tell me her life-story in every detail.'

'She was also shrewd enough to ingratiate herself with the members of your family. She acted as Eva's madame, corrupted your son, and talked Felix Frost into a sordid adventure. If that wasn't brazen, what is?'

'I don't think you see it in quite the right light,' Morgenrot said, almost sadly. 'Sabine began by arranging certain business deals for me. That led to the forming of a certain friendship and eventually to plans for marriage.'

'And also to a sort of pact between Sabine and your son, no doubt. Eva's existence robbed them both of a million-dollar future. As a result, they formed a temporary alliance, possibly in bed as well.'

Morgenrot smiled. 'You're letting your imagination run away with you a little, Wander. You mistake the mentality of a woman like Sabine. When such a person recognizes the true promise inherent in a calculated course of action, no sacrifice is too great. From the moment when I asked Sabine to become my wife – and I did so after the most mature consideration – she became a model of ladylike decorum. Nothing will convince me otherwise.'

'You're aware, of course, that she was Feldmann's mistress?'

'Of course. She told me about that too. She slept with Feldmann and did business with Krug. That's one of the main reasons why I owe her so much – my acquaintanceship with you included.'

'I seem to have done more than underestimate her,' Wander said thoughtfully. 'I obviously misjudged her.'

'Sabine was worth her weight in gold. She not only knew how to set up valuable contacts – she also had ideas. From a certain point of view our operation was one of them. However, she must have made some crucial error. The question is, what was it?'

'Perhaps she overlooked Felix Frost. Or didn't take him seriously enough.'

'Wander,' Morgenrot said, 'if you can get rid of that scheming swine I'll double the value of your cheque – no, treble it.'

'How did he get to Eva in the first place? Why did she allow herself to get mixed up with a man like Frost? Just to provoke someone, and if so, who? You, your son, or Sabine?'

'Your question warms my heart,' Morgenrot said. 'It implies that even you, who have been at the centre of all these events, don't have the least idea of what really happened.'

'Perhaps your son could produce a satisfactory answer.'

'Quite possibly, but I don't propose to press him on the subject. It might destroy our relationship of mutual trust. After all, Martin is my sole heir now.' Almost proudly, Morgenrot senior added: 'That's what he was aiming at, quite obviously, and he's done it.'

'Take care he doesn't do you too, one fine day.'

'I always take care, Wander. I'm counting on Martin's intelligence – a quality he has demonstrated only too clearly. Martin knows his money is invested in the factories I control – without me, he's a dead letter.'

'In your place, Herr Morgenrot, I wouldn't be too sure.' Wander stared at him provocatively. 'Eva's death may have been a communal effort, but why did Sabine have to die too?'

'Because Martin wanted it that way, you mean?'

'He can prove that he wasn't implicated, quite apart from the fact that it may genuinely have been an accident. There are other complicating factors – Feldmann, for instance, whose power and prestige were at stake, or Krug, whose business ventures looked threatened, or Sobottke, who simply gets a kick out of beating people up. Then there are your son Martin and your prospective son-in-law Felix Frost, both of them intensely interested in financial gain. Finally, don't forget me.'

'All you want to do is cash in,' Morgenrot said. 'You're even prepared to blacken my son's character in the process.'

'He does that without any help from me,' Wander retorted. 'Your son and Felix Frost can prove that they were in Düsseldorf at the time in question, in a club for homosexuals.'

Morgenrot veered towards the door, where he nervously fingered the handle. He stared at Wander with a helpless expression.

Wander rose, picked up the cheque, folded it carefully, and put it in his pocket. 'I don't know who actually killed your beloved bride-to-be, but I hope and expect to be able to present you with his name very soon. You can have it free of charge. This business may well cost you more than enough as it is.'

*

Marlene Wiebke having paved the way, Konstantin Krug received Wander in his office with every appearance of cordiality. He now sat enthroned behind his desk like a mail-order Buddha, wearing the semblance of a friendly and obliging smile.

'Are you worried about something,' he inquired, 'or did you come to say goodbye?'

'I'd like you to clarify a couple of points.'

'By all means, my dear fellow, if you still consider it necessary.'

'Unavoidable would be a better word.'

'Call it what you like,' Krug said. 'Let's stick to essentials, though, if you don't mind. I'm extremely pressed for time, largely thanks to your hard work.'

Krug devoted the next few minutes to further pleasantries of this kind, spoke about the campaign that owed so much of its initial success to Wander's efficiency, and expressed the hope that it would continue to progress at the same tempo.

'Your contribution has been far from negligible, Herr Wander. I recognize that and so does the Minister. Incidentally, he asks me to convey his thanks and express his appreciation of your efforts. As you probably know, there's a specially adjusted fee waiting for you.'

'What am I supposed to have done to earn it?' Wander demanded. 'My efforts weren't aimed at making Feldmann the next Minister of Defence.'

'Ah, so that's the trouble!' There was relief in Krug's voice. 'My dear Wander, it was never for a moment envisaged that Herr Feldmann would take over the Ministry of Defence.'

'So I firmly believed.'

'And rightly so.' Krug raised his hand like a witness taking the oath. 'As you were more than once assured, this campaign was launched at the secret instigation of the Chancellor, who considered it to be politically expedient. We were loyal enough to shoulder the burden, swallowing our personal misgivings for the sake of Party and country. Our complete disinterest . . .'

'Disinterest?' Wander exclaimed. 'You don't know the meaning of the word!'

Krug's face was a frozen mask, but his voice lost none of its cordiality. 'You must try to view this issue more dispassionately. You, in particular, ought to welcome it if Herr Feldmann becomes the next Minister of Defence – not that it's a foregone conclusion. He's making every effort to decline the responsibility.'

'I know, he's bridling like a bashful virgin. After all, he can't very well admit that his only motive in smashing so much china was to take over the whole shop at a knock-down price. He wants people to go on their knees to him first.'

'Herr Wander,' Krug said quietly but distinctly, 'you're obviously suffering from strain. You've taken too much on yourself. We all appreciate your unstinting devotion to our cause, but now you ought to unwind a little. A few days' relaxation would soothe your nerves. And if you care to return – say in a week or two – you should with luck be able to go straight into the Ministry of Defence. A special adviser's post might suit you.'

'Under Minister Feldmann, with Keilhacke as Inspector-General and you chairing the Defence Committee? What the hell do you take me for?'

'Not a fool, anyway,' Krug said. 'I've never taken you for one yet, so please don't disillusion me at this late stage. To make my meaning even plainer, rest on your laurels and consider yourself fortunate that we don't hold your outside activities against you.'

'In other words, I'm to make myself scarce and keep my mouth shut so that you and Morgenrot have a completely free hand.'

'There you go again!' The reproach in Krug's voice was still tinged with benevolence. 'Those uncontrollable impulses of yours, that dangerously deficient sense of proportion – think of all the trouble they've got you into already! Never mind, as I've told myself repeatedly, the man's efficient, talented and hard-working, so do your best for him.'

'By presenting the police with circumstantial evidence of an incriminating nature?'

'What an appallingly biased attitude to take! You're blinded by your own stubborn prejudices, Wander. Of course I had to supply the police with information when I was questioned. I did so in your interests – in fact, I spoke up in your defence.'

'And drew your fee from Morgenrot, no doubt.'

'Continue in this vein, Herr Wander, and you'll begin to annoy me. Then I might genuinely feel tempted to hand the police some of the more damning material I have on you. One item is a sworn affidavit which could gravely implicate you in Eva Morgenrot's death.'

'Who thought that one up?'

'Baroness von Wassermann-Westen lodged it with me a few days before her death.'

'And even that failed to save her?'

'That's enough, Wander!' Krug said sharply. 'You're on the point of trying my patience too far, and nobody ever did that with impunity.'

'Not even Sabine, you mean? Strange how conveniently she died, just before concluding a big deal on which you now stand to collect without her. That boosts your share of the profits, doesn't it? Poor old Sabine, she's certainly worth her weight in gold as a corpse.'

'Get out of here, fast!' Krug's hands had begun to tremble. 'And forget your foul insinuations or I'll hand you over to the police without another thought.'

*

'Call this beer!' Peter Sandman shuddered. 'It smells like horsepiss.'

'Like corruption,' Wander said mournfully, 'or fog, or loneliness – it all depends on your mood. I've grown used to it.'

'It's a drink you have to smell and taste simultaneously,' Detective Chief Inspector Kohl declared. 'Then it's more like a mixture of milk, honey and blood.'

They were sitting at the corner table in Mutter Jeschke's, chatting with exaggerated casualness about nothing in particular. They had already discussed the weather, which was bad, the level-crossing barriers in the centre of the city, which were nearly always shut, and the Rhine, which had stunk like a gigantic sewer lately.

They had met to raise a last glass to Kohl's departure. The policeman was glad that Sandman had come too. The two men knew and liked one another.

Wander said: 'I've got a farewell present for you, Kohl. It isn't for you personally – I couldn't manage that – but it may help you off to a good start in Neuberg.' He produced a pale blue slip of paper and pushed it across to the policeman. 'A cheque for ten thousand marks.'

Kohl took the slip and unfolded it incredulously. Sandman craned over his shoulder. They first checked the figure and then tried – successfully – to decipher the signature.

Kohl gave a low whistle. 'How did you pull it off? Maybe I shouldn't ask, though.'

'No reason why you shouldn't. I'll even give you a straight answer. I earned that cheque by sticking to the truth for half an hour.'

'Congratulations,' Sandman said. He sounded relieved. 'At least your efforts here haven't been a complete waste of time. Taking Morgenrot for ten thousand is an achievement.'

Wander smiled. 'You're overestimating me again, Peter. Unfortunately, I got the impression that the ten thousand was a reward for stupidity. The longer I told Morgenrot the truth, or what I thought was the truth, the more delighted he became. There couldn't be a surer sign that I've overlooked something vitally important.'

He drained his glass and asked Mutter Jeschke to refill it. She did so with a touch of uneasiness. Wander had already disposed of two stouts in the last fifteen minutes and she wondered if he would last the evening. Sandman and Kohl eyed him appraisingly.

'You earned the money one way or another,' Kohl said. 'Why not keep it yourself?'

214

'That's just what Morgenrot hopes I'll do. If I decide to wash his dirty linen in public, he wants to be able to prove that I was on his pay-roll. That's why I'm asking you to use this cheque as you think fit, Kohl. It needn't necessarily go straight into the police welfare fund. You could bring a little sunshine into an orphanage, or something.'

The policeman nodded with uncharacteristic enthusiasm, but Sandman asked sharply: 'What was that about washing dirty linen in public? I hope I misunderstood you.'

'You're entitled to hope anything you like,' Wander said.

'Haven't you had enough, for Christ's sake? You've already been played for a sucker and thrown out on your ear – what more do you want?'

'I've also been very generously paid. Other people usually pay good money for the sort of entertainment I've had. I'd like to go on enjoying the show for a while longer if there's any chance of it.'

Sandman glanced inquiringly at Kohl, who eyed Wander for a moment and then asked: 'Did your conversation with Morgenrot yield any pointers you haven't told us about yet?'

'Gentlemen, gentlemen!' Sandman broke on. 'Can't you restrain yourselves. I thought we'd gotten together for a quiet farewell beer, and what happens? Wander dreams up brilliant new schemes, Kohl insists on raking over past history, and I do my damnedest to prod you into a little common sense.'

Kohl gave an appreciative nod. 'What you're trying to do, Mr Sandman, is to lead an ox to the slaughter and simultaneously persuade us that you're doing it at the ox's request. A fine bunch of friends you've picked yourself, Wander!'

'All right,' Wander said, 'let's talk about Morgenrot. My conversation with him showed that our theories were more or less correct, Kohl. Apart, that is, from a few minor points which we couldn't have known and one detail which might have helped you if you'd known about it in time.'

'Start with the minor points.'

Wander ordered another beer and drank half of it. 'When it comes to business,' he went on, slurring his words slightly, 'Morgenrot's the sort of man who's prepared to auction off his foster-daughter and his future wife and see his beloved son and heir get away with murder. He's even proud of the fact.'

'So it was all to do with Eva's inheritance,' Kohl said. 'Morgenrot not only let the Baroness loose on her but gave his son carte blanche as well. If they wanted to inherit they had to do something to earn it.'

'That's it more or less,' Wander confirmed. His voice sounded increasingly weary. 'It was just a business venture, really – a speculation promising maximum returns. He was ready to use anything and everyone that came to hand – son, daughter, bride-to-be, business partners, friends in the Party, members of the government, even the army . . .'

'Don't forget yourself, Karl,' Sandman said.

'How could I? I was fattened for slaughter, just in case it became necessary to buy off the wolves.'

'Hence Krug's comprehensive dossier on you,' Kohl put in.

Wander nodded. 'Yes, except that I prematurely stumbled across a girl who'd been beaten up. I suppose that's why I'm still at liberty. At least I can still drink a beer with my friends.'

'Without enjoying it,' Sandman said. 'What's worrying you? Is it Sabine?'

Wander shook his head. 'You've never had the misfortune to cross swords with a woman like her or you'd go easier on me. One thing's certain – Sabine realized that marriage with Feldmann was out of the question, whereas Morgenrot seemed willing and able. So she duly tried to keep both of them happy by reserving herself for Morgenrot and recruiting a team of substitutes for Feldmann, Eva Morgenrot among them.'

'Was that deliberate or coincidental?' Sandman asked.

'How the hell should I know?' Wander shrugged. 'There's

always been a wall between me and the truth – literally. All the real action took place in the apartment next door, perhaps while I was asleep or talking to one of you.'

'I haven't been idle on my last day in Bonn,' Kohl said sadly. 'Here's what I found out: it isn't beyond the bounds of possibility that Feldmann visited Apartment 205 on the night Sabine died, but he wasn't there at the time of her death. Reliable witnesses are ready to swear to that.'

'What about Krug?' demanded Wander.

'He claims to have been attending the same series of talks as Feldmann. Various members of parliament were there too, so he isn't short of witnesses.'

'This Apartment 205,' Wander said, 'who did it really belong to? Who had access to all the keys?'

'All that I can say is, there were probably three of them. One I found among Eva Morgenrot's effects and another was in Wassermann-Westen's handbag. Not in No. 205, though. It was upstairs in No. 304, her official apartment.'

'That means someone must have been using the third key. Who has it?'

'I don't have the time or opportunity to find out.'

'You give up, you mean.'

'Detective Superintendent Traugott is taking over the case. Traugott's the ideal man – a real demolition expert. He'll happily get you off the hook unless it proves absolutely essential to find a guilty party. Then he'll flatten you like a steamroller.'

Sandman gave a worried frown. 'You're exaggerating, Kohl. Wander's under the aegis of Krug and Feldmann, and they can't afford to have one of their closest associates involved in a scandal.'

'No,' Kohl said, 'but what if their close associate deliberately provokes the scandal himself?'

'They'll still try to cover him and hush things up – at this stage of the game they don't have any choice. Another two or three days and they'll have the army in their pocket. All hell can break loose after that, for all they care, but not *until* then.'

'Except that plenty can happen in the next two or three days,' Wander said. 'Those two gentlemen are quite capable of following my advice and taking a leaf from Clausewitz's book. Attack has always been the best method of defence.'

'Is that just conjecture, Karl, or something more?'

'I had an interview with Krug since I last saw you – bullied him into seeing me.' Wander stared drunkenly from one worried face to the other. 'I had to find out what I was involved in.'

'That was asking for it,' Sandman said, and Kohl shook his head grimly.

'I asked for it and I got it,' Wander mumbled. 'Rushed in with fists flying and got smacked on the nose for my pains. He tried to soft-soap me at first – even expressed his thanks and appreciation – but ten minutes later I got an earful. They might be compelled to throw the book at me, he said. Coercion, attempted extortion, deliberate misrepresentation, false pretences, multiple embezzlement – the lot.'

'That,' the policeman said, 'is bad.'

'Bad for whom?' Wander retorted defiantly, before he started to slide under the table.

*

Marlene Wiebke opened the door and let Wander in. 'There you are,' she said. 'I was expecting you earlier than this.'

'Don't offer me any black coffee,' he groaned. 'I've already had pots of it poured down my throat by two so-called friends of mine. I only came because I thought you'd enjoy a laugh at my expense.'

'I'm not going to do you the favour,' Marlene said. 'Anyone would think you had a death-wish, the way you've been acting lately. You can't win, you know.'

Wander flopped on to her bed and cradled his head in his hands. 'You see before you, madam,' he said in a mock fairground barker's voice, 'the celebrated donkey that ventured on to thin ice, intending to feast on its own beauty. It smiled at its glorious reflection and the ice broke. Well, what do I do now?'

'Maybe donkeys can swim – maybe the ice broke at a place where the water isn't very deep.'

Wander studied her earnestly. 'You really do look gorgeous, even when you're pretending to be severe. Your eyes sparkle in the most seductive way. Why not take off those glasses and come here?'

Marlene frowned at him. 'If you came here for consolation you've got a long wait ahead of you. If you came to pick my brains you'd need a lot more time than you've got. If you've made up your mind to do something and came here to sleep on it, go somewhere else. I don't go to bed with supermen.'

'Who, then? Party secretaries?'

'I see you haven't lost your sense of humour, but it's wasted on me. You'd far better tell me what you came here to talk me into. Who knows, I might be agreeable.'

'That fraud you work for, Marlene – get away from him. You just don't fit into this political bargain-basement.'

'Can you suggest something better?'

'It shouldn't be too difficult.' Wander leant over and switched on her television set, which stood on a table by the bed. 'Use some discrimination, that's all. Your idol is currently cultivating his image as a serious politician, respected statesman and avowed champion of democracy. He's taking part in one of those tailor-made press conferences aimed at arousing universal goodwill. Journalists ask polite questions and politicians give noncommittal answers. Here's an opportunity to admire his technique.' He pointed to the screen.

Konstantin Krug's head materialized out of a sea of darkness, gaining definition as the light lapped round it. His bald dome gleamed faintly but commandingly as he inclined it for the sake of effect. His keen eyes were veiled and his voice had dulcet overtones. He was expounding his views on the relationship between human morality and political expediency.

Krug's television image said: 'There is no need for morality and expediency to conflict. They must not be allowed to conflict, nor do they in fact – not for those who endeavour to fulfil their obligations with the necessary sense of responsibility, disinterest and devotion to duty. To them, nothing can be politically expedient unless it is also ethical, and politics have to serve human beings. I and the other members of our party . . .'

'Does he talk like that in the office too?' Wander inquired.

'I take down what he dictates. I book appointments and keep files, make 'phone calls and draft memos. That's how I earn my salary. I used to work in the advertising department of a detergent firm. It was a sobering experience.'

'And it never irritates you, working for a long-playing record like Krug?'

'It never did before you came, Karl.'

'What's changed?'

'Nothing definite, yet.' Marlene leant back in her chair. 'So far, I've never heard you give vent to anything but requests and demands – things that concern you alone. You seem blind to anything but yourself, your problems, your ideas, your version of truth and justice. Is that enough?'

'Not quite. Not now. I can look beyond all those things and see something else, something more important. You, Marlene.'

'And what do you propose to do, now that you've had this blinding intuition?'

'Badger you into a decision. One you shouldn't find too hard to make, now.'

Konstantin Krug's harshly defined television image had just been asked to describe how it envisaged the future of the army. It said: 'The army is an instrument, as essential as it is indispensable, for the defence of our freedom, our people and country. We hope that we shall never be forced to employ it, but, should that day come, we must be able to rely upon it with full and complete confidence. That, however, can only come about if we entrust this costly and sophisticated instrument to the safe-keeping of a man who merits, and can count on, our unqualified trust and support – my esteemed and universally respected fellow Party member, Minister Feld . . .'

Wander switched off the set.

Konstantin Krug's image swiftly lost its clarity and dwindled to a mere speck of light. Marlene smiled.

'What was that supposed to prove?'

'His mendacity, for a start.'

'You call it that. Other people call it tactics. Everybody lies in this world, out of expediency, calculation, love, sympathy, even pity. You insist on the one and only ultimate, definitive truth, but you've no idea what it looks like.'

'You're a cunning little devil, Marlene,' Wander said with cheerful indignation. 'You only want to see how far I'll go for the sake of some information about those keys.'

'Well, what lengths will you go to?'

'All right, Marlene, I like you and I'd like to sleep with you, but I'm damned if I'll say the one thing that would really make you laugh. I won't say I'm in love with you.'

'Why not?'

'Because I've never said it to any woman in my life.' Wander felt a sudden urge for ice-cold water. He jumped up and made for the bathroom, but Marlene barred his way. She had removed her glasses and was looking up at him with a smile.

'The key business is quite simple,' she said. 'There are three keys to each apartment including No. 205. Two of them were issued to Sabine von Wassermann-Westen. One of these she kept for her own use and other for temporary loan to understudies like Eva Morgenrot. Apartment 205 was the rendezvous, and its immediate proximity to yours wasn't as coincidental as you may think.'

'So Feldmann has the third key!'

'No, he didn't need any key. The Baroness's specially trained and selected stand-ins used to wait for him there.'

Wander pondered hard without coming to any apparent conclusion. 'But who held the third key? Not Krug, surely?'

'You've got it. I could never have told you, of course, but how could I guess you'd be so quick on the uptake? Just to confuse the issue, Krug holds six keys, not one.'

'Six?' Wander asked in bewilderment. 'What on earth for?'

'Organization,' Marlene explained. 'As you probably know, Krug's a so-called sleeping partner – and a pretty influential one – in a number of private finance and property companies, one of which happens to own the apartment house you're staying in. Krug has reserved six of the apartments for his private use – for accommodating business contacts and friends of the Party, temporary employees like you, deserving political associates and their playmates, and so on.'

'And 204 is another of these apartments?'

'Of course. Krug can walk into your love-nest any time he wants. The six apartments administered by him personally are Nos. 203–4–5 and 303–4–5. All the keys belonging to them were in his safe this evening. Whether that was so before this happened, I can't say. Now work it out for yourself.'

'I'm trying to,' Wander said. 'So only Krug . . .'

'Don't underestimate him, Karl. Don't forget about me either, if you can help it.'

'How could I do that?'

'I'm ready to go with you, Karl. At once, without any conditions. Wherever you suggest. Would you like that?'

'Why ask? I'd like it better than anything in the world, but I can't.'

INTERIM REPORT No. 10

BY THE MAN KNOWN AS JEROME

on human foibles and the merits of indulging in them occasionally.

The stage came when many things seemed clearer, at least in a few important respects. The charge that it was already too late cannot be made against me or my department, especially as we succeeded in pulling off a neat little coup of our own just before the stable door was finally bolted.

One or two people did, of course, burn their fingers, not to mention certain other important parts of their anatomy, but that was in the nature of an occupational hazard.

Quite a few contemporary politicians appear to spend most of their time founding mutual insurance corporations with limited liability. They gloss over their problems rather than air them and compromise instead of grappling with things. In short, they expend their combined energies in reducing a contemporary evil to the most innocuous common denominator possible.

Steel-nerved gamblers like Feldmann and skilled manipulators like Krug take this into account from the start. Their political PR work is carefully calculated. Out come the great big, beautiful, meaningless phrases, and always with the same underlying intent: sound adamant but never commit yourself, inspire trust but leave the object of that trust vague. Above all, never utter a word against any larger and more powerful corporate body.

To illustrate this, a member of Feldmann's party declared that it was 'to the Minister's credit to have confronted such a thorny situation courageously and with determination . . .' A member of the current coalition: 'While conceding that this step was justifiable, if not essential, we hope and expect that it was

223

taken in full consideration of our security requirements ...'
Finally, a member of the so-called Opposition: 'We cannot
refrain from uttering a word of warning, not that this should
under any circumstances be interpreted as a rigid and wholly
unfavourable attitude ...'

All of a sudden, apparently from the Chancellor's office, a
confidential ruling went out. In the future, nothing was to be
exaggerated or unnecessarily played up. Public disquiet must be
allayed as far as possible, because the enemy – i.e. Communists
of every conceivable species and subspecies – were attempting
to use this temporary weakness, which was really a democratic
strength, for their own sinister ends. 'A development which we
refuse to tolerate!'

'True character,' declared Feldmann, 'reveals itself only in
the hour of trial.' Numerous individuals suddenly betrayed an
urge to demonstrate this invaluable quality – one on which they
pinned considerable hopes. Every potential victor acquires a
cadre of camp-followers.

It isn't that I deplore these things – why should I? I'm an
intelligence expert, not a philanthropist. As such, I know that
every conceivable power set-up has its hangers-on and fellow-
travellers, its propagandists and theoreticians, its poets and
priests. If fate so decrees and circumstances are more or less
favourable, a nation can become inured to virtually anything,
even – to state the obvious – mass murder.

But who ever learnt from the past, whether recent or remote?
Four or five thousand years of bloodshed have taught us
nothing. Not even the atom bomb has been able to deter the
human herd from its preoccupation with the slaughterhouse.
People are like that, and every day simply brings further confirmation of it.

So much for the era of progress which we hail with such
enthusiasm.

Peter Sandman was unable or unwilling to accept this. Karl

Wander actually suffered from his reluctance to come to terms with reality, ably assisted by people like Kohl. Germany, rather than America, has always struck me as the land of boundless opportunity.

I often felt an urge to laugh at this. After all, what more can an inveterate tilter at windmills like Wander evoke – at best – than a pitying smile?

I tried to form an appreciation of Wander and failed. Which means, in practice, that even a man of my calibre has his foibles.

What's more, I indulge them.

Chapter 11

'My name is Traugott,' said the man who looked like a postman off duty, good-natured, unassuming, and discreetly cheerful. 'Detective Superintendent Traugott. I'm here on a special assignment. I don't attach any importance to being addressed by my rank – I imagine that's all right with you, Herr Wander.'

Wander eyed him without enthusiasm. 'So you're the man who's been detailed to sort out this mess.'

'Call it what you like,' Traugott replied smoothly. He was a thin man of medium height with the irritatingly respectable air of an honest bureaucrat. 'I make it a rule never to quibble over turns of phrase. They're largely a question of temperament and personal values. To you, this is a mess to be sorted out; to me, it's a problem to be solved. The final result will be the same, I assure you.'

A special office in Precinct Headquarters No. 3, presumably that of the station officer, had been placed at Detective Superintendent Traugott's disposal. It was not an uncongenial room. Carefully tended flowers in plastic pots stood around, selected with a loving eye to specialization. There were dozens of varieties of violets – pale-blue, sky-blue, aquamarine, twilight-blue, midnight-blue.

A frown of concern clouded the serenity of Traugott's brow. 'I trust the officer who conveyed my invitation to you behaved with due courtesy?'

'He was alarmingly polite,' Wander assured him. 'An English butler of the old school couldn't have done it better.'

'Delighted to hear it,' said Traugott. 'I'm a stickler for

politeness. By the way, if there's anything you'd like before we get down to business – cigarettes, coffee, sandwiches – one of my men will be only too happy to oblige.'

Wander shook his head. 'Thanks all the same, but I'm not planning to picnic here all day.'

'So much the better. That means we'll be able to deal with this matter quickly.'

'And thoroughly, I hope.'

'Your hopes are well-founded, Herr Wander.' Traugott's tone was almost cordial. He placed his hands palm downwards on the desk-top, which was entirely bare. He had small, dainty, supple-looking hands, like those of a boy-juggler. 'I imagine we can dispense with the usual preliminaries – your particulars are known to me, also full details of the events in question. All that remains for me is to dispel any misunderstandings, prejudices or erroneous ideas.'

'Why don't you do that?' prompted Wander.

'Well, let's start with the suicide of Fräulein Morgenrot.'

'One minor point, Superintendent, if you don't mind. Do you intend to lecture me on your personal or official views, or am I allowed to ask an occasional question?'

'But Herr Wander!' Traugott registered dismay. 'This is a friendly talk, purely for your information. Ask anything you like and I'll answer to the best of my ability.'

'Good. The first thing I'd like to know is, why do you describe Eva Morgenrot's death as suicide?'

'Because it was suicide, plain and simple.'

'I don't find it as plain and simple as all that.' Wander was not wholly unimpressed by the Superintendent's tone of gentle authority. 'But perhaps you aren't aware of certain peculiarities in the Morgenrot family set-up.'

'Certainly I am,' Traugott assured him. 'I'm thoroughly conversant with all the information on record. It's not only plentiful but in most cases extremely well-documented. The material was prepared by a respected colleague of mine, Chief Inspector Kohl, whom I believe you know, and Kohl is nothing if not thorough. The information at my disposal includes guesses, conjectures and suspicions as well as proven facts. I've taken all those things into account.'

'I venture to doubt that.'

'And I venture to suggest that your attitude will change,' Traugott retorted, if anything more courteously than before. 'What particular objections do you feel obliged to raise?'

'To proceed systematically, point by point: Eva Morgenrot was attacked – beaten up, in fact.'

'Most regrettable, to be sure, but of no concern to the police because no complaint was made by the victim of the attack. No such complaint is on record nor was ever intended to be. And since the assailant was Fräulein Morgenrot's brother – yes, I know, stepbrother – the whole thing should really be regarded as a family matter. As you're probably aware, everyone in this constitutional State of ours has a legal right to be beaten up by anyone he pleases. You may deplore that, but you can't change it.'

'I gather you intend to dispose of my objections piecemeal – you don't seem to be interested in possible connections between them. Isn't that an over-convenient method?'

'Not over-convenient, Herr Wander. Appropriate and logical would be a better description. In any case, I shouldn't like you to think I'd overlooked any of the possibilities that suggest themselves. Suicide is always an isolated factor because the sole responsibility invariably rests with the person who commits it. If a suspicion arises that someone may have driven someone else to suicide, experience shows that the circumstances must be grossly exceptional. Convincing proof is seldom if ever forthcoming.'

'Not even in this case?' Wander said defiantly. 'Do you really expect me to believe that?'

'I can guess what you're alluding to.' Superintendent Traugott smiled confidentially. 'According to the records made available to me, you seem to believe that Fräulein Morgenrot was systematically maltreated. Have I quoted you correctly? I have? Thank you. Systematically maltreated by her stepfather, her stepbrother, a self-styled woman-friend, and one or more lovers.'

'Don't forget another possible candidate – Felix Frost.'

'The man who called himself her fiancé? No, I haven't overlooked him either. In fact he never was engaged to Fräulein Morgenrot – he simply claims to have been, and only by implication. Surely you wouldn't make a legal issue out of that?'

'Not out of that alone,' Wander said vehemently. 'Frost deliberately hounded Eva and then turned on me.'

'In your opinion, perhaps. But even if your extremely bold assumption is correct, how do you propose to prove it? It's no use juggling with imponderables – surely you see that?'

'I'm not doing anything of the kind. You're the one who refuses to see straight.'

'Please don't vent your prejudices on me, Herr Wander. I concede that your attitude may be fully justified – something terrible may well have occurred here, but only of a purely human, psychologically complex nature. It would never be possible to prove such things to complete satisfaction even if they came within the scope of laws currently in force, which they don't. One can't punish a man for his thoughts, desires and expectations, however reprehensible they may be. To simplify the present issue slightly: when a girl commits suicide for emotional reasons, the man responsible for her emotional state cannot be held accountable for his actions before a criminal court.'

'What about the size of her inheritance? Wasn't that motive enough for a crime of violence?'

'To the best of my knowledge, no crime of violence has yet been committed by means of an overdose of sleeping tablets. Suicide is generally attributable to depressive tendencies of a deep-rooted and often complex character.'

Wander had some difficulty in restraining himself. He was obviously butting his head against an india-rubber wall. 'But Dr Barranski's alleged findings are in doubt. According to Dr Bergner's testimony . . .'

'No, no!' Traugott interposed, all courtesy and concern. 'I'm afraid I must disabuse you on that point too. Look at it this way. Barranski may, in one genuinely demonstrable instance, have committed some minor breach of the Dangerous Drugs Act, but the fact remains that he is a distinguished and respected member of his profession. Dr Bergner, however estimable his character and motives, could never prove otherwise however hard he tried.'

'I see your tactics now, Superintendent. You're giving me the salami treatment – slicing my suspicions so thin that they amount to nothing.'

'Sorry to have to disillusion you yet again, Herr Wander, but I'm no tactician.' Traugott looked disconsolate and folded his boyish hands neatly on his lap. 'You might, with a little of the generosity which I'm sure you possess, describe me as an upholder of justice. Please don't think I'm talking in idealistic terms – I'm referring to concrete things such as laws, directives, regulations, and so on.'

'Things you're privileged to interpret at your discretion, for the benefit of the existing order and to the advantage of those who temporarily represent it.'

'Please don't try to provoke me, Herr Wander – you'll never succeed, believe me. I understand you and your reactions only too well. You're obviously a person who abhors, despises – indeed, hates – anything which strikes you as profoundly immoral and unethical. To you, immorality is synonymous with criminality, but it needn't be – not in this instance nor in the eyes of the law. My duty is to the laws currently on the statute book, and I shall naturally stand by them.'

'No matter who bites the dust, I suppose! As soon as a dead woman fails to fit neatly into one of your legal pigeonholes, she ceases to exist from your point of view.'

'It isn't as simple as that, Herr Wander.' Detective Superintendent Traugott remained unswervingly patient and polite. 'Dead bodies are all in a day's work to us, which means that our approach to death is neutral, free from thoughts of revenge, devoid of hidden guilt complexes or other essentially romantic undertones. Dead bodies are simply objects of research, and research is a specialized skill. Our inquiries show, for instance, that the death of Baroness von Wassermann-Westen was almost certainly accidental.'

'You don't believe that yourself,' Wander said brusquely. 'Sabine Wassermann procured Eva Morgenrot for Feldmann. She herself did business with Krug but then tried to outsmart him, possibly with Morgenrot's help. So she became an embarrassment and had to be eliminated. It's the only logical explanation.'

'That's your theory, Herr Wander, and you're entitled to it. It says much for the ardent moralist in you but little for the coolly analytical brain which I'm sure you also possess.'

'You seriously intend to bury something that stinks to high heaven, merely because it affects people in high places?'

'All credit to your highly individual moral code, Herr Wander, but really! Unlike yours, my reaction to this affair is wholly objective. It's a matter of complete indifference to me who sleeps with whom and in what circumstances. It's equally immaterial to me whether the man in question is a municipal dustman or a cabinet minister – the equality of all individuals, races and religions finds particularly strong expression in bed.

231

We do not at present subscribe to any laws or regulations prohibiting intercourse between consenting adults.'

'What are you driving at?' Wander demanded.

'You occupy Apartment 204,' Traugott said gently. 'It is decorated and furnished exactly like Apartment 205, almost down to the last detail. Have you noticed the rug, probably of Persian origin, which lies near the window and immediately in front of the radiator? It is possible to slip up on that rug – I carried out some experiments which demonstrated that beyond doubt. Anyone who fell awkwardly could strike the base of his or her skull on the radiator ribs – which are extremely sharp – thereby sustaining fatal injuries. That is the only possible explanation.'

'The only explanation? Isn't it also conceivable that Sabine was helped into the hereafter by me, Superintendent? Isn't it possible that, as a spurned ex-lover in the grip of an uncontrollable obsession, I killed her and tried to pin my crime on others – Krug and Feldmann, for instance – because I hated them for reasons which are immaterial?'

'Don't bother to go any further. I've no intention of making out a case against you, easy though it would be. I'm simply trying to demonstrate that one death was suicide and the other an accident, nothing more. I trust you take my point.'

'What about the joint attempt to murder me on the Rhine Bridge by Martin Morgenrot and Felix Frost?'

'Yet another of your delusions,' Traugott declared sadly. 'I've re-examined all the sworn statements on the incident – your testimony being contradicted by that of two independent witnesses. You obstructed the road and were overtaken in violation of the highway code. A collision resulted. The case will sooner or later be decided in court.'

'I was meant to be killed – why?'

Detective Superintendent Traugott thoughtfully studied the profusion of potted violets around him. Then he said: 'Harsh as it may sound, some people might call that remark a symptom of paranoia.'

'Why should you cover for a couple of bastards like Morgenrot and Frost?'

'My dear Wander, you're a man of considerable intelligence. Use it! Try to recognize the pointlessness of further opposition. Give up – either play along or fade out of the picture gracefully.' Traugott's expression was full of understanding. There was even a hint of compassion in his eye. 'Very well, I shall close the files on these cases, once and for all.'

'You really think I'll give up?'

'What other choice do you have? After all, you're not the suicidal type.'

*

Two moves by Karl Wander, then two interludes, then two further moves – such were the immediate results of this informative conversation with Detective Superintendent Traugott, Christian name Christian.

While Traugott was engaged in closing his files, Wander was trying to put the clock back. Both men were convinced that no other course of action was open to them.

Karl Wander's first move . . .

He paid another call on the Chairman of the Defence Committee.

The Chairman's opening words: 'What more do you want?'

'Only one thing – to stop trampling around on your bad conscience.'

The Chairman of the Defence Committee buried his angular chin in his chest and toyed with a pencil. 'I did as much as I could – as much as I could afford to do. I communicated my grave misgivings, submitted the details that had become known to me for consideration. I even passed on the incriminating facts about the Bölsche Corporation to the Chancellor direct.'

'And all because you were afraid of what a potentially hostile witness might say in court?'

'I was finally convinced by the arguments put forward by my fellow Party members Feldmann and Krug,' replied the Chairman, clinging to the tattered remnants of his dignity. 'I now support them, in principle.'

'And you'd continue to support them even if you didn't have to?' inquired Wander.

'How do you mean?'

'Your successor as committee chairman could be a gentleman by the name of Krug, provided Feldmann succeeds in becoming Defence Minister – it doesn't take much mathematical ability to work that out. Set that possibility against the following fact: the man whose testimony you're afraid of is dead.'

'You mean it, or is this just another of your tricks?'

'Dead men can't talk, so hang on to your integrity – and the chairmanship of the Defence Committee too, if you're clever. Here is a photograph of a grave, here is a copy of a death certificate, and here are two sworn affidavits. You're in the clear.'

'Can I rely on that?'

'You can,' Wander assured him. 'You don't have much time to mull it over, though. In other words, you must act fast.'

'But how?'

'By making the most of your advantages. To be practical, you must prevent Feldmann and Krug from destroying your political prospects. You wouldn't want them to do that, would you?'

'Of course not,' the Chairman replied. 'After all, the country has entrusted me with responsibilities of a grave and exceptional nature. I cannot shirk them.'

Karl Wander's second move . . .

He went to see the parliamentary Defence Commissioner, who greeted him in identical fashion.

'What more do you want?'

Wander, standing near the door, said: 'You have recently given your support – unqualified support, in a manner of speaking – to Feldmann and his cronies. Why, exactly? Have you suddenly seen the light and decided that political considerations require it? Or are you, to use a vulgar but graphic expression, shit-scared?'

'How could you ask me that – you of all people? I left you in no doubt about my abhorrence of Feldmann's methods and those of his clique. His accession to the Ministry of Defence would strike a death-blow at all our ideals, all our hopes for a sound, clean, modern army. But what else can I do if I don't want to risk a term of imprisonment?'

'That would be asking too much of you, naturally. Who cares if the army you love so much is auctioned off for scrap as long as you and your pals keep your jobs. However, just assume that I have a lousy memory – suppose I don't know of any charge that could land you in court.'

'There'd still be the evidence you compiled.'

'Here it is,' Wander said.

He produced the originals which Fünfinger had given him and laid them out on the Defence Commissioner's desk. 'One diary, various letters, a few literary exercises, and several addresses. It's all there. What more do you want?'

The Defence Commissioner stared at his visitor incredulously. Then he said: 'What's your asking price this time?'

'A little integrity – whatever you understand by the word. Surely you haven't abandoned all your ideals?'

First interlude . . .

'Here I am again!' Sobottke proclaimed staunchly. He was sitting in Wander's apartment.

'At your service!' he added.

'What is it this time?' Wander demanded. 'Come to give me a hand with my packing?'

'Be glad to,' Sobottke said promptly. 'My car's downstairs, tanked up and ready to go. I could get you to Munich before the night's out. You'd be bound to feel more at home there.'

'Sobottke,' Wander said, studiously casual, 'don't bother to put on a private performance for my benefit. Krug sent you here. He gave you a key to this apartment and told you to see me off the premises. How do you propose to set about it? Think twice before you turn this place into a shambles. I have a friend who's a divisional boxing champion. One word from me and he'll knock your teeth out – if I don't manage to do it myself.'

Sobottke looked hurt. 'You really shouldn't talk to me like that – it isn't fair. If you want to know, I came here off my own bat. Nobody told me to. So why did I come? Because Herr Krug's such a decent sort, that's why.'

'You don't say!' Wander's amusement was tempered with uneasiness.

'A decent sort,' Sobottke repeated, crowding Wander into a corner, 'that's what Herr Krug is. He took me on just after the war, when I was down and out. He didn't say: Sobottke, what have you done? He just said: Sobottke, what can you do? And I said to him: For you, anything! That's the sort of man he is, get it?'

'I'm gradually beginning to understand a lot of things round here.' Wander assumed a meaningful expression. 'Including a couple of things about you.'

'About me? What sort of things? Who told you, anyway?'

Wander stared into Sobottke's muscular face with an air of pity. 'It has been intimated to me that I could incriminate you without any difficulty whatsoever. It might even pay me to.'

'Me?' yelped Sobottke.

236

'You're an ideal subject,' Wander told him gravely. 'The perfect man behind the scenes, that's you. You do your employer's dirty work, beat up anyone who gets in his way – especially young girls.'

'That's a filthy lie!' bellowed Sobottke.

'Was it you who beat up Eva Morgenrot?' Wander inquired. 'Was it you who finished off the Baroness, for whatever reason? They'll have to pin it on someone some time, so why not you? Of all the likely candidates, you'd be the easiest and most convenient scapegoat.'

'You bastard!' Sobottke snarled. 'Don't ever say that again! What are you trying to do – set me against Herr Krug?'

'Go on, you know damn well he'd sell you down the river tomorrow if it was worth his while.'

'You dirty, conniving little bastard!' Sobottke could hardly control himself now. 'Stop trying to soften me up! Krug would never dare get rid of me. I know too much.'

'So do I, probably. Isn't that reason enough?'

Second interlude . . .

A telephone call made from a public call-box at lunch-time on the following day. The speakers: Karl Wander and Marlene Wiebke.

Wander: 'Are you alone, or do I have to phrase my questions so you can answer yes or no? Did I dial the wrong number? No? Good. Well, how does my stock stand?'

Marlene: 'It isn't quoted any longer. In other words, this office never officially listed it. Do you know a man called Traugott?'

Wander: 'As well as I want to. Have they turned him loose on me?'

Marlene: 'They tried to, but he declined with thanks. Very politely intimated that he didn't feel competent to intervene. When they tried to badger him into filing a series of charges against you, his only reply was: muck-raking and criminal investigation are two different and mutually incompatible forms of activity – said he wasn't the man for the job.'

Wander: 'Remarkable man, Traugott. Another thing – did Krug 'phone Keilhacke to tell him that I'd been blackballed from the club?'

Marlene: 'He tried to, but the General wasn't available.'

Wander: 'It would be preferable if the General's number remained unobtainable – till this evening, say.'

Marlene: 'Anything else?'

Wander: 'Yes, at the risk of annoying you – I love you.'

Marlene: 'It doesn't annoy me. Tell me again.'

Wander: 'I love you.'

Marlene: 'I know it's crazy in the circumstances, but I'm so far gone I don't want to hear anything else, ever. We can't afford to dwell on the subject, though. After all, there's always tomorrow. Do you have anything else on today – anything important?'

Wander: 'I've fixed up an interview for Peter Sandman. General Keilhacke will see him at four p.m. Could you ring Sandman – I'm short of time – and give him a message? Tell him to spin out the interview for at least an hour and take a photographer along. Tell him I think I can offer him something rather special.'

Karl Wander's third move . . .

The man he sought was not hard to find. His name was in the telephone book and his office in the new skyscraper near the Beethovenhalle, with a view of the Rhine. The Bölsche Corporation of Munich employed him to represent its interests in the West German capital.

Wander was shown in at once, not because the receptionist took him for a VIP but because her boss was not overloaded with work. Her boss turned out to be a young man with an ageing face, ultra-fashionable clothes and a smile that would have done credit to a hair-cream advertisement.

'Well,' he inquired amiably, 'what can I do for you?'

'Nothing,' Wander replied, no less amiably. 'I propose to do something for you. To be precise, I'm going to pass on some information.'

'Pass or sell?' asked the PR man. His smile did not alter.

'Call it an unsolicited gift. Don't bother to wonder why – it wouldn't be worth it. Let's stick to facts. Your client has been under tremendous pressure here for the past few days, isn't that so? Please don't try to deny it – I know what I'm talking about, and don't expect me to tell you how I know. I shouldn't be surprised if the Chancellor hasn't already sent for Herr Bölsche and requested a full report on his government contracts. I'm right, aren't I? Well, do you know who started it all?'

The smile temporarily froze. 'If that's the nature of your information,' he said, 'I have to concede that we're . . .'

'In the dark. I know. You've merely found out that a file on the Bölsche Corporation exists – production figures, development costs and financial plans. What you don't know is the actual identity of the supplier of this information. Right?'

The PR man nodded. 'Right.'

'In that case, you don't know which direction to operate in, what counter-measures to take and whose services you may have to enlist in order to buy a little time, if nothing more.'

'Right again, I'm afraid.'

'Then listen to this. All the information was supplied by one of your competitors. It came straight from Morgenrot's, from the managing director's office.'

'Sounds logical,' said the PR man, beaming like a child with a new toy. 'But why tell me all this? What's it worth to you?'

'What price-tag would you put on a clear conscience?'

'You've got me there.'

'Quite so. I'm simply trying to enlighten you, that's all.'

'And very grateful I am too – really very grateful, even if I haven't quite worked out the most effective way of using your information.'

'No difficulty there. Simply trace the possible contacts and connections between your sphere of interests and Morgenrot's. The safest way would be to run a check on personnel records. Aren't you with me yet? I'm talking about staff members who've gone over to the opposition, Bölsche employees who have been wooed away or offered bigger money by Morgenrot's. Their inside information would have gone with them.'

The P R man's expression conveyed injured innocence and reproach. 'It's unethical, the whole thing!'

'But profitable too – always has been. And you can save your righteous indignation for someone else.'

Karl Wander's fourth move . . .

This had been planned and prepared by Corporal Fünfinger. Wander had christened it 'Operation Keilhacke'.

It had come to Fünfinger's ears that several of the more ingenious members of a neighbouring armoured unit had hit on a remarkable way of taking the elbow-grease out of vehicle cleaning. They simply drove their armoured car to the nearest garage and put it through the automatic car-wash. In the interim, they repaired to the café opposite for a couple of leisurely beers.

This, as Fünfinger had unerringly realized, was grist to Keilhacke's mill. The General's attention having been drawn to this irregularity, he could once more demonstrate that nothing escaped his eagle eye and that no candidate for the Inspector-Generalship was more perfectly fitted to wield a new broom than Keilhacke himself.

So there they now stood, surrounded by the dismal concrete and asphalt of the suburban landscape, waiting for the General's arrival. In the foreground, a dully glinting armoured car poised at the narrow entrance to the automatic car-wash; a little to one side, glancing at his watch, Karl Wander; in the background, the gleefully expectant figure of Corporal Fünfinger.

Alerted by a 'phone-call from Wander, the General roared up in his Mercedes almost exactly on schedule. He was accompanied by an officer and two civilians, namely, Sandman and a newsphotographer. Keilhacke climbed out, greeted Wander cursorily, and marched over to the armoured car. He halted in front of it, hands on hips, and glared. The photographer caught the pose.

'This is incredible!' the General bellowed in the parade-ground tones appropriate to the occasion.

'Interesting spectacle!' Sandman whispered to Wander.

'There's more to come,' Wander assured him.

Keilhacke sent his escorting officer to look for the crew of the armoured car. He personally summoned the garage attendant, who had been suitably primed and rewarded in advance. A lively dialogue developed. The General posed questions and received prompt replies. 'How long has this crate been standing here? What's it doing here? How often has it been brought here? When was the first time? Are other military vehicles brought here? What sort and when?'

It took Keilhacke less than three minutes to compile a whole catalogue of misdemeanours. The offences in question ranged from 'insufficient attention to duty', via 'conduct prejudicial to combat readiness', to 'suspected sabotage' and 'abetting espionage'. Skilfully concealing his deep satisfaction, Keilhacke gravely gazed round him. The photographer captured him in this pose too.

Then, dictating for the benefit of Sandman, who duly took down every word, the General declared: 'Yet another piece of evidence to support my contention that the army is becoming riddled with carelessness, irresponsibility and negligence – the result of too much soft treatment. The only thing that will stop the rot is iron discipline and warlike morale!'

Wander had meanwhile climbed into the armoured car, remarking in an undertone: 'Let's see just how rusty I've become.' With a nod and a grin to Sandman, he squeezed in behind the wheel and started to fiddle with the controls.

'Would you mind repeating that last phrase, General?' Sandman asked, in an effort to distract Keilhacke's attention. 'Did you say warlike discipline and iron morale or vice versa?'

'Eggs and ham, ham and eggs – what the hell does it matter which way round you say them?' Keilhacke was slightly indignant at having to repeat himself. 'Morale and discipline, those are the key words.'

He was now standing directly in front of the armoured car with the air of one intending to conduct a thorough inspection. Suddenly, Wander found the starter and the engine roared into life. The vehicle began to inch its way forward. The General hurriedly took evasive action, instinct telling him to retreat. Although he failed to realize it at first, this took him down the blind alley which led straight into the automatic car-wash bay. The electronic eye at the mouth of the installation, thoughtfully switched on by the garage-hand, emitted a sinister red glow.

'Hey, you!' Keilhacke called indignantly to the oncoming vehicle. 'What are you playing at? Stop that damn thing at once!'

But nobody seemed to hear. The armoured car continued to bear down on him, engine roaring. He retreated again, backing steadily down the blind alley, closing inexorably in on the electronic eye. Sandman stared open-mouthed, and the photographer, with a professional's sense of occasion, took one shot after another.

'I won't stand for it!' Keilhacke bellowed, trembling with outrage and the first faint stirrings of fear. He began to realize his predicament. In front of him he could see the armoured car, on either side of him blank walls, behind him the gaping jaws of the car-wash bay. 'Switch that machine off at once. That's an order!'

His order fell on deaf ears, or, rather, seemed to bounce off the armour-plating like a ping-pong ball. The engine noise drowned it. Inch by inch, with unnerving slowness, the vehicle bore down on him. He tried vainly to elude it, made as if to stem its advance by main force but quickly realized how pointless that was and retreated still farther down the bay, straight towards the electronic eye.

'Have you gone crazy, man?' Keilhacke screamed. He stumbled, stared aghast at the wheels threatening to run him down, and fell back again, gasping: 'You can't do this to me!'

He had now interrupted the beam which initiated the washing cycle. The installation was a fully automatic device imported from the USA. Electrical circuits sprang to life, releasing a succession of impulses. Jets of water leapt hissing at Keilhacke from all sides, soaking him to the skin. He collapsed on to the conveyor-belt, was drawn through a hot bath, buried in clouds of foam, pummelled by rotating nylon brushes, rinsed off, buffeted by gales of warm air, and finally ejected. He sat up helplessly and remained sitting there, stunned.

'My apologies, General!' Wander called in tones of profound dismay. He had brought the armoured car to a halt and was peering out of the driver's slit. 'I'm terribly sorry but I couldn't get the hang of the controls. A bit rusty, I'm afraid.'

The escorting officer had hurried up and was regarding his general with utter bewilderment, unable to believe his eyes. 'What happened?' he asked ponderously.

Fünfinger, who had also hurried up, sniffed the air. 'The General seems to require a change of underpants, sir. That's all.'

*

'They're fantastic!' exclaimed Sandman. He was looking at

the prints which he brought with him. 'Almost too good to be true!'

Wander forced himself to smile rather than spoil his friend's delight.

'You obviously don't share my amusement, Karl,' Sandman said. 'Why not? Are you afraid Keilhacke will make a political issue out of the incident?'

'He can, for all I care – it makes absolutely no difference to me.'

'He won't, though. He comes out of it too badly – these pictures make him look ridiculous. You don't need to worry.'

Wander stared into space. 'I admit it amused me at the time. Then I realized it was just another Punch-and-Judy show, and that's not enough. It isn't enough, I tell you!'

They were sitting in Mutter Jeschke's bar, drinking a feather-light Moselle instead of the usual Irish stout. It went down like lemonade.

'What more do you want, Karl?' Sandman looked perplexed. 'You've put one gigantic spoke in Feldmann's wheel. You've nudged the chairman of a parliamentary committee into doing the right thing, stopped the Defence Commissioner from having nightmares, effectively mobilized Morgenrot's most influential competitor. And to cap it all off, you've just succeeded in putting the loudest-mouthed of all Hitler's World War Two left-overs out of commission. Doesn't that amount to something?'

'Not enough,' Wander repeated. 'Feldmann and Krug are tough nuts. They won't give up so easily, not when they're within spitting distance of success. Maybe someone ought to go to the Chancellor or to the President and put them in the picture. My connections don't reach that far, unfortunately, but yours do.'

'I might be able to arrange something – dinner with our ambassador, say. Old John is a nice guy. He's also under a kind of debt to me – I let him beat me at golf from time to time. You couldn't expect him to commit himself or come out into the open, but that's not to say he wouldn't drop a casual hint to the Chancellor a couple of days later.'

'That would be something.'

'Too little and too late, though, from your angle. You don't have much time.' Sandman sat back and drew a deep breath. 'I guess there's nothing else for it. I'd better introduce you to Jerome.'

'Who's Jerome?'

'I mentioned his name once before, the first time we met here in Bonn. You obviously don't remember.'

'Should I have?'

'And how!'

'Is he a friend of yours?'

'God forbid! Jerome's one of the toughest agents this side of the Iron Curtain. He'd wring my neck without a moment's hesitation if circumstances demanded it. Fortunately, there wouldn't be much point at this time.'

'And you propose to put me in his clutches?'

'Maybe you're there already,' Sandman said. 'What's more, I'm tempted to say you deserve it.'

＊

Jerome appeared in Mutter Jeschke's bar exactly half-an-hour later in response to a telephone call from Sandman. 'What gives?' he demanded, and sat down between Sandman and Wander without any further preamble.

The man known as Jerome looked even-tempered, mechanically amiable, stolid and noncommittal. His smile matched his appearance, and he used it most of the time.

'My friend Karl Wander has a problem,' Sandman explained.

'No problems are insoluble,' Jerome observed calmly, 'not in my business. What's this one?'

'It's a long story,' Wander said.

'I'm not interested in stories,' Jerome told him. 'Facts are all I care about, documented facts, photocopied facts and figures, names and numbers. Stick to facts, Herr Wander.'

Jerome accepted a large brandy and drained it like mineral water. He then demanded the bottle it came from. 'Part of my daily routine,' he explained. 'Don't let it bother you, Herr Wander – I'm listening.'

Wander embarked on an account of recent events, trying to keep it as succinct as possible. Jerome listened without a trace of expression. After three minutes he said: 'No guess-work, please. Stick to what you think you can prove.' After a quarter of an hour he said, insistently: 'Go on!' Another quarter of an hour, and his only comment was: 'Be more precise!' By that time the brandy bottle was half empty.

Wander did his best to avoid looking at the irritatingly vacant face beside him, but failed. Peter Sandman looked slightly exhausted. Lethargy seemed to hang in the air. Wander heard his voice droning on with the persistence of a steady downpour.

Jerome suddenly emerged from his apparent day-dream. 'Stop!' he said. 'Repeat what you just told me.'

'You mean about the information supplied by Morgenrot?'

'Exactly.' Jerome's manner was brisk now. 'How was it transmitted – by telephone, in person, or on paper?'

'It was a sort of file containing data-processed material, at least six pages of it. About new weapons. Technical information, details of development costs and how they were arrived at. That sort of thing.'

'Was it passed on direct, or did they use a middleman?'

'As far as I know, Morgenrot passed it to Krug direct. Krug informed Feldmann and probably the chairman of the Defence Committee too, so that the latter could notify the Chancellor. They must have used notes, transcripts or photocopies.'

The man known as Jerome eyed Wander hopefully. 'That would mean the originals weren't distributed but kept somewhere. Any idea where?'

'In a safe in Krug's office.'

'Who has access to it?'

'Only Krug himself.'

Jerome ruminated for a moment. 'We ought to be able to do something with that.' He nodded at Sandman and then refocused his attention on Wander. 'Are you familiar with the contents of the file?'

'Not in every detail. I only know the bare bones. For instance, I saw figures relating to the production of magnetic warheads for short-range rockets, also reports on errors of planning in the development of a guidance mechanism known as the Z69. Then there were some notes on the inadequacy of security-measures for a secret project bearing the code-name Focus X.'

'Not bad,' Jerome said to Sandman. 'We might really do something with that.'

Sandman said: 'Then get cracking, Jerome.'

Jerome nodded and turned back to Wander. 'Know something? You look just the way I'd pictured you. Don't take that as a compliment, though – I never give compliments. Sandman here knows me well enough to confirm that. If I understand you right, Herr Wander, you want to see this man Krug immobilized.'

'Yes. Feldmann too, if possible.'

'One of them could bring the other down,' said Jerome. 'It might not even stop there. However, we should be able to hit your primary target without too much difficulty.'

'How are you going to do it?' asked Sandman.

'By starting a chain reaction – just the sort of process which happens to gibe with my present approach. I'll have to ask you a favour in return, Peter. OK?'

Sandmann nodded. 'When can you deliver?'

'Three hours or so,' Jerome replied. 'I'll turn Samson loose on it.'

*

A little less than three hours later the man known as Jerome reappeared in Mutter Jeschke's bar. The room was thick with tobacco-smoke and four empty bottles stood on the table in front of Sandman and Wander.

Jerome resumed his place between them and called for another bottle of brandy. Mutter Jeschke served him in silence and brought another two bottles of Moselle in as well. Then she locked up and retired behind the bar.

'Well,' Sandman asked eagerly, 'did you have any luck?'

'Yes and no.' Jerome smiled sardonically and poured himself a drink. 'It didn't go quite the way I expected – even better, maybe. There's one fly in the ointment, but minor flaws are the imponderables of my profession. They even take me by surprise, sometimes.' He drained his glass and refilled it. His deceptively ingenuous face looked as mellow as a sunset. 'I entered Samson for the race, as I said I would. Samson's been champing at the bit for days. All he needed was a flick of the whip.'

'Since when did you keep horses, Jerome?' inquired Sandman. 'I thought your outfit confined itself to breeding rats.'

'Samson's a rat as well,' Jerome said. 'A goddamned efficient one too. Samson's the code-name of an agent who's worked for us for several years, and successfully. For the last few months he's also been working for the opposition, that's why his time's up. We'd already made preparations to turn him over to the West German security people – as a friendly gesture repayable in due course. But decoys like Samson have to be fleshed out to be really effective – fattened up with tasty bits of information.'

'Like the Morgenrot file, you mean?'

'In this case, only as an addition to his diet and because it was such a perfect opportunity.' Jerome drank with relish.

'Anyway, I arranged for Samson to be offered the Morgenrot material – implied that we could actually deliver. He turned it down, though. And why? Even I failed to answer that one right away, but the solution was downright simple. He was familiar with Morgenrot's information, down to the last detail.'

'The man must have been bluffing.'

'I'm afraid not,' Jerome said. 'However, since Operation Samson was already rolling according to plan, the only course open to us was to drop our esteemed West German colleagues a few discreet but unmistakable hints about the Morgenrot bombshell. It turned out that they knew about it too.'

'How did they know? Who told them?'

'It shouldn't be too hard to find out,' Jerome replied casually. 'We know the source, Wander included. My West German business partners only knew the nature of the information. What they didn't fully appreciate was where it came from, who it was meant for and where it was meant to be passed on to. Maybe it suited them better to remain in the dark for the time being.'

Wander gave a worried frown. 'It's like living in a jungle.'

'Where else do you think we are?' Jerome demanded, faintly amused. 'Anyway, I went out of my way to be helpful to the boys from the Federal State Security Service – always acting on the assumption, Peter, that your friend Wander isn't a nut.'

'He's just the opposite,' Sandman said earnestly.

Jerome nodded. 'I was banking on that. From your description of him, Wander, Morgenrot's no fool – the fact that his information gave no clue to source or destination proves that in itself. So Morgenrot knew very well that the facts he had assembled and passed on were dynamite, also that they mustn't fall into the wrong hands.'

'The basic plan was to make it a question of national security,' Wander said. 'You can justify virtually anything on those grounds.'

'Which is what they proceeded to do.' Jerome carefully refilled his glass. 'The only trouble was, events didn't follow anything like a normal course. It wasn't just a question of settling an account, making a deal. Emotional factors were involved too – plenty of them. Also, human vagaries and all too human errors. And unpredictably, some of the fingers in the pie turned out to be daintily feminine. Baroness von Wassermann-Westen's, for example.'

'It can't be true!' Wander exclaimed.

'If it is,' Sandman said, 'what was involved? Espionage on behalf of foreign interests, preferably East European and best of all Chinese? Was it treason, in fact? If not, what was it?'

'A host of attractive possibilities, aren't there?' Jerome said. 'The one fact which springs to mind is this: the Baroness knew where the dynamite was kept and only she could have gained access to it.'

'Why only her?' Wander asked.

'Eva Morgenrot may also have stumbled on some document or other, but she's dead. Maybe that's why she died. Another possibility is Felix Frost. Remarkable type, Frost. Said to be a millionaire, also a Communist. However, he's out of reach now – developed a sudden overpowering urge to visit South America.'

'It all sounds intriguingly complicated,' Sandman remarked, not without a glimmer of hope.

'It is,' Jerome said. 'Eva Morgenrot's dead. Whatever she took from her father can't be found. We can assume that the Baroness took charge of it, but she's dead too. The State Security boys will merely note the fact and do nothing more, that's for sure. They'll grab at anything tangible they can lay hands on.'

'Krug, you mean?' Wander asked.

The man known as Jerome nodded. 'I've already set the wheels in motion.'

'In that case,' Wander said gratefully, 'you've achieved more in three hours than I did in a week, in spite of all my efforts.'

'Don't rejoice too soon,' Jerome advised. 'Remember these boys can be knocked over as many times as you like. They always bounce back as long as they know the rules of the game.'

'That could take time, though,' Wander said. He still sounded confident. 'Krug will be temporarily immobilized. That's good enough to be going on with.'

Jerome stared at him with something like compassion. Then he said: 'Neutralizing Krug isn't the equivalent of crippling Feldmann. It's conceivable that he'll find himself in a heap of trouble, but he won't be the only one.'

'Let's stop juggling with possibilities,' Sandman cut in hastily. 'You're letting your imagination run away with you, Jerome.'

Jerome shook his head. 'I'm afraid not. Look at it this way: Morgenrot delivered the goods and Krug sold them at a profit; Eva Morgenrot tried to interfere and the Baroness planned to collect, preferably from both sides; Martin Morgenrot and Felix Frost were systematically exploited. And your friend Wander, Sandman, acted as an intermediary. It doesn't matter two hoots in hell whether he did so voluntarily or involuntarily, deliberately or accidentally, willingly or under duress.'

Sandman looked shocked. 'You mean he's cornered?'

'I'm afraid so.'

'But that's just what I've been waiting for,' Wander insisted, 'a chance to unload!'

'You're an idealist,' Jerome said drily. 'I hope you aren't a fool as well. My only advice to you is, hide out for the next few weeks.' He turned to Sandman. 'Make him listen to reason.'

'But that would be like running away,' protested Wander. 'It might even be taken as an implicit admission of guilt.'

'Sandman,' Jerome said, 'I was right – this guy is a nut after all, so don't expect me to put on a white coat and humour him. Talk some sense into the man. Nobody can turn his back on reality for ever.'

'My dear Karl,' Sandman urged, 'if you don't make yourself scarce quickly, you can take it for granted they'll lock you up and isolate you to give themselves time to build up a case. Surely you don't want to risk that?'

'I'm not aware of having committed any crime,' Wander said.

'I realize that.' Sandman could scarcely conceal his agitation. 'Who do you hope to convince, though? I'm beginning to doubt whether a Don Quixote can survive in this day and age – Kohl realized that too, and we always did our best to act like friends.'

'Don't overrate friendship,' said Jerome. 'The longer I live, the less I can afford to indulge in it. In your case, Wander, the temptation is minimal.'

Wander gazed round him helplessly. 'What am I supposed to do?' he demanded. The question sounded as if it was addressed to himself. 'I know, I can give in. I might even save my skin without ever knowing what it was really worth.'

'I wouldn't invest a dime in it myself,' Jerome observed, turning to Sandman. 'Really, the man's a hopeless idealist.'

'You may be right,' Wander said slowly. 'However, I don't want to involve anyone else. You're the last person who ought to risk any trouble on my account, Peter.'

'I'm fireproof, Karl. After all, I not only play golf with the US ambassador – I even try to do business with Jerome here, and Jerome occasionally produces bombshells, even if they do have minor defects.'

'Well, what are you waiting for, Wander?' Jerome drained his latest brandy. 'Can't you bear to say goodbye to this beloved country of yours?'

Wander raised his glass. 'You're probably right. I was

dreaming so I must have been asleep. I'm awake now, but I'll have to get used to the feeling first.'

'Try!' said the other two.

Karl Wander tried. He only had a few hours to spare and he failed.

Soon afterwards, he was arrested.